THE GODSLAYER

STAR CROSSED CROWN
BOOK ONE

ALINA KRAMER

For Devin, the raven to my raptor.

CONTENTS

PROLOGUE

Lyanndra

Embers swirl as the flaming blade sizzles through the air above me.

The weapon traces a vicious diagonal arc toward my head. It's a death blow, if it connects, one designed to sever the skull from my spine in one clean, efficient motion.

Ducking low, I roll out of the way a split second before the sword crashes into the ground where I was just standing. Flames choke out in the ankle-deep ash with a serpentine hiss.

I'm safe, but not for long.

I'm losing steam, and we both know it. My muscles scream from the effort it takes to swing my greatsword and dodge the savage blows of my opponent. Smoke chokes my lungs and prickles my eyes. Though the worst of the flames can't penetrate the dragonhide leathers I wear beneath my armor, the heat still simmers through my veins, cooking me alive.

Not for the first time, I wonder how in the stars I've ended up here.

This is not the life I'd been slated for. By all rights, I should still be in my village on the outskirts of the Southern Caldera, married off to a farmer or a merchant and raising a hefty brood of children in the shadow of the mountains. After all, good women aren't supposed to don their father's armor and ride away in the night to seek their fortunes. Good women don't slay great beasts or joust against the finest of the Celestial Knights.

Good women don't fight. Good women don't kill.

But I am not a good woman.

I clutch the handle of my greatsword tightly, the metal scales of my gauntlets biting into the worn leather grip of the weapon. Blinking rapidly to clear the sweat and soot from my eyes, I study my opponent.

It's the first time I'm able to get a good look at him since he initially engaged me on the battlefield in a swirl of fire. He's tall, towering over me by a good foot. He wears the gleaming golden armor of the Celestial Court, as though I need the reminder that he's a Demigod. He certainly fights like one, with flames seething out along his blade and surging from his fingers like the striking fangs of a great serpent. A red mantle, the edges charred, flutters at his shoulders. Above that, an inlaid helm protects his face, but it does little to hide his identity.

The distinctive metal work depicts a vibrant constellation of falling stars, a retelling of the birth of the Demigods that harkens back to the old legends. That helm is sacred to the Demigods, and there's only one man–one *god*–who would be allowed the honor of wearing it into battle.

The Flaming God, the King of the Celestial Court.

Rage flares in my chest, hotter than the fire that flickers in my peripheral vision. It surges through my arms in an unexpected torrent of strength. How many of my people have died at his hand? How many of the Starless have been slaughtered on his orders?

A bellow erupts from my throat, a war cry that rolls across the smoldering planes of the battlefield as my aching shoulders flex beneath the weight of my greatsword. I cleave the hunk of metal through the steaming air, deliberately aiming a few inches shy of my opponent's plated chest.

He reacts exactly as I'd hoped. His longsword, shorter and lighter than my blade, flashes in a quick parry. The force of the clashing metal spins me around in a tight circle. My feet kick up a cloud of ash, momentarily blinding both of us.

But I don't need my eyes for what comes next. I open my fingers, allowing the momentum to carry the weight of the greatsword from my palms and away from me. The huge blade flies into the plume of soot, falling to the earth seconds later with a dull thud. I'm hoping the Flaming God thinks he's disarmed me completely.

Still obscured by falling ash, I draw my emptied hands down to the sheathed dagger that's strapped to my thigh. The dragonhide leather of the scabbard is cracked and brittle from the heat. Panic rises in my throat like bile as I scrabble blindly at the clasps thinking that I won't be able to get them undone in time, but then they slide apart, and the hilt of the blade sits solidly against the palm of my gauntlet.

I've drawn the dagger not a moment too soon. Somewhere in the gloom, fire sparks. Orange light flickers off golden armor as the Flaming God materializes over me, a great monster lurching through the fog. He raises his blade, his intention clear.

One of us is going to die.

Any normal opponent would attempt to dodge the blow by moving backward or sideways. It's exactly what the Flaming God would predict, but I've never been the type of woman to meet anybody's expectations. Instead, I wait until the longsword starts to drop, and then I dart forward, confident that I can move faster than the falling steel.

He doesn't have enough time to change the trajectory of his swing or to get out of my way. I skid into him in a chaotic clatter of armor, sending him stumbling backward.

Propelled by the weight of us both, he falls heavily onto his back. My helm slams into his golden chest plate as I land on top of him. The sound of it rings around my head, and for a desperate moment, I feel like I might vomit into my visor, but then the hiss of flames brings me back to reality.

I'm flush with the Flaming God's chest. Heat rolls off him in great waves, choking the air from my lungs. At this angle, I can just barely see up through the slits of the visor of his helm. I catch a glimpse of a pair of green eyes, wide with surprise, shockingly human.

There's no time to hesitate. I've fought Celestial Knights before. I know where the gaps in their armor lie, where the mail beneath is thin. I can only hope that their king is no different.

This time, there's no war cry as I bring the dagger down. There's just the short hiss of hot metal through the festering air before it hits home in the weak spot just beneath the King of the Celestial Court's left arm. The heated blade slides easily through the exposed mail, sinking down to the hilt with barely any resistance until it pierces his heart.

I'm not sure what I expect the Flaming God to do next. Part of me thinks he'll erupt in a flash of fire, taking me with him, until we're both nothing but a pile of smoldering ash.

But he simply lets out a pained exhale and falls still.

The king is dead.

The ringing in my ears is back. My breath escapes in short, panting gasps as the air begins to noticeably cool around me. Ash falls like black snow, dotting the golden armor of the fallen Demigod in sullen flecks. For the first time since our deadly dance began, the smoke of the battlefield is starting to clear. Shapes loom through the haze, and it takes me a moment to realize that they're people.

I barely register that the fighting around me has ceased. Soldiers, Starless and Celestial Knights alike, stand in a tableau of disbelief. Murmurs rise in a speculative tide as I stare down at the lifeless form beneath me.

I've heard the stories about the Flaming God, about his cruelty and his anger. Elders would often huddle around cooking fires and muse in low voices about the monster sitting on the throne of the Celestial Court. Even his own warriors whispered about how they believed him to be immortal.

Fear grips me now. Is it possible that he's not really dead?

I have to make sure.

I reach down with shaking hands. My gauntlets are slick with blood, so I pull them off to reveal the worn dragonhide gloves I wear beneath. With stiff fingers, I push the smoldering mantle aside to reveal the pale column of the Flaming God's neck. Logic whispers in the back of my mind that he must be gone. No king would bare his jugular to his enemy like this. But the animal part of me, all instinct and superstition, needs to be certain.

It's a challenge to find and release the leather strap that secures the helm to the Demigod's head, but I manage it. The breath catches in my throat as I slide the gleaming metal up, inch by inch.

His mouth is revealed first. I've always imagined it would be pulled into a stern, cruel line, but his lips are now slack and speckled with blood. His nose comes next. It's hard to imagine what it would have looked like since it's now nothing but a broken mess. Did I do that? Or perhaps one of the Starless soldiers he'd slain before me was the one to inflict this particular damage.

And then there are those eyes. Green. Empty.

Gone.

I slide the helm the rest of the way off, allowing a shock of red hair to escape. The Flaming God's head drops the last inch into the ash, his lifeless gaze turned toward the heavens he so fervently worshipped.

This Demigod died like any other man.

Was he ever anything but?

A strangled noise escapes me, a choked sound that falls somewhere between a sob and a laugh. A fresh wave of rage forces through me, but it's followed by an echoing pang of sorrow.

Is this what we've all died for?

I don't have time to ponder that question any further. The shuffle of boots through ash tugs me from my thoughts as the surrounding soldiers creep closer, their voices curling on the wind in shocked snippets.

"Is he alive?"

"Blood! I saw blood!"

"It's the king!"

I glance around. Curious, desperate faces peer at me from all directions. I'm hotly aware of how my hands shake as I grip the golden helm with numb, tense fingers. Weak light filters down onto the inlaid stars, lending them an ethereal glow.

My armor clatters against the king's as I rise. Everything seems to swim around me. My heart pounds in my chest as though the battle is still raging, as though I didn't just do the impossible.

And then silence swells as I lift the golden helm as high as I can, stretching it to the heavens.

When I finally speak, my voice is hoarse, barely recognizable, but it booms across the battlefield as surely as kindling flares from a spark.

"The Flaming God is slain!" I proclaim. "The king is dead!"

For a moment, nobody moves. But then the tenuous peace that's descended upon the battlefield is broken when a Celestial Knight, resplendent in gold, breaks through the front of the crowd.

The knight has lost his helmet somewhere in the fighting, revealing a grizzled face streaked with soot and blood and grief. His azure mantle tells me that this man is not one who wields fire like his king, but I'm far more distracted by the halfhand sword he swings as he barrels toward me.

"Godslayer!" he howls. The word is somewhere between an accusation and a curse. Madness shines behind his eyes as he repeats, "Godslayer!"

I have no weapon, but I'm not defenseless. I shove the king's golden helm out to meet what would have been a nasty strike. The halfhand blade sinks easily through the outer plating but barely dents the steel beneath.

The Celestial Knight has no time for a second swing. Several Starless soldiers swarm forward to grab him, absorbing him back into the crowd. I know what will happen to him now.

Behind the safety of my visor, I shut my eyes. I don't need to see any more bloodshed today.

But his screams still carry over the ashen battlefield as he's dragged away.

"Godslayer! Godslayer! Godslayer!"

Even when the man's wailing cuts off in an abrupt and jagged peak, the word still rings in my ears.

An accusation.

A curse.

Godslayer.

CHAPTER 1

Lyanndra

The tavern is bustling with activity tonight.

I'm under no illusions that the villagers who have crowded into the small, murky room are here to catch a glimpse of the Godslayer. In fact, I'm counting on it.

Tucked away in a gloomy corner, I lean back in my chair and wait. I'm not wearing my distinctive armor, which took on an eerie black sheen after the Flaming God's onslaught last year. Instead, I'm lounging in my dragonhide leathers. They're just bulky enough to hide the curve of my hips and the swell of my bound breasts, creating the illusion of masculinity. I've wrapped a dark kerchief loosely around my face. My hair, braided back into a long plait, is tucked away in the shadows of a large hood.

I could be anybody.

But it's the helm that sets me apart from any normal traveler. While I've left the rest of my armor tied to Barra's saddlebags in the stable next door, the golden helm rests on the table in front of me, glimmering in the muted candlelight. There's a sizable chunk taken out of the overlay from where the halfhand sword struck it only a year prior. The naked steel beneath gleams like bone.

Wearing the helm was simply a practical decision at first. After the war, after the king lay dead at my feet, I was taken to the healers' encampment on the outskirts of the battlefield, where I secluded myself away in a tent. A powerful wave of nausea rolled over me in that calm silence, too unyielding to ignore. My hands shook so severely that I was unable to wrench my own helmet off in time. I ended up retching black bile, clotted with soot, through the thin slats of my visor.

It was a hellish mess to clean up with just a small basin of cloudy water. I felt certain that at any moment, a healer would barge in only to find a woman instead of a knight, and so in a panic, I hastily traded my soiled helm for the golden one to buy me some time.

The strategy paid off–in more ways than one. Walking around the encampment in the golden helm and my blackened armor secured my reputation as the Godslayer. Later, as I aimlessly wandered the Alastrian countryside, I realized that word of my deeds preceded me. Whole villages met me with enthusiasm and celebration and, eventually, requests for assistance.

It started with a bandit who was stopping merchants on one of the high roads leading off into the northern mountains. He fell to his knees with absolutely no resistance upon catching a glimpse of that golden helm.

After that, there were others. With the Demigods of the Celestial Court sequestered away to lick their wounds in their capital city of Nexus, crime flourished in the impoverished Starless strongholds throughout the land. Nature, too, encroached on the outskirts of villages and towns, and rumors of strange beasts attacking in the night ran rampant. No matter where I wandered, there was always some threat, some menace that needed culling.

I've never turned down a request. I tell myself that it's only fair. After all, the Starless denizens of Alastria always greet me warmly since the war. They feed me without compunction or charge. All taverns are open to me. Any inn I enter has a room waiting for my arrival. And if the people won't take my silver, then service is the only way I can repay them.

But in a way, haven't I already settled that debt?

An image of two green eyes, wide with shock and fear, floats through my mind. Those eyes, like twin coins more valuable than any golden helm, should have been enough.

I draw in an uneasy breath. The fabric of the kerchief that covers my mouth is damp and humid against my lips. The sudden urge to tear it away, to reveal the truth of me, flashes through my fingers, but then it subsides as quickly as it comes.

I may be the Godslayer, but sometimes I am also a fool.

A quick glance around the pub reveals that nobody seems to have noticed my brief affair with madness. Chatter rises and falls, and I allow the snippets of conversation to tug me along in their gentle undertow.

Over by the bar, one grizzled old man says to another, "Three sheep. Heads ripped clean off! Can you believe it?" His companion shakes his head and mumbles something too quiet to hear. This piques my interest. Perhaps this is what I've been waiting for.

Only time will tell.

Seconds later, a chorus of braying laughter pulls my attention to one of the establishment's two long tables. Several young men loll on the benches with mugs of ale clutched in their hands. As one of them regales the rest with a tale of his exceptional strength and bravery in battle, I resist the urge to roll my eyes.

Unimpressed with their drunken nonsense, I instead look to the second table. This one is much quieter, populated by several fresh-faced maidens who, by their flat expressions, are about as enamored with their male counterparts as I am. They gossip easily amongst themselves, their voices just loud enough to carry below the enthusiastic ramblings of the other patrons.

"It's tonight, isn't it?" one redheaded woman asks.

Another girl, this one blonde, shakes her head. "Tomorrow, I think."

"It's always on the full moon," a third, raven-haired maiden chimes in while the rest of them nod sagely. "So it must be tomorrow."

"What do you think it'll be like?"

The redhead breaks out a dreamy grin. "It must be very romantic," she sighs. "I would love to see it."

The second girl's eyes narrow, and I get the sense that she doesn't like her fiery-haired companion very much. "As if you'd ever be invited to the Ceremony of the Crossed Stars," she scoffs.

Beneath the shadows of my hood, my expression darkens. I almost forgot about the Ceremony of the Crossed Stars. Is it really happening so soon?

My mood sours even further as I realize what this means. The Crown Prince of the Celestial Court must be preparing to take over the throne.

"Only Demigods are allowed to go," another woman, this one older, adds in an attempt to soften the blow.

"Go *where?*" a new voice asks. It belongs to a young girl who looks to be no older than ten. She's far too young to remember the last Ceremony. Even I'd missed it by a few years, though I grew up with the stories.

The older woman in the group turns to her and replies, "The Ceremony of the Crossed Stars. This one is for the prince."

I listen as she explains what I already know, that the Demigods believe that some of them are so special that the very heavens have blessed them with a perfect mate, their crossed star. The Ceremony helps the crossed stars find one another and binds them together.

"It's like a betrothal," the blonde butts in. "But worse. You can break a betrothal, but once you find your crossed star, the magic is binding. And if your crossed star rejects you, something bad happens."

"What? What happens?" The little girl gasps, equal parts intrigued and horrified.

The maiden offers her an unkind smile. "You *die.*"

"Enough of that," the older woman admonishes, but it's too late. The little girl's face crumples into a mask of dread.

I can't blame the child for her disgust, though the rumors I've heard are a little different. Back before the war, there was relative peace between the Starless and the Demigods. I regularly sparred with Celestial Knights that I'd met on the road, and it wasn't unheard of for us to share tales over a campfire now and then.

Those lesser Demigods told me about the custom. The subject of the Ceremony performed the rites beneath a full moon, pleading to the stars to reveal his or her mate and offering a ring. When the full moon reached the highest point of its journey in the sky, the ring disappeared and reappeared on the finger of the subject's crossed star.

According to the stories, the binding was absolute. The crossed stars were unable to remove the ring. The magic was so powerful that suicide or self-harm was impossible, and death of either party caused the survivor to go mad.

It's a barbaric ritual, in my opinion, to be matched in such a way by some cold, unearthly force. It's a small mercy that the Starless have always been excluded from such ceremonies.

I think I'd rather die than be betrothed to a Demigod.

But the redheaded woman doesn't seem to share my distaste. "What do you think would happen if I woke up tomorrow with the prince's ring on my finger?" she asks. "I hear he's quite handsome."

Her blonde friend spears her with a withering look and says, "I imagine the prince would run away screaming. And besides, only Demigods can be chosen. No Starless has ever been bound to a Demigod."

"I don't think I'd want to be bound to a Demigod," the little girl murmurs. "Even if he is a handsome prince."

I share that sentiment. How could any Starless woman want to be with a Demigod who so despises their kind? But it's the child's final comment that sends a sharp needle of unease through my heart, and I can't help but wonder if this handsome prince, the son of the Flaming God, has his father's eyes.

Green eyes.

Dead eyes.

My stomach lurches. Phantom heat, a memory of the battlefield, curls around me. I'm done eavesdropping, I decide. I've been sitting in this tavern for hours waiting for somebody to ask me for help, and all I've gotten for my troubles is some foolish gossip and indigestion.

I stand and heft the golden helm into my hands. Voices drop to quiet murmurs as I ease my way between the two long tables. I can feel the patrons' eyes on me, which only deepens the heavy dread that has lodged itself deep in my gut.

"I bet that the Godslayer's handsome too, under that hood," one of the women giggles. If I were in a better mood, I might turn and nod my head toward her, keeping up the ruse of manhood that I work so hard to perpetuate. But tonight, I simply ignore it.

I step out from between the narrow pass of the tables, skirt the two old men sitting at the bar, and stride out into the night.

The air, still warm from the midsummer's sun, is blissfully clear. I suck it down greedily, resisting the urge to rip the kerchief from my face as I fill my lungs.

Behind me, the tavern door creaks open and then slams shut again. Footsteps, barely audible on the packed dirt, approach me carefully, as though I'm a wild animal that may lash out with tooth and talon at the slightest provocation.

I blink slowly, hoping desperately that it's not one of the women, and then turn around.

The louder of the two old men from the bar stands before me. His eyes dart nervously between my shadowed face and the helm I still clutch in my hands.

"You're the Godslayer," he says finally.

It's not quite a question, but I answer it anyway with a slow incline of my head. As far as anybody knows, I've been mute ever since I proclaimed that the king was dead that fateful day on the battlefield. In truth, I never quite got the hang of lowering my voice to a deep enough pitch to be convincing, and so I long since decided not to speak at all.

If the old man is perturbed by my silence, he doesn't show it. "Is it true what they say?" he presses. "That you… help?"

I nod again.

"There's a wyrm in the mountains," he tells me. "It's been killin' livestock here for weeks now. The bastard got three o' my sheep just yesterday." He pauses, as though waiting for me to answer. After a long moment, he seems to understand that he'll get no words out of me, so he continues, "I know where the bastard's hidin'. If I tell you where, will you help me get rid o' it?"

To this, I nod a third time.

Relief passes over the man's face like a caul. "I'll pay whatever you like. I haven't any silver, mind you, but I've got sheep and all that comes from 'em. Name your price and it's yours."

For the first time in our exchange, I shake my head. I know the likelihood is high that I'll walk away from this with some wool or dried lamb jerky, but I'm not going to ask for it.

As the man relays his directions to the creature's lair, the dread that's built up inside of me begins to loosen and shake apart like a clod of dark earth. The prospect of a good hunt is the distraction I need.

By the time I've started toward the stables to fetch Barra, I've barely thought about the prince at all.

The only thought I've spared for him is to pity the poor wretch who ends up as his crossed star.

CHAPTER 2

"What do you think, my Lord?"

Drawing in a deep, grounding breath, I turn to the gilded mirror to study my reflection.

Too much of my father stares back.

The line of my jaw is from my mother, but the stern set of my mouth and the neat triangle of my nose are both gifts from the former king. My eyes, green as clover, are his too, along with the flaming red of my hair.

My father, who stepped into the role of the Flaming God with terrifying vigor, was not a good man. I'm his only child, his only heir, but even that didn't protect me from his wrathful hand.

I wonder if I will ever escape the memory of him.

"Are you pleased, my Lord?" the servant asks, gesturing to the black mantle he's affixed to my shoulders.

"Yes, thank you," I say, if only to get rid of him faster.

He bows and sweeps out of my chambers, leaving me alone at last.

Well, almost alone.

Torran remains seated in the corner with his brittle hands

steepled over his lap. His blue eyes, strangely young for such an old and wizened face, find mine in the mirror.

"You look like a king," he offers in a voice that reminds me of wind through river reeds.

"I will feel much more like one after this farce is over." I sigh.

An impish grin curls across the old man's face. "If you are so afraid of what the stars may reveal, you could always run away."

I roll my eyes at Torran's reflection. "I've never been one for court affairs, but this is one duty that I cannot avoid. The Ceremony of the Crossed Stars may be a formality at this point, but I'll be ineligible to take the crown without it. So I'll dress up like a good little prince in my royal armor. I'll smile and offer the ring. I'll act dismayed when nothing happens. And then the path to the throne will be clear."

By this time next month, I'll be crowned King of the Celestial Court, King of Alastria.

I will finally put my plan into motion.

Once again, I survey myself in the mirror. I'm wearing the golden armor of the Celestial Court. Shined to a high polish, the metal shimmers with an eerie liquidity in the candlelight against the matte black backdrop of the mantle. The whole ensemble makes me feel like a glittering star teetering on the precipice of some great and unknowable void.

Is this how my father felt all those years ago, waiting for his own Ceremony?

I shake my head. The less I think about the former king, the better.

As if he senses the dangerous trajectory of my thoughts, Torran rises and clasps an ancient hand over my shoulder. When he speaks, I feel like a babe again, visiting the old man down at his hut by the woods with my mother.

"You will be more than your father ever was," he says quietly.

"That shouldn't exactly be a challenge," I reply.

The Flaming God ruled over the Starless with an iron fist. When I was a small child, I'm ashamed to admit that I viewed those who hadn't been graced by the heavens as no more than animals, as foreign creatures who squabbled over scraps in the mud outside the city gates. But as soon as I was old enough to venture outside the sparkling streets of Nexus, I realized that perhaps they were out there not because they deserved it, but because my father had *put* them there. They didn't possess the riveting powers of the Demigods, but they wanted the same things as us: food, shelter, safety.

Peace.

And by the time I reached adulthood, I came to understand that the Starless would only be the enemies of the Demigods if we made them so.

My father had certainly made them his enemies.

The Flaming God waged war against the Starless. Demigods and Starless alike were churned into the great meat grinder of the battle-field in order to fertilize the never-ending animosity. While the Demigods possessed sheer power, the Starless had the numbers.

And they had something else.

Someone else.

The Godslayer.

My mouth—my father's mouth—turns down in a sneer at the thought of the Starless knight that did the impossible and felled a god.

I was there the day my father died. As his only heir, I wasn't allowed to fight. He planted me on a high bluff overlooking the battlefield alongside his generals, who were explicitly instructed to hold me back by any means if I tried to join the carnage.

From my vantage point, I watched as he fought and felled dozens of Starless soldiers. It was easy to follow the beacon of his flames as he slashed his way across the battlefield.

By the time the short knight with a hulking greatsword came along, I was barely concerned. Fighting my father was like staring down the sun. He was unyielding, unbeatable, inextinguishable.

Until he wasn't.

At first, the Flaming God was beating the smaller knight back. The Starless man was flagging, clearly outmatched. And when the knight misjudged the distance between them in what should have been a fatal swing of that monstrous greatsword, I was certain that he'd be dead in seconds, especially when his blade went flying.

I'm still not sure what happened next. The knight stumbled, kicking up a great puff of soot that momentarily obscured both of them.

And when it cleared, my father was dead.

The Godslayer held up the king's helm. I imagined the smug grin he must have worn on his face as he announced what he did.

I wanted to kill him.

Now, standing in my chambers on the cusp of my own rule, I understand why the Godslayer did it. He sent a message to his people and to ours. As much as I hate him, I can respect his motivations.

I would have done the same.

Torran's fingers dig into my shoulder. "Don't lose yourself like he did," the old man warns. "You'll have a chance to face your enemies, but you don't have to burn the world down in the process."

Anger bristles through me. Not for the first time, I wonder how he seems to know the thoughts that churn ceaselessly inside my mind. "I would like some privacy," I snap, but my words lack the teeth to really bite.

The old man's gaze is calm as he says, "The stars will show you your path." And then he turns in a swirl of purple robes and disappears through the open doors.

When I'm sure I'm alone, I hold one hand out in front of me and call the fire.

A flame, black as midnight, flickers to life in the crease of my palm. I can feel the heat of it, but it doesn't burn. It's comforting, familiar.

"Beautiful," a voice sighs from behind me.

I whirl around at the sudden sound, the flame frothing outward in a cruel whip, ready to strike at any potential threat.

But there's no enemy there ready to stick a knife in my back.

It's only Ressa.

My body sags in relief. "By the stars, Ressa, you know better than to sneak up on me like that." I sigh.

My betrothed smiles placidly. "You would never hurt me."

I shake my head as I pull the flame back in toward me before quenching it in my curled fist. "You shouldn't be here," I tell her. "You should be down in the cathedral."

Ressa's demure expression falls. Anxiety flashes through her dark eyes as she crosses toward me.

I catch a glimpse of the two of us in the mirror. We make a proud couple, I think. She's got all the makings of a queen. She's tall and willowy, with dark hair and porcelain skin. She's wearing a silvery gown that probably costs more than any Starless would see in a lifetime.

I draw her close and press a chaste kiss against her painted lips. When I pull back, the worry in her eyes has only deepened.

"You don't need to do this," she insists in a low voice, as though she expects servants to be listening outside the door.

"I do," I tell her firmly. "If I'm to take the throne, I have to complete the Ceremony. You know that."

She shakes her head. "But what if…?"

I hold up a hand, cutting her off. I know what she's afraid of, that somehow I have a crossed star out there, just waiting for me.

All of the powerful Demigods have a crossed star. At least, that's what Torran taught me.

But there were no other Demigods born under my star sign.

There was no crossed star out there for me.

It alarmed my parents at first, but they quickly found a solution. They betrothed Ressa to me when I was only three years of age. Without a crossed star, a betrothal was the next best thing.

As a child, a part of me wondered if there truly wasn't another soul out there for me. At first, I held out hope that, someday, another Demigod from a far-off land would step forward to announce herself as my crossed star, but that has never come to pass.

Now, I am at peace with the idea that the stars, for whatever reason, have set me on this path. I've made an effort to grow closer to Ressa, who is as sweet and loyal as any man could wish.

I look down at her now, hoping that her anxiety isn't mirrored in my gaze. "We just need to get through the Ceremony," I soothe. "This will be behind us, and then I'll be king."

Something flashes behind Ressa's eyes. "And I'll be your queen?"

I swoop down to capture her lips in another kiss, this one more passionate than before. I trace the curve of her mouth with my tongue, waiting until her lips part before pulling away.

"How cruel," she pouts, and I laugh lightly.

"Perhaps I'll show you how cruel I can be later," I tease, though my heart isn't fully in it. Something within me is uneasy, curling in my gut like a great serpent awakening from a long hibernation.

Ressa offers me a sly smile, but it quickly falls again. "Just tell me," she pleads. "Tell me that nothing will happen tonight."

"Nothing will happen tonight," I assure her. I feel flat as I say it, as though I'm reading lines from a book. "No other Demigod was born under my star. I have no crossed star."

"Are you sure about that?" she presses. "Couldn't your parents have made a mistake?"

I shake my head. "No. Not with this."

"Then say it," she insists. Her eyes are large, almost manic. "Say it, please."

For a moment, the answer sticks in my throat, but then it comes tumbling out all at once.

"I do not have a crossed star. Nobody will come between us."

The words hang between us like soot on the battlefield, obscuring everything underneath.

Ressa's expression softens, and my guilt flares.

Because I don't believe those words, even as they echo in my chambers.

Because somewhere deep inside of me, down at the flint in my soul, I feel a spark.

CHAPTER 3

Lyanndra

The sun has already risen and set again by the time I find the wyrm's lair.

It's right where the old man said it would be, a craggy hole chiseled into the barren hillsides a few miles out from the village. The mouth of the den glowers angrily through the gathering darkness, illuminated faintly by a pulsing red glow. It could easily be mistaken as the welcome flicker of a cooking fire, but anyone foolish enough to make that error would find themselves being served as dinner rather than eating it.

Barra seems to know this too. The monstrous steed snorts and dances beneath me, her giant hooves scraping at the rocky ground in excitement. I sink deeper into the saddle to encourage her to settle.

She's not afraid.

She's *hungry*.

Leaning forward, I kick one leg over her broad hindquarters and then slither down her side to the ground. When she turns her head to look at me, her fiery red eyes spark like coals in the night.

"Easy," I tell the kelpie as I smooth a gloved hand over the dolphin-like hide of her neck. "Stay here, and I'll bring you something good to eat."

Barra whickers but doesn't move as I rifle through the saddlebags.

"Let's give this a try," I murmur as I pull a thin crystal phial from the depths of one of the packs. Icy cerulean liquid swirls within. A crone from one of the eastern roosts gave it to me many months ago, claiming that it would coat my blade with frost. I've never heard of such a thing, but it piqued my interest enough for me to want to test it out now.

I'm already encased in the sturdy shell of my armor. The gold helm rests on my head, secured by a thin leather strap beneath my chin. I draw my greatsword from its sheath on my back and heft it in my palms before placing it down on the rocky ground.

Using the sharp edge of my dagger, I pry the cork from the slim neck of the phial. It jumps free with a dull pop. The scent of pine and fresh snow wafts up as I shake a few beads of the brilliant blue liquid onto the greatsword.

The effect is as immediate as it is surprising. The substance hisses when it hits the metal. I expect the droplets to run down the steel, but instead they creep out into a latticework of frost until the entire blade is crusted in a vibrant, icy husk.

"By the stars." I grin. I can feel the cold radiating from the greatsword even as I stand above it. It certainly is a wonder.

After corking the phial and replacing it safely in the saddlebag, I retrieve my weapon from where it lies on the ground. I don't stop marveling at the frozen glow of it as I pick my way across the rocky terrain toward the mouth of the cave.

It's only when I'm close enough to the entrance of the den to hear the slither of serpentine scales from inside that my focus narrows. The ruddy glow paints the walls of the opening with lazy color, but the wyrm itself casts a great black shadow against it. It looks to be about the size of Barra—and just about as deadly.

I glance around at the moonlit landscape. It's barren except for some scraggly scrub clinging desperately to the rocky soil. A wyrm won't do well out here in the open. They're burrowing creatures that generally prefer to lay low in caves and crevices, only venturing out at night to snag their prey. If I can lure it out here, it'll have nowhere to hide.

Hefting the flat side of the greatsword onto my shoulder and ignoring the chill that surges through me at the contact, I stoop down and select a large, jagged stone from amidst the smaller pieces of gravel. I take a moment to squint up at the mouth of the cave, plotting the trajectory.

And then I throw the rock.

It arcs up high into the air before it plummets down into the ground a few feet before the den's entrance, clattering loudly against the boulders until it comes to rest amidst the scrub.

A strange, dry rattle echoes from the cave. The light from within grows in intensity as the wyrm slithers closer and closer to the entrance until I finally see it looming halfway up the hillside like something out of a nightmare.

It's like staring down a colossal earthworm. A maw filled with several rows of serrated, triangular teeth juts out from its eyeless face. Its rust-colored scales rustle as it approaches the spot where the rock landed to investigate the source of the noise. A tiny, atrophied pair of wings flutters in excitement, producing the same parched rattle. Aside from the heat that puffs off the wyrm's body in that eerie crimson glow, the wings are the only visible reminder that this thing is distantly related to the great dragons that once populated the skies.

Moving carefully, I pluck a second stone off the ground. The wyrm, even with its sharp sense of hearing to offset its blindness, doesn't seem to notice.

This time, I toss the rock away from the mouth of the cave. It lands only a few feet away from me, a little too close for comfort.

The wyrm rattles its wings again and slides toward me. My grip tightens on the handle of my greatsword as the beast whispers closer. I draw in a breath and hold it, willing myself to stay calm. The scaled coils of its body come within inches of my feet, and I feel a scream building in my chest as its sinuous tail nearly smacks my greaves, but then it's past me.

I raise the blade from my shoulder in a smooth, soundless motion. I'm now between the wyrm and its den. It has nowhere to go.

Using all of my weight for leverage, I slam the sharp tip of the greatsword down into the root of the wyrm's tail. The icy steel steams as it drives through the wyrm's rusty scales and down into its flesh. No sound comes out of the creature's mouth. It writhes and tries to loosen the blade, its broad teeth gnashing silently in the night.

When I wrench the greatsword loose, a great sulfurous cloud shoots up from the gash in the great creature's hide. Coughing, I stumble backward. That instinctual reaction saves me as the wyrm's tail whips over the ground where I was just standing, sending up a shower of gravel.

I dart back into the fray, this time hacking the greatsword down just behind the atrophied wings. The joint there is articulated, which makes severing it all the easier. My blade cleaves through the wyrm's body, catching briefly on the cartilage before neatly severing the creature in half.

The smell is nearly unbearable as the back end of the creature thuds to the ground in a lifeless coil. It reeks of sulfur tinged with a sharp edge of iron. I retch inside my helm, but manage to swallow the bile back down. This fight isn't over yet. I can be sick when it's done.

Unlike its other half, the head of the wyrm is still very much alive. Without the rest of its body, it isn't very mobile, but its mouth still works. The teeth glimmer in the dull red light as it snaps at the air, confused and in pain.

I approach it cautiously. It hears me coming and lashes out, but I quickly sidestep the strike. "I'm sorry," I murmur sadly to the creature as I raise my greatsword up on last time for the killing blow. "I know you were only trying to eat."

Gravity draws the blade down with a sickening thud.

It's over.

I lay the sword on the ground and then flop down beside it. A deep sigh escapes my lips and streams through the visor of my helm as weariness threatens to overtake me. I was hoping to ride back to the village tonight, but the thought of all those miles in the saddle has me squinting through the darkness toward the hillside where I know I can take shelter in the wyrm's den.

Wyrms like warm, dry places. Its den will make for a comfortable camp.

Groaning, I sit up. My armor clangs as I scramble to my feet and retrieve my greatsword. The vibrant blue of the frost is gone, replaced by a sticky coating of the wyrm's sulfurous blood. I don't dare replace it in its sheath like that, so I drag the blade behind me as I clamber up to the opening in the rock.

"Barra!" I call over my shoulder.

The kelpie heeds my voice. She moves through the night like it's water, moonlight rippling over her tough hide as she picks her way up the incline toward me. She stops beside me and waits patiently as I unbuckle the saddlebags and the bedroll, though her eyes dart eagerly over to the wyrm even as I pull off her saddle and slide the bridle over her head. Once freed, she trots away toward the corpse of the wyrm without so much as a glance in my direction.

My stomach clenches.

At least one of us will eat well tonight.

I drop Barra's tack just inside the cave's entrance. It's so dark in here that I can barely see my own hand in front of my face. A fire is in order.

I've got some kindling stashed away in the saddlebags, so I pile it up a short distance into the cave before taking out my flint and striking it off the edge of my sword. Eventually, the sparks catch, washing the stone space in a warm, flickering light.

Just as I predicted, the wyrm's den is surprisingly comfortable. I even feel safe enough to shed my armor, since the scent of the creature will keep predators away.

Once I've stripped down to my dragonhide leathers, I get to work cleaning my greatsword. It only takes a little water from my flask and a couple of rags to divest the weapon of wyrm's blood. I toss the soiled scraps of fabric into the fire, flinching slightly as the flames momentarily leap, and then replace the blade in its sheath.

Finally, I spread out my bedroll on the cold stone floor and crawl inside. I know I should eat something, but the lingering stench of the wyrm makes my guts churn. Hopefully, sleep will take me before my stomach revolts.

It's warm inside the bedroll. Not wanting to spend my night sweating, I pull off my gloves to reveal the pale skin of my palms. Shadows dance over my knuckles as I stretch my fingers out.

These are women's hands, hidden beneath the armor of a knight. They're calloused and scarred from battle and travel, but the truth is undeniable. What might they look like if I had stayed in my little village in the Southern Caldera? I scrutinize my left fourth finger in particular. Would there be a ring there if I hadn't left to become the Godslayer?

My dozing mind wanders to the previous night at the tavern. Those women talked about the Crown Prince's Ceremony of the Crossed Stars, about how it would feel to look down and find the Demigod's ring on their finger, as though that was something to aspire to.

A ring like that would be a curse.

Something glints out of the corner of my eye, and I realize that it's the golden helm flashing in the firelight. The inlaid stars wink lazily at me, reminding me of the old Demigod legend they depict.

It's said that thousands of seasons ago, there were no Demigods or Starless. People were just people. As the story goes, one night the gods looked down and saw that some individuals were superior, so the heavens sent a shower of stars down to earth as a gift. Those chosen by the gods inherited great power from the fallen stars, thought to be the spark of divinity itself. Those who were lesser did not receive those blessings and were shunned as Starless. Over time, the Demigods' power had coalesced into the rule of the Celestial Court while the Starless such as myself had been pushed to farther and farther extremes of society.

It's not a story I choose to believe, but it's probably gospel to the Crown Prince. His father before him was certainly willing to kill in the name of the legend, to wage war against the Starless and lay waste to much of Alastria.

Will the Flaming God's son follow in those same footsteps?

If he does, I'll kill him too.

My stomach roils again, and this time, it has nothing to do with the festering corpse of the wyrm outside. I feel sick for the woman who ends up bonded forever to the son of such a tyrant. I'm only glad that, as a Starless, I can fall asleep tonight knowing that I'll still be free when I wake up in the morning.

Still, that queasy feeling doesn't quite fade, even as sleep presses me to her bosom.

Whoever that poor woman is, she's doomed. After all, who could ever love a Demigod?

I think I would rather die than be bonded to the Crown Prince of the Celestial Court.

CHAPTER 4

SYRAN

"Breathe, cousin," Kartas whispers from beside me. "It wouldn't be very kingly of you to pass out on your big night." He punctuates his words with a discrete elbow to my ribs.

I keep my eyes fixed straight ahead and school my features into an emotionless mask.

From my other side, Ressa hisses, "Quiet, you idiot."

Even though I can't see him, I know my cousin is probably grinning in that sly, foxy way of his. It's an expression I'm quite familiar with, one that carries trouble in its wake. Even now, after so many years spent growing up and becoming men together, Kartas is still the same as he always was.

It seems that some people never change.

With great effort, I shift my focus back to Torran. He's reciting script from an ancient, leather-bound tome. Both the elderly Demigod and the book look like they could crumble to dust at any moment. Snippets of the language are vaguely recognizable, but most of the chanting means nothing to me. It's the tongue of our ancestors, prose forgotten to time and the stars.

I suppress a sigh. This part of the Ceremony of the Crossed Stars is the most tedious. I've sat through many of them as the Crown Prince of the Celestial Court, and it's no more interesting now at my own than it was at anybody else's.

But on the other hand, I'm dreading the moment that Torran's droning ceases. That's when I'll be called to play my reluctant part in this charade. Of course, most of the assembled courtiers are aware that none of the other Demigods were born beneath my star sign. My relationship with Ressa, superficial as it may be, is common knowledge in Nexus. The actual rites will only be for show, nothing more.

There will be no surprises this night.

My gaze wanders over to the crowd. The cathedral is full to bursting, with bodies packed between the marble columns and lining the stone pews. Everybody in attendance is draped in jewels and fine fabrics that glimmer in the dim candlelight. I'm sure that the less fortunate citizens of Nexus are swarmed outside in a similar manner, waiting with bated breath as the moon rises to its highest point in the sky. Some of the more devout members of the court have their heads tipped forward in silent prayer, but most of the Demigods are watching the proceedings with the same polite boredom as I am.

After several long minutes, Torran finally recites one last, unintelligible phrase, pauses, and then gently places the book on a nearby podium.

I risk a glance over at Kartas, whose smirk has only intensified, and Ressa, who looks about as sick as I feel, before I turn back to face the old Demigod.

"Syran, Crown Prince of the Celestial Court, Lord of the Midnight Flame," Torran booms, "approach the altar."

I do as he instructs. My feet are leaden, matching the weight that dampens the pit of my stomach. The few steps across the dais feel interminable, and yet I reach my destination far too quickly.

"You carry the gift of the gods," Torran proclaims as I stand before the altar. It's a pedestal of moonstone, carved hundreds of years before I was born. The top is concave, and the material is crudely chiseled and chipped in many places. Runes, some faded beyond recognition, line the base of the bowl, but I can't make any sense of them. In the glittering, smooth splendor of the Celestial Court, there's something troubling about this flawed and rough-hewn basin.

"The gods have blessed me," I say, reciting the words that Torran taught me. My voice rings hollowly through the eaves of the cathedral like a death knell. "Now, I ask the stars to bestow their virtue unto me."

"Offer your flame," the elderly Demigod prompts. He gestures to the moonstone bowl with frail fingers.

It is through sheer will that my hand does not shake as I raise it to the altar and call the fire. It curls to life in my palm, as black and depthless as the mantle I wear at my shoulders. I tip my hand and release the flame, allowing it to flow like water from my skin into the depths of the ancient basin.

The fire leaps within the confines of the altar. Black facets flash through the moonstone and cast flickering shadows across the faces of the amassed courtiers. Perhaps it's a trick of the light, but I think that I see fear in some of their eyes.

Torran steps toward me. In the glow of the dark blaze, his skin seems more sallow now, though his blue eyes shine as bright as flints. "The rings," he states gravely as he passes me a small wooden box.

I take it readily and pop the inlaid lid open. Two rings, one sized to my finger and the other much smaller, glitter in the curling light. The larger piece of jewelry features a large, square-cut onyx set into a wide gold band. The surface of the stone is carved with a delicate, twisting serpent, the insignia of the royal family. The other gold piece matches it perfectly, a miniature replica, albeit with a slightly thinner band.

"Place the ring on your finger," Torran instructs, as though he and I hadn't rehearsed this very scene a dozen times in the last fortnight.

Forgoing the urge to grit my teeth, I slip the band onto the fourth finger of my left hand. The metal is cold and heavy, unfamiliar against my skin. It weighs far more than I ever would have imagined.

Torran nods in satisfaction. "You may now present your vows to the stars."

The sour ball in the pit of my stomach writhes like a living thing. It hisses and spits, urging me to keep quiet.

But I can't.

My throne depends on this moment.

I open my mouth and let the words tumble out, just as I learned them.

"I offer my flame in penance to the stars. I offer this ring in supplication to the gods. Grant me wisdom for my faith. Reveal to me the soul who shares the heavens with my spirit, my crossed star. Bind us in honor and in death, in mind and in madness. Behold us as one beneath your moon and sky."

And this time, I can't stop my hand from shaking as I pluck the second ring from the box and drop it into the fire.

Nothing happens.

A sigh builds in my chest at the sight. My parents were correct.

I really don't have a crossed star.

The Ceremony is over.

I turn toward Kartas and Ressa. Kartas' smirk still remains, while my betrothed regards me with stark relief written plainly across her regal features. I take one step toward them, fully intending to sweep out of the packed cathedral with the two of them on my heels, when a startled gasp from Torran spins me back around to face the altar.

The flame, which had just been fluttering so demurely in the moonstone basin only moments before, has risen up into a gnarled, serpentine blaze.

My blood freezes at the sight. The very air around me seems to coalesce, dredging the breath from my lungs. My heart hammers against my ribs as I try desperately to make sense of the scene before me.

The fire crests in a hissing roar, nearly licking the high peak of the ceiling, before it's sucked back into the bowl, where it crumples into itself until there's nothing left but ash.

I peer down in the altar, but I'm met with the dreadful realization that I already know what I'll find once the smoke clears.

The bowl is empty.

The ring is gone.

Whispers surge through the spectators. They echo off the marble walls and froth together into a shambling mass of noise. There's a flurry of motion as the assembled Demigods check their hands for the missing ring. I half expect there to be a shout from one of them, some sign that my crossed star is in this room, but there's no joyous declaration, no victorious exaltation.

"Syran?" Torran's voice cuts through the rumble of unrest. I whip around to face him, desperate for answers, but his face is inscrutable.

"This wasn't supposed to happen," I mutter frantically as I scan the crowd with renewed desperation. "How could this be?"

Kartas materializes at my shoulder, where he always is in times of trouble. "I can't say I saw this coming," he admits in a low voice that's too quiet for the crowd to hear.

"It's not possible," I insist.

"And yet the stars have deigned it so," Torran cuts in. "The situation is clear. The ring is with your crossed star now."

I shake my head, refusing to believe it. "But Ressa...."

"She isn't wearing the ring," Kartas says softly. "I'm sorry."

The thought doesn't pain me as much as I had imagined it would. Instead, I feel a curious tugging feeling in my chest, though panic swiftly overrides the sensation.

"Then who is?" I snap.

My cousin glances at the murmuring Demigods in the pews before fixing his gaze on me. "Not anybody in here," he states firmly. "Let's send guards out to check the city. Somebody must be wearing the ring. Whoever it is, we'll find them. Maybe they're even on their way here as we speak."

I don't want to believe that this is even happening, but I find myself nodding along with Kartas' plan. Part of me hopes that the guards will find the ring discarded somewhere, the result of some faulty magic or machination of the stars.

With my blessing, Kartas rushes off to facilitate the search.

Ressa quickly slides into the spot where he stood. Tears track down her face, painting rivulets of kohl across her cheeks. Her dark eyes are wild with disbelief as she pushes past me to stare down into the empty moonstone basin.

I reach for her, but my hand stops on its own accord when I catch sight of the ring that now sits solidly on my own finger.

"No," Ressa sobs. She paws at the bowl, as though she might find the missing band if she were to look hard enough. "No!"

"Ressa," I plead. I'm not sure what to say. "Please calm down."

Those were the wrong words to utter. She whirls around, her delicate skirts fanning out as she fixes me with a scathing glare. "I will fix this," she hisses. "I *will* be your queen."

Before I can respond, she shoves past me and runs from the dais, where the crowd swallows her up like an eager beast. I open my mouth to call out after her, but Torran's hand on my shoulder stops me.

"Let her go," he says quietly.

"But..."

"Let her go. She'll need time," the old man insists. In contrast to my own flustered demeanor, Torran looks positively calm. While the chaos seethes around us, he's the eye of the storm, steady and dependable.

Black embers smolder in my palms. I want to explode, but I need to keep myself together.

I need to act like a king.

I draw in a deep breath and ask, "What does this mean?"

Torran's eyes dance in the candlelight.

"You'll find out soon enough."

CHAPTER 5

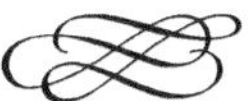

Lyanndra

None of this is real.

The dry warmth of the cave is gone, replaced by the cool, fragrant air of the midlands. The world is awash in moonlight, though the corners of the balcony I find myself on are draped in the beckoning lace of shadows.

I grip the iron railing with my bare fingers as I lean slightly over the edge. Below lies a magnificent garden bursting with all sorts of wondrous blooms. The night mutes the colors and transforms the flowers into a patchwork of grays and blacks, but the shapes of the petals and the outlines of the leaves are more than enough to impress me.

That's how I know that this is a dream, no matter how awake I feel. There are no flowers like this in Alastria. Save Nexus, I have wandered every inch of the continent, and never in my life have I seen anything so otherworldly as this.

I'm so enraptured by the scene that spills out beneath me that I don't notice I have company until the stranger steps up behind me.

In the waking world, I would be on the newcomer in a flash with my dagger pressed into his neck. But this is a dreamscape where impossible flowers bloom in the liquid silver moonlight. The certainty that nothing can harm me here is absolute.

The man is so close that I can feel the smooth planes of his bare chest against my back. The scent of ash and kindling clings to him, strong and distinct, but not unpleasant. He moves his hands to my waist, where his fingers splay hotly against the swell of my hips. I shiver, though there's no chill in the air.

Nobody has ever touched me this way.

That's when I realize that I'm no longer wearing my dragonhide leathers. Instead, I'm draped in a gauzy white nightdress and nothing else. The fabric is the finest thing I've ever seen, right down to the silver embroidery that decorates the low, plunging bodice. My long hair, usually constrained tightly in a plait or braided close against my crown, hangs loose over my shoulders in honeyed waves.

"Welcome home," the man murmurs. The words curl along the shell of my ear, igniting something deep inside of me that sets my blood on fire. Even in the heat of battle, I've never felt anything like this, and for the first time in this moonlit dream, I feel a sharp pang of fear.

"Who are you?" My voice, which once heralded the death of a god, comes out as little more than a whisper.

"I am yours," he breathes. His tone is sinful and full of dark promise. "I have always been yours."

I don't understand. I open my mouth to ask him once again, but the question melts on my tongue as he dips his head and presses his lips to the pulse point where my neck and shoulder meet.

Goosebumps dance across my skin where his teeth graze my flesh. My warrior's instinct urges me to push him away from my most vulnerable point, but something deeper, something buried, makes me tip my head to the side to allow him more access instead.

He rewards my compliance by drawing me closer so that I can feel every angle and every plane of his body through the thin fabric of my nightdress. A moan tumbles from my lips as the heaviness of his arousal presses against the small of my back.

I do not like to think of myself as naïve. As a knight, I've seen men stand naked before me, more times than I care to remember. I've sat through countless boasts of sexual prowess and endowment, of conquests and lovemaking. I've even had the intense misfortune of walking in on a fellow soldier relieving his own lust on one occasion.

But I have never once lain with a man.

The risks of revealing the truth were always too great. I could be a knight, or I could be a woman, but I could never be both.

But here, in this impossible world, I don't have to hide. My armor is gone, banished to reality with the golden helm, my greatsword, and the rest of what makes me the Godslayer.

Here, I am just Lyanndra.

And I know now what I want from this dream.

I turn in the man's arms to face him. He's so much taller than me, towering over me by more than a foot. His chest and shoulders are wide and muscular, and I wonder who he is, if he's a warrior. Looking down, he wears nothing but a pair of trousers.

I tilt my head up to catch a glimpse of his face. The darkness cloaks his features in shadow, but something deep in some forgotten corner of my mind whispers that I know him and that he knows me. It feeds me the courage I need to raise onto my toes and press my lips against his.

His mouth meets mine with barely concealed hunger. The kiss is bruising and leaves me breathless when he pulls away seconds later. I lean in again, eager for more, but he steps back, breaking the contact between our bodies.

Shame floods through me as I wonder what I did wrong to cause such a quick retreat. But that embarrassment quickly twists into desire as he once again closes the distance between us, this time to grasp me around the middle and fling me over his shoulder like I weigh nothing at all.

I gasp at the sudden motion, and he chuckles in response. It's a dirty sound, a promise that has me squeezing my thighs together as he carries me from the balcony and into the room beyond.

The chamber we enter is as lavish as the gardens below. Marble walls seem to glow in the moonlight. We pass a huge onyx fireplace, the grate cold and empty, before we reach the bed. It's massive, trimmed with black silk and golden accents that dance amidst the shadows of the night.

The man tosses me unceremoniously onto the mattress. I barely have time to appreciate how the luxurious sheets slide against my skin before he's on top of me, claiming me with his mouth and tongue.

There is nothing gentle about this kiss. The taste of him stokes the frenzy of desire that burns deep in my core. It's overwhelming, consuming. And just as I think that this must be the unspeakable pleasure that men fight over and women beg for, the stranger starts to touch me.

His fingers brush the swell of my chest, tracing the outline of my breasts through the thin material of the nightdress. Pleasure sparks across my skin, and I instinctively arch into his touch, wanting more.

He wastes no time in obliging. His palm skims over one breast, where he teases my taut nipple through the fabric. At the same time, his mouth leaves mine to trail a scalding path down my neck and into the hollow of my collarbone before his lips move lower to nip at the skin just above the bodice of my dress.

Siren sounds spill from me as he grasps the edge of the thin garment and pulls. The material tears cleanly down the middle to expose my bare breasts to the cool night air and his mercy.

The man doesn't give me the chance to feel self-conscious. His mouth immediately closes over the bead of my nipple, hot and desperate, while I arch into him, hungry for more. Now free, his hands wander shamelessly over my body to clutch my thighs and the curve of my ass.

At one point, his fingers graze the very edge of my core, drawing a moan from me. Bewitched by his ministrations, I thrust my hips up in a desperate plea for more friction.

He does not deprive me. A growl rolls from his chest as he sits up and grinds against me, and for the first time, it strikes me that perhaps I can offer him the same pleasure he's teased from me.

I start slow, running my hands up the smooth, corded muscle of his arms. Even though his face is still hazy with shadow, I can feel his gaze locked on me, as sharp and hot as flame. Emboldened, I continue my explorations along his shoulders and pecs, then down his abs toward the low-slung waist of his trousers.

But when I reach for the laces, he catches both my wrists up in one hand and pins them over my head, far from temptation.

The sudden loss of control should frighten me, but instead, I find it exhilarating. My heart thrums in anticipation as he uses his unoccupied hand to tug the laces free and push his trousers down to reveal his cock.

I eye his length warily as he strokes it. It's bigger than I had imagined it would be, especially for a maiden such as myself. Anxiety skitters down my spine for a moment before I remind myself that this is just a dream.

He won't hurt me.

Picking up on my sudden trepidation, he moves his hold from my wrists and instead trails his fingers down until they come to rest on the hem of my nightdress. A casualty of our passion, the long skirt is now hiked up high above my knees, well past the point of decency.

He continues to pump his cock even as he dips his hand beneath the edge of my dress. I squirm, hesitant, until his fingers brush up against the sensitive flesh between my legs.

Pleasure ricochets through my nerves at his touch. I press my hips into his palm as he curls one finger into my wet heat, stretching me in a way that's both foreign and delicious. The sensation is unreal, churning the flames inside of me until I'm squirming and panting against him.

I cry out as he adds a second finger. He coaxes ecstasy from my small frame, all the while pleasuring himself to my wanton moans. The tension builds, curling through my limbs as he draws me closer and closer to *something*, and just when I think I'll snap from the pressure, he pulls his hand away and leaves me shaking and gasping for air.

The respite only lasts long enough for him to grab my hips and pull me down roughly toward him. The tip of his cock sits heavily against my entrance.

My mouth opens in a soundless groan as he thrusts into me with a slow, calculated roll of his hips. There's a twinge of pain as something inside me gives, but the hot friction as he sheaths himself in me quickly overshadows the sensation.

I've never felt so full. He stills for a moment, allowing me to adjust to the size of him, before he pulls out. A hiss escapes him as he impales me on his cock once more, and then again, and again.

Fresh pleasure courses through me with every thrust, and soon, my hips rise to meet his. His mouth finds mine and he nips at my lips before capturing me in a grueling kiss. He's everywhere inside of me, consuming me like kindling in a bonfire, igniting me until I'm on the edge of something I don't understand, something bright and wild, something ablaze.

And then I shatter beneath him with an unbridled cry.

The world swims around me as he rolls his hips once, twice, and then one last time before he, too, finds his release. He growls into the darkness while he pulses inside me, claiming me as his own.

But it's not dark anymore, not completely.

The watery light of dawn is starting to filter in through the open doors of the balcony. With it comes a strange tugging in my chest, as though I've forgotten something important.

I gaze up at him, hoping to finally see his face clearly, but his features are smudged like smoke. I can't even tell what color his hair is. Even his outline is hazy and undefined, dissolving in the growing light.

"Wait," I plead. I try to grasp his arms, but they're no longer solid. He's just an outline now. "Wait!" I cry, reaching for him, reaching…

And then I'm awake.

I sit up, blinking hard.

The wyrm's den solidifies around me, warm and close. The fire has dwindled down to embers that glow softly in the thin gray light of early morning. Inside my bedroll, I'm fully dressed in my dragonhide leathers, save for the gloves that lie beside me on the ground where I left them the night before. The weight of the man is gone, but the pleasure he gave me is still present in the slick ache between my thighs.

I sigh and bury my face in my hands. I don't know whether to feel satisfied, humiliated, or both.

It was just a dream.

A weird, sensual dream.

I decide to put it out of my mind and just get started with my day. Even though it's early, it's still a long ride back to the village. I'll confirm that the job is done, collect whatever reward the old man is willing to give me, and move on.

Feeling a bit steadier, I reach over to grab my gloves. But something on one of my hands catches in the low light, something that wasn't there the night before.

Confusion swirls through me as I lift my hand closer to my face and squint at the object that now sits on my left ring finger.

And then a bubble of horror bursts in my chest as I realize that I'm looking at an onyx ring.

The ring.

The ring of the Crown Prince of the Celestial Court.

CHAPTER 6

Syran

I saw her.

I saw her!

My heart thunders in my chest as I startle awake. I'm in bed, alone, in my private chamber as I have been since I retreated here last night after the shocking results of the Ceremony. Black silk sheets pool around my waist, though the fabric does little to conceal the evidence of last night's spent desire.

I blink against the burgeoning sunlight that trickles in through the open balcony doors and try to picture the woman from my dream, my crossed star. But my impression of her physical form is vague and clouded by heady arousal. All I remember is the smell of her, a strange mix of horse, leather, and metal, and the feeling of her small, calloused hands against my skin as she massaged my cock in the velvet grip of her womanhood.

A growl of frustration snarls from my throat.

Who is she?

She's not a Demigod, of that I am sure. Her hands were not soft like those of the fine noblewomen who grace the halls of the Celestial

Court. She didn't carry the scent of any flowery fragrances, nor were her chipped and quickened nails painted in delicate colors.

She was like no woman in Nexus.

And that could only mean one thing.

I squeeze my eyes shut, banishing the very notion of it. I can't bring myself to even think about the consequences such a thing would have for me, her, or Alastria.

But she's still powerful, somehow. I felt it in her grip, in the lithe way she moved beneath me. And there was something else about her, something deeper…

I shake my head. I'll have all the answers I need once I find her, but how can I possibly figure out who she is?

There's only one person who can help me now.

I jump out of bed, stumbling slightly as my legs tangle in the sheets. I wash and dress haphazardly, throwing on the first tunic and pair of trousers I find before yanking my boots on without doing up the laces properly. Satisfied that I look presentable enough that I won't scare the servants, I stride out of my chambers in search of Torran.

I find him in the first place I look. He sits at the long table in the royal dining room, which is set for breakfast. A tome, the same one from the Ceremony, is cracked open before him, and he's so engrossed in the text that he doesn't seem to notice my arrival.

Kartas, however, does. He's lounging at the setting closest to the head of the table with his feet resting easily on the wooden surface. Several plates of food are stacked before him, and he looks to be about halfway through the process of devouring them all, including the one balanced precariously on his lap.

"Cousin," he greets me. "Did you sleep well?" His tone is far too innocent for my liking.

I narrow my eyes, and he grins.

"It seems that the legends are true that your crossed star visits you in your dreams if you don't find them right away," he says slyly. "From the sounds you were making, you two got on quite well."

"Don't say another word," I warn him as a mix of anger and

embarrassment flushes through me. If anybody else had needled me like that, they'd be skewered upon my black flame in an instant. But Kartas' words never come with any ill will, annoying as they are.

"You saw her?" Torran asks, breaking me from my fantasies of revenge.

I glance over the old Demigod, who's finally registered my presence, and nod. "But she was... unclear."

"How so?" he queries. His eyes are bright and wide now that his full attention is fixed upon me.

"Her features were like smoke," I explain. "But it was her. I'm sure of it."

"And you didn't recognize her?" Kartas butts in.

I shake my head. "No."

Torran's gaze sharpens at this new piece of information, but it's my cousin who speaks first.

"Perhaps she's some Demigod from beyond the continent?" he suggests. "Or from a family that's somehow lived in secret outside of Nexus?"

I open my mouth to answer, but my voice catches in my throat. How am I supposed to explain my impressions without revealing what I fear most?

But my silence is an answer too. Incredulousness dawns across Torran's face, though Kartas just watches me expectantly, not yet making the connection.

Finally, I stammer, "She's... I don't think she's a Demigod, exactly."

Kartas' mouth falls open in shock, and I thank the stars that he isn't in the middle of chewing another mouthful of his breakfast. "Starless?" he gapes. "Your crossed star is *Starless*?"

"Quiet," I hiss, but it's already too late. Any servant or courtier within a five-mile radius probably heard my cousin's little outburst. Within the hour, everybody in the Celestial Court will be aware, if not the entirety of Nexus. I turn to Torran, hoping that he can give me some answers before this all gets out of hand. "Is that even possible?" I demand.

"Of course it's not possible!" Kartas counters before the old man can speak. "Only Demigods have crossed stars. Even children know that!"

Torran holds up one frail hand to stop my cousin's tirade. He motions down to the book before him. The pages are filled with delicate symbols transcribed in dark ink, all of them unreadable to me. The old Demigod, however, seems to have no trouble deciphering the ancient code.

"This is the incantation from the Ceremony," he explains as he runs one finger beneath one sloping line of text. In the next breath, he utters something unintelligible, though the sounds themselves are slightly familiar from the many times I've sat through the Ceremony of the Crossed Stars.

"Well, that really clears things up," Kartas grumbles before shoving a forkful of eggs into his mouth.

I roll my eyes at him, but Torran doesn't react. He's still watching me with that careful gaze, the one that makes me wonder exactly how much this old man knows.

"Do you understand what that means?" he asks. When I shake my head, he offers, "It's written in the sacred text that crossed stars are matched in power."

"Power?" I muse.

Torran nods. "Most scholars interpret this passage as referring to the power of the stars, of divinity. A Demigod who has been blessed by the heavens could only be matched to somebody of similar power," he explains. "And thus, the crossed star of a Demigod could only ever be a Demigod. Divinity begets divinity."

"That's just a fancy way of repeating what I just said," Kartas argues.

"No," Torran denies patiently. "It's not." He points back down to the writing in the book, as though we'd suddenly be able to make sense of it. "That is how the passage is interpreted, but that is not necessarily what it *means*."

"Power," I say again, this time in realization. "You're saying that this woman is just as powerful as I am?"

The old Demigod smiles thinly. "Perhaps not through divinity, but through other means."

"Like what?" Kartas demands.

"Alas, you ask for answers I do not have. But there is one who does possess them," Torran replies sagely. "Syran's crossed star."

Both men look at me expectantly, as though I'll summon this mysterious woman out of thin air for them. When I don't, I break the silence and ask, "How am I supposed to find her?"

Kartas sighs. He's clearly not happy about the idea that my crossed star could be Starless, but he's still my closest ally. He would do anything for me, including this.

"Messengers," he suggests after a brief moment of rumination. "Send them out to every corner of Alastria. Have them spread the word that whoever finds the ring on her finger should come to the Celestial Court in a fortnight's time, where you will welcome her with a grand celebration."

I consider this carefully. It's not a bad plan. The kingdom is large, but the network of messengers that run intelligence, correspondence, and proclamations is both vast and efficient. The news will spread quickly, even among the Starless. It's a better option than riding out myself to check every last hovel for my crossed star.

"Do it," I command. "And if she requires an escort or more time to travel, it shall be granted."

Kartas, whose jovial manner has slipped into the cool demeanor of my most trusted general, bows his head in acknowledgement. He doesn't even gripe about not finishing his breakfast. Instead, he strides out of the room with great purpose. Seconds later, the sound of his voice barking orders to various Demigod knights drifts in through the open doors of the dining room.

With a sigh, I sink down into the chair at the head of the table. My stomach growls, and I realize that I haven't eaten anything since the previous evening. Not bothering to wait for anybody to serve me, I fill up my plate and pour myself a cup of hot tea from a silver urn.

"You'll find her," Torran assures me once I begin to eat.

"Perhaps. But the Starless hate the Demigods. There's no guarantee that she'll receive the message or heed it if she does," I fret. "What Starless woman would come to me willingly?"

"If the stars have crossed you, there must be a reason," he answers in a measured tone. "You will know more once she's here with you."

I don't want to ask what will happen if she doesn't come to me, so I instead pose, "What of these powers? I've never heard of any Starless on par with a Demigod."

Torran shakes his head. "I wish I knew," he admits. "I've never heard of any other match than between two Demigods, but it is possible that this has happened before. I will consult the archives. Perhaps I can find something to help explain this."

"Thank you."

The elderly Demigod smiles fondly as he stands and gathers up his book. "Have hope, Syran," he urges. He offers me a reassuring squeeze of the shoulder before exiting the dining room, presumably to dig up more musty tomes.

And then I'm alone, with only the faceless specter of my crossed star for company.

All I can do now is wait.

CHAPTER 7

Lyanndra

The ring will not come off.

I glare down at the slender golden band that sits flush against my skin. The onyx stone is as dark as my mood and shines innocently in the glare of the morning sun.

Now that the initial shock has worn off, I'm slowly but surely attempting to remove the ominous portent from where it lingers.

I tug at it again, willing the ring to slide up and over the joint. But it doesn't budge. It's as though the band is affixed to my finger, even if there's no pain as I attempt to twist it loose.

Frustrated, I decide it's time to resort to more drastic measures. I kneel with my knees in the dirt and splay my left hand on the ground before me. With the right, I select a particularly hefty rock from the surrounding scrub. Before I bring it down on my finger, I grit my teeth.

This is going to hurt.

Gravity takes over as I hammer the stone down. I expect a bolt of pain, maybe some blood, but the rock just ricochets off the gold and onyx ring, missing my hand entirely.

The stone slides from my grasp and clatters back to earth beside my outstretched fingers. There's not a single mark on the gleaming band or my skin, not even a bruise.

Dread twists my insides into a tight knot. If I can't damage the ring, will I be able to get it off? I can't let myself consider the possibility.

Not ready to give up quite yet, I backtrack into the cave. The embers of last night's fire still glow amidst the spent kindling. I scuff my boot through the ashes, kicking up sparks. Perhaps a few coals will be hot enough to soften the gold?

I find my answer after several boring and overheated minutes. I'm not sure if it's the metal itself or the magical properties imbued within, but the band doesn't so much as tarnish. The onyx, too, doesn't crack or warp. By the time I finally shake the embers off the ring and back into the dying fire, the cursed piece of jewelry isn't even scorched.

"If fire won't do it, maybe ice will," I hiss as I stalk over to Barra's saddlebags, which are still where I left them the night before by the mouth of the cavern. It only takes me a moment to fish out the delicate crystal phial that I have in mind. The remains of the frosty liquid swirl within and cast a strange blue glow across my fingers. I uncork the thin vessel and am met with that same fresh, pine needle scent as before.

Recalling that only a few drops of the concoction were enough to freeze over the blade of my greatsword in my standoff against the wyrm, I shake a single bead of effervescence out onto the onyx. I wait for frost to crackle forth, but nothing happens.

By the stars, I don't even feel a chill.

Anger rears within me as I cork the phial and drop it back into the saddlebag. The blue liquid slides easily from the ring at the sudden movement, easing across the gem into free fall. The droplet bursts against the stone floor of the cave, sending an eruption of ice skittering across the ground.

Something about the sight of it drives me into a panic. The need to remove the ring now is suffocating, overwhelming. Even though I'm not wearing the golden helm of the Godslayer, I automatically reach up to pull it off. The very air around me is closing in, and the claustrophobia creates a deafening roar in my ears. My lungs feel frozen, as though I drank the icy potion instead of applying it to the onyx.

The weight of the ring is unbearable now. Who knew that gold could be so devastatingly heavy?

I need to get it off.

I need to get it off *now*.

Moving in a blind frenzy, I burst out of the cave into the midmorning sun. My boots slide over stone and scrub as I reach for the dagger I keep strapped against my thigh. The cruel blade, the same one that killed the king, flashes in the light as I release it from its thin scabbard.

I swipe the sharp edge violently at the base of my finger. I don't care anymore if my flesh rends, if blood spatters. All I care about is flaying this damned ring off of my finger, off, *off*...

The dagger's blade slides against my skin as though it were marble.

The ring does not move.

"Fuck!" I howl. The sound rings across the arid landscape, echoing off the high hills. Barra, all but a sleek outline in the distance, starts in surprise at my outburst.

I sink down onto my haunches and stare down dejectedly at the gold band.

How is this possible?

My mind is lost to a tangle of dark theories, of curses and revenge.

I only look up again when Barra's muzzle nudges my shoulder, drawing my attention. She huffs out a stagnant breath that reeks of sulfur from her late night meal, and the smell is enough to draw me out of my agonized stupor.

"What cruel jest is this?" I ask in desperation. "Is this my punishment for slaying a god?"

The kelpie blinks her wide red eyes. Below them, I catch a glimpse of the curve of her jaw, which is lined with yellowed, shark-like teeth. A horrible idea takes root inside of me at the sight.

So far, I've been the one to try to remove the ring. Is it possible that somebody else, or perhaps *something* else, would have more success than I?

I stretch my fingers out. Barra's gaze follows my action.

"Do you see this?" I ask, tilting my hand so the sun catches tantalizingly on the gold and onyx.

My trusted mount stares at it, which I take as an affirmative answer.

"Could you... could you bite it off?" My stomach churns at the words that tumble from my lips, but I have to ask. Losing a finger, or even several, to Barra seems a kinder fate than the alternative.

The kelpie, never one to pass up a meal, darts her head forward, her mouth gaping wide in a broken crocodile grin. Her teeth snap shut over my finger and then...

My hand slides from her maw.

She squeals and rears back, her great hooves kicking out between us, and I realize that her teeth have simply slid off the skin of my finger the same way the dagger did.

The last of my hope slithers away.

I am doomed.

The rest of the morning passes in a blur. I retreat into the safety of habit. My first order of business is to pull on my dragonhide leather gloves. Covering the ring allows me to breathe the smallest sigh of relief, but the weight of the band is still there, unforgettable.

Next, I head to the cave, where I kick some dirt over the campfire to extinguish it fully. Then I don my armor, ease my greatsword into the sheath on my back, and grab the saddlebacks and tack.

By the time I rejoin Barra, she's calmed down to her usual stoicism. As a peace offering, I toss her a chunk of dried meat from one of my bags, which she snaps up easily from its midair trajectory. I can't tell if she's totally forgiven me, but she does stand patiently while I tack her up and secure the saddlebags.

After checking the girth one final time, I grab the horn of the saddle, jam my foot high up into the stirrup, and heft myself up onto the kelpie's back.

I'm in no rush to get back to the village, so I let Barra set the pace at a leisurely walk. Lulled by the smooth rocking of her gait, my mind wanders back to the omnipresent squeeze of the gold band on my finger.

My first thought is that I should kill the Crown Prince.

After all, he's probably the same type of cruel tyrant that his father was. I haven't heard much of him since the war, but that's not surprising given that most of the Demigods retreated to the safety of Nexus, the cradle of the Celestial Court, after the fall of the Flaming God. That doesn't mean much, though. He's probably just biding his time before he can ascend to the throne and unleash some fresh hell upon the Starless.

In a way, slaying him would be a mercy.

But as much as I'd like to plunge a dagger into his heart for binding me to him, I'm not sure that it would accomplish anything. I recall the Demigod legends about crossed stars, the ones that reveal that when one crossed star dies, the loss will drive the other to madness.

I won't take the risk that this is true. I refuse to live as a shell of myself, as an easy target for Demigods seeking revenge.

Murdering the Crown Prince of the Celestial Court is not an option.

Neither is taking my own life, I realize. I wasn't able to harm myself to remove the ring, which only lends credence to another part of the Demigod stories surrounding the crossed stars: neither crossed star can do themselves harm.

I close my eyes and sink deeper into the saddle in defeat. It seems that no matter which course of action I consider, the stars are determined to stand in my way. But surely there is some way to be rid of this curse?

It's only a matter of finding it.

Hours later, as velvet darkness closes in around us, and the lights of the village twinkle in the near distance, I still haven't found a solution. My head aches dully beneath the golden helm, and my body aches from the long ride.

Just as we pass the first buildings that mark the outskirts of civilization, a courier on horseback gallops out of the night toward us, heading out in the direction from whence I came. His eyes widen as he processes the sight of my helm, and he dithers for a moment as though he's unsure whether or not he should stop.

His job gets the better of him in the end. He reins his horse to a halt, though the creature prances uneasily in place in Barra's shadow.

"Godslayer," the courier says. He nods his head but his eyes never quite leave my distinctive armor. "I ride with news from the Celestial Court."

My heart jumps in my chest at the mention of the seat of the Demigods' power. The ring suddenly seems far too bulky beneath my leather gloves and the plated gauntlets that are layered on top. Even though the man can't see my face, I try to keep the fear from creeping across my features.

When I don't say anything, the rider's eyes dart back and forth before landing back on the façade of my helm. "The Crown Prince seeks his crossed star. He calls for her presence at the Celestial Court in a fortnight. The court will gather to receive her."

Beneath the anonymity of my helm, I suck in an inaudible breath. We're almost a week's distance from Nexus, but this messenger carries this news faster than it could possibly travel. It strikes me then that Demigod magic must be responsible.

As though he senses that I'm making this connection, the courier nods once again and then urges his horse forward. The nervous animal surges to a gallop, and within seconds, the man has faded into the darkness at our backs. Was he a Demigod or just carrying the message of one?

On a normal night, I would consider pursuing him and finding out. But this evening, my brain is working far too quickly for me to bother.

A diabolical plan begins to take shape.

In two weeks' time, the Crown Prince and his court will gather to meet his crossed star. They'll all be expecting a lady, fine, refined, and as harmless as a church mouse.

But what if the Godslayer arrives instead?

The son of the Flaming God will never suspect that there's a woman concealed within my armor. If I play the part of the Starless hero, could I goad him into a duel?

Could I trick him into killing me?

The cost would be great, there's no denying that. I possess the survival instincts of a warrior, but this wouldn't be giving up, not if my sacrifice would also drive the Crown Prince to madness. And with the Demigod's ruler incapacitated, the infighting over the throne would fracture their ranks enough for the Starless to start testing those weaknesses.

If I let my crossed star slay me in battle, the Crown Prince goes mad, and the Celestial Court will fall.

As sick as the thought makes me feel, I'd rather be dead than chained to a Demigod for eternity.

This is a sacrifice I'm willing to make.

CHAPTER 8

SYRAN

The welcoming Ceremony is only days away, yet there is still so much more to be done.

At present, I'm in the grand ballroom with Kartas, where the palace kitchens have laid out an impressive spread of dishes on one long table. We're in the process of sampling each of them in order to determine which ones we will feature at the great feast after my crossed star is received in the courtyard.

"This one definitely has to go on the menu," my cousin remarks through a mouthful of stewed lamb.

I nod in agreement, though I honestly couldn't care less about what will be served at the welcoming Ceremony's feast. Instead of the fragrant plates of food before me, all I can think about is my crossed star.

Ever since that first night, the mysterious woman has plagued my dreams. None of the encounters were clear or physical, and I'm not even sure that they were real. By the time I woke with the dawn each morning, my recollection crumbled into vague impressions and fleeting outlines, teasing but never fully revealing the truth that I so desperately seek.

Do I come to her in sleep too? When she opens her eyes to the sun, does she think of me with fondness?

But even with only that tenuous connection between us, I feel strongly that my crossed star is making her way toward Nexus, toward *me*.

Kartas' hand finds my arm and a small jolt of electricity courses through me at the touch.

I jump back from him in a decidedly undignified way, rubbing my skin where he shocked me

"What was that for?" I growl.

My cousin grins. "You were mooning over your Starless woman," he teases. "I asked you to try the prawns three times, and you just stood there drooling like a love-struck fool."

"If any other Demigod used their powers on me like that, I'd have their head," I snap. It's true, and we both know it.

Kartas holds his hands up in surrender. "Really, Syran, I'm trying to help! Daydreaming won't get her here any faster. And think about how upset she'll be when she gets here after such a long journey, and there's nothing to eat because you couldn't be bothered to approve the tasting menu!"

I roll my eyes, though I have to admit that he has a point. I reach down and pluck a prawn off the plate he offers and pop it in my mouth. Flavor dances over my tongue. It's delicious.

"They're good, right?" my cousin prods.

"Yes." I sigh. I hate it when he's right.

We move down the table slowly but surely, sampling each dish as we go. By the time we've reached the dessert spread, I don't think I could eat another bite.

The sounds of heels on the polished marble floors echoes through the hall in a welcome distraction. I turn from the table to greet the newcomer, but my heart sinks as I recognize the willowy form of Ressa striding toward us.

We haven't spoken since the night of the Ceremony. At first, I sought her out in hopes that we could at least still find friendship in each other's company. She was unwilling to see me, however, and her entourage of Demigod noblewomen ushered me away from her each time I tried to talk. I gave up after that, figuring that she would come to me when she was ready to speak.

Now, she approaches without her constant companions. She's wearing a dress in shimmering silver with her dark hair coiled atop her head, and while I can acknowledge that she's a beautiful woman, nothing inside of me sings at the sight of her.

"Ressa!" Kartas greets her. I know him well enough to understand that he's trying to diffuse any tension before it starts, but something tells me that he won't be successful today. "I fear that Syran has overindulged on the main courses, and now he won't even try dessert. Perhaps you could offer me your expert opinion on this meringue?" He holds a plate out to her like a man attempting to placate a great beast.

Ressa does not look amused. She spares Kartas a sour frown and then turns to me in a swish of silver skirts. "May we speak?" she asks me. Her voice is high and cold, and a vein of venom runs white-hot underneath.

"We may," I grant her formally.

Her eyes flicker over to Kartas, who is in the process of stuffing three meringues in his mouth at once. "Alone?" she demands.

"I can take a hint," he grumbles through a mouthful of sugar. Snatching the plate of remaining confections, he retreats across the ballroom.

Once he's disappeared through the tall double doors, Ressa turns back to me. I'm surprised to see that her eyes are rimmed with tears.

"How can you do this to me?" she hisses. "To us?"

I've been dreading this conversation. In the safety of my chambers, I planned out what I would say, how I would soothe her feelings of anger and betrayal. Now, those words all leave me.

"This wasn't… I didn't mean for this to happen," I stammer. "I didn't know, Ressa. I swear I didn't know!"

She shakes her head violently. "You promised!"

Guilt strikes me directly through the heart because she's right. "I shouldn't have," I admit. "It was cruel of me. But I never thought that this would happen. You have to know that!"

"Cruel?" she howls. "That's all you can say? You're mine! We were *betrothed*! You were going to make me your queen! And now, you're going to, what? Throw it all away for some… some common Starless whore?"

Something snaps inside of me at her words. Black flames gather in my palms as anger coils in my veins. The urge to strike out at her lights through my brain, but I push the instinct back.

I will not allow myself to act like my father.

I will not become a tyrant.

Instead, I curl my hands into tight fists by my side, extinguishing the serpentine fire that threatens to erupt. I draw in a deep breath and then exhale fully before I speak again.

"I was never yours," I snarl, unable to keep the venom from seeping into my voice. "I understand your pain, and I'm sorry for leading you on. It was wrong of me. But know that if you *ever* disrespect my crossed star again, I will not tolerate it."

Hurt flashes across Ressa's face as my words sink in. For the first time, I realize that she was hoping that I would pick her over my crossed star. But how could she uphold such a foolish hope that either of us would be able to defy the heavens?

And after seeing Ressa act like this, I don't think I would even if I could.

"But I love you!" she shouts. Her words are punctuated with a sharp, stinging tap of her heel against the marble floor. She stares up at me with desperate, dark eyes, searching from any sign that I share her affections.

"Our parents betrothed us to one another when we were children," I answer. "Whatever was between us was born of convenience and fondness, not love. Never love."

In the beat of silence that follows, Ressa goes still. For a moment, I think that my sentiment has hit home, that she finally understands how I've felt about her this entire time.

Then her pale, delicate hand flashes up, striking my face with a resounding slap.

The sound echoes through the vast, empty ballroom like a thunderclap. Pain, minimal but stinging, flashes through my cheek where her palm connected with my jaw.

The serpent of rage that I keep coiled tightly inside of me lashes out, and this time I cannot stop it.

Maybe a small part of me wants it to be free.

So fast that she barely has time to react, my hand darts out and loops tightly around her wrist before she can hit me again. Anger seethes through me, and I know by the way she flinches away from me that it's written plainly across my face. It's all I can do to keep the fire contained. The last thing I want to do is burn her wrist with my flame, which is known to be lethal even to Demigods.

I stare down at her. She looks to be caught somewhere between fear and triumph.

"I knew you'd fight for me," she goads.

Disgusted by her twisted logic, I quickly release her wrist and take several steps backward. "Make no mistake, Ressa," I warn her, "I am your king. Strike me again, and I will make sure that you have no home here in the Celestial Court. Do I make myself clear?"

Her face hardens with determination. It's such a foreign expression, one I've never before seen cross her delicate features. In that moment, I realize that perhaps I never really knew Ressa at all.

She gathers her skirts and storms toward the doors. Just before she reaches them, she glances back at me, her eyes flashing. "I will not let you go that easily," she resolves.

And then she pushes the double doors open. They part to reveal Kartas lingering just beyond the threshold. She shoots him a withering glare before she shoves past him.

Kartas and I stare at one another as her footsteps fade into the distance.

When she's finally gone, my cousin lets out a low whistle. "Did you know you have a handprint on your face?"

"Leave me alone." I growl. The rage is slowly trickling from my body. I expected pushback from Ressa, perhaps some tears and hysterics, but not whatever that was. Has she always been that way? Have I just been too blinded by her beauty and her careful noblewoman charm to notice?

"The stars did you a favor," Kartas drones. "Imagine if you had married her?"

I don't want to hear it. I don't want to think about it.

"Get out!" I snap.

Realizing I'm serious, my cousin hesitates. When he speaks again, all of the jest is gone from his tone. "I'll go down to the kitchens and tell them you approved. You're supposed to decide on the color of the bunting in the courtyard too. Would you prefer that I go in your stead?"

I tip my head in approval.

"Ressa will cool off," he says as he starts to back out the door. I turn away from him, wishing he would stop talking, but he doesn't. "But be careful, Syran. Broken hearts have the power to topple kingdoms. Even yours, if you're not careful."

His words ring through the ballroom long after he's gone, and I know he speaks the truth.

I'm going to have to keep a careful eye on Ressa.

I don't trust her.

Not anymore.

CHAPTER 9

Lyanndra

On any other day, the Starless are forbidden from entering the Demigod city of Nexus, so it is with the greatest satisfaction that I guide Barra through the grand arched gate that marks the boundary between the midlands and the sprawling marble architecture of the Celestial Court.

The first thing I notice is that there are *streets*. These are not the muddy roadways or dirt tracks that I'm used to. They're wide and clean, lined with smooth white cobblestones that glint like quartz under the radiant noonday sun. Barra's wide hooves clop wonderfully against them as we journey beneath the unattended archway and into the conclave of the city limits.

The buildings that rise up around us are splendid and surreal. Marble, moonstone, and quartz decorate the stone facades of the homes and businesses. My jaw drops beneath the safety of my golden helm as I realize that some of the structures are four or five stories tall, rising into the sky like the great glittering teeth of some forgotten beast.

I drag my gaze forward, where the long street curves upward. Buildings line either side of the cobbled road. Signs, hammered out on bronze and copper, swing from hooks and advertise all manner of establishments in looping, colorful letters. I note a butcher, a florist, and a blacksmith as I ride past, though all of the businesses seem dark and silent within.

It strikes me then that I have not yet seen a single soul here, not even a guard at the gate. Where is everybody? Are they really all gathered to meet their crown prince's crossed star?

The silence makes me feel uneasy, but I push my anxiety down. After all, I've come here to die. Perishing at the hand of my crossed star would certainly be poetic, but meeting my end on the spear or sword of a Celestial Knight would certainly still get the job done.

Still, I can't shake my disquiet as we venture farther up the main thoroughfare.

In the distance, the glittering outline of the Celestial Court rises above. Towers of marble topped with golden spires seem to glow in the sunlight. It looks ethereal, like something out of a story. Awe swells in my chest as I drink in the lavish sight, but it's quickly chased off by the realization that this opulence has existed in Nexus this whole time while Starless peasants have toiled and suffered for centuries with nothing to show for it. Why have my people gone without so that the Demigods could have so much?

I silently curse the stars for their favoritism. How could anybody look upon such splendor and not want to share it with those in need? If I were to rule over such a rich kingdom, I would not allow even the most lowborn Starless to go hungry.

Fresh anger swirls within me, steeling me for what's to come.

I'm riding to my righteous death.

If my demise drives the crown prince mad, then I will have made the ultimate sacrifice for my people. The cruel fist of the Demigod's rule will crumble with his mind, and I have no doubt that the Starless forces scattered across Alastria will rise to claim our justice.

It's a reckoning centuries in the making.

If my death is all it takes, then it's worth it.

But that surety doesn't quell the quiver of fear that thrills through me at the thought of dying, of what does, or doesn't, come after.

I squeeze my eyes shut beneath the visor of the golden helm, only opening them when we reach a round plaza about halfway through the city. The sound of burbling water catches my attention and I turn my eyes to the sight of a tall, golden fountain in the middle of the open space.

My breath hitches in my throat as I realize that the metal is fashioned into the likeness of the Flaming God, the fallen king. A replica of the helm I wear, which rests in the crook of the figure's arm, is unmistakable, as is the blank staring visage that gazes down at me.

Memories of flames and ash threaten to choke me. The urge to rip off my helm, to *breathe*, is overwhelming, but I do not give in.

This statue is nothing more than a phantom.

He's already dead, and now I'll destroy his legacy too.

With this fresh resolution, I ease Barra past the ostentatious statue to continue up the main street. From my vantage point, it's a straight shot to the Celestial Court.

The palace rises up on the horizon in impossible, jagged peaks, reminding me of the stalagmites I once saw growing deep inside a cave as a child in the Southern Caldera. The marble edifice sparkles in the light, effervescent against the mild blue sky. Each gleaming tower is capped with gold that winks in the afternoon sun.

I gaze at the structure, raking my eyes down from the buttresses and cut glass windows to the golden gate that surrounds the palace. Beyond that border, the grounds are bursting with Demigods dressed in every color I can imagine as they patiently await their crown prince's crossed star. They're too far away to make out any details, and I know that I must look like little more than a dot in the distance to them.

And as I contemplate the unsuspecting crowd, one of the assembled Demigods notices me.

A cry rings out through the buzzing silence, audible even from my position further down the hill. Every head turns my way as the Demigods move like one, pushing toward the gate to get a better view. I don't see the crown prince, but I'm certain he's there, waiting.

Cheers of excitement rise over the crest of the hill as I approach. A song has broken out, too, though the patchy melody is nearly drowned out by the rest of the noise. It's joyous, celebratory.

They have no idea of the grim deeds that lay ahead.

I urge Barra to a canter. The sooner I close the distance between myself and the palace, the less chance I have to reconsider my convictions.

Her hooves boom on the cobblestones as her stride eats up the ground. The sway of her gait is familiar and soothing, and I lean forward to pat the sealskin of her neck. The realization hits me that this is the last time I will ride the kelpie. Out of everybody and everything in this world, she is my closest companion.

Tears prickle the corners of my eyes as we streak ever forward toward my doom, but I blink them back. I don't have time to mourn. I only have time to die.

As Barra surges toward the golden gate, the tone of the crowd starts to shift. Perhaps those closest to the street have caught sight of my monstrous mount, or maybe they'd recognized the glint of my distinctive helm. Either way, the excited cheers have become confused and alarmed.

And then the sweet cry, music to my ears, sounds out clearly as we finally approach the gate.

"Godslayer!" somebody shrieks. "It's the Godslayer!"

The name pierces the afternoon like a curse, and I grin beneath the golden helm. The cheers have now fully morphed into a fearful fever.

There's no turning back now.

The great gates are in front of me, open to receive the crown prince's crossed star. Several guards dart through, their golden chest plates gleaming as their colored capes flutter behind them. I unsheathe the greatsword, holding the blade aloft. Sitting high up on Barra, I have the advantage here, regardless of these Demigods' powers.

The knights create a defensive line in front of the gate as others within work to close the massive gap in their defenses. Even as the Demigods draw their weapons, the kelpie doesn't slow. She barrels through them like a charger, easily crushing through their formation. Two men get caught beneath her hooves. The rest scatter, shouting and rolling away from the rampaging beast.

Now it's my turn. I swing the greatsword in an arc, simultaneously striking three men in the torso. The impact shudders up my arms and into my shoulders, but my grip on the weapon doesn't falter. I use the momentum to carry the sword up and safely over Barra's head before striking down at the closest knight on the other side. The hit doesn't land, though. One of the others lifts his hands and sends out a gust of wind that pushes my target just out of range of my blade.

It's a small frustration, but it doesn't last for long. Barra, unfazed by the skirmish, pushes forward, carrying me away from the line of Celestial Knights and up to the gate. Others inside shove at the golden barrier, but it's not quite closed.

Barra rams through the barricade. I wince as my left leg catches on the metal, but the thrill of the fight quickly masks the pain.

Chaos greets us in the courtyard. Celestial Knights swarm, but none of them are mounted. The surging, screaming crowd of Demigods rushing between them prevents them from executing any coherent defense.

I ignore all of them as my eyes scan the crowd, hunting for my target.

He stands on a dais on the far side of the courtyard. For a moment, my heart stutters as I'm sure that it's the Flaming God, back from the dead. But then my brain kicks into gear, and I realize that this is his son, the crown prince.

He's the spitting image of his father. Tall and broad, he stands dressed in the golden armor of the Celestial Court. The mantle that flutters at his shoulders is black as pitch, probably a nod to his title as Lord of the Midnight Flame. His red hair is pulled back from his face and topped with a jagged black crown. His handsome features are curled into a scowl.

Green eyes lock onto mine.

For a moment, there is nothing else.

Something unknown pulses through my gut. The ghost of his

touch runs over my skin beneath my armor as his hands did in the dream. How could this Demigod who glowers at me with such hatred also be that same man who brought me to such heights only a fortnight ago?

He deceived me somehow, I decide.

He won't get a chance to try it again.

I urge Barra forward, using her body to cut through the crowd until we're in front of the dais. The Demigods are terrified and unprepared. They push backward, effectively creating a clearing between the crown prince and myself.

When I'm only a few feet from the Lord of the Midnight Flame, I draw Barra to a halt. She paws at the ground but obeys. At the same time, the crown prince raises one gloved hand, and the crowd stills to silence.

My heart thuds against my ribs as I dismount. Before I can lose my fortitude, I slap Barra on her hindquarter. She whinnies and rears up before galloping away toward the gate. Nobody stops her as she goes. The sea of Demigods is focused only on my target and me.

The crown prince speaks then, his rich voice twisted with hatred. "What trickery is this, Godslayer?" he demands. "What have you done with my crossed star?"

I smirk beneath my helm. There are so many insults I'd like to hurl at him, but I hold my tongue. If he wants to hear my voice, he's going to have to earn it.

And earn it he shall.

I plant my greatsword in the ground before me. A ripple of confusion rolls through the assembled Demigods as I reach to my right hand and slide the gauntlet off to reveal the dragonhide leather glove beneath.

Without removing my eyes from the crown prince's face, I toss the gauntlet down between us.

The crowd gasps as the Lord of the Midnight Flame's expression hardens.

The challenge is clear.

We will fight to the death.

CHAPTER 10

The Godslayer is smaller than I remember.

He stands before me, and I am struck by how diminutive the legend really is. He's a head shorter than I, though the bulk of his armor makes it challenging to get a good read on his form beneath.

He wears a ragtag ensemble of steel, all of it sporting a strange blackened, opalescent quality that could only have come from bearing the brunt of extreme heat. Where the gauntlet once sat on his right hand, a glove that looks to be fashioned from dragonhide obscures the skin. That strikes me as unusual. Dragonhide is difficult enough to come by for Demigods who can afford the steep price. How could a Starless hero come to possess such a rare and valuable item?

As I study the rest of my opponent's defenses, my eyes linger on his helm.

My father's helm.

Fresh rage surges through me in a torrential wave, but that anger is tipped with white-hot fear. Where is my crossed star? What has this Starless devil done with her?

Before his arrival, I was certain that my crossed star was on her way, growing closer and closer with every passing second. So how is it that it is the Godslayer who has come in her stead?

He's tricked me somehow.

I will not let him make a fool of me or keep my crossed star away.

I glance down at the gauntlet on the ground between us. More than anything, I'm itching to fight the Godslayer, to force him to admit his deception. But I know that to meet this challenge, I risk another war between the Demigods and the Starless.

Kartas, lingering on the edge of the dais, catches my eye and nods. I understand why. If I back down from this fight in a desperate bid to preserve the tenuous peace between the Nexus and the rest of Alastria, my own people will ridicule me. They will deem me unfit to rule, and I cannot risk giving up my throne so easily.

Faced with an impossible choice, I decide to give into the rage, to the part of me that wants to avenge my father's murder.

I will show the hero of the Starless why they call me the Lord of the Midnight Flame.

Without any more hesitation, I leap from the dais and into the clearing, meeting the Godslayer on even ground. At the same time, I draw my sword in a flash of black flame. Dark embers swirl between us as the air heats to a shimmer.

It's a fierce display, yet the Godslayer does not back down. I recall how he engaged my father on the battlefield a year prior and how I marveled at the time that he was either very brave or very stupid.

Perhaps he's both, I realize as I take one menacing step forward. The black fire flickers, but he appears unafraid. Does he know that the color of my flame is due to the poison that lies within?

Regardless, his challenge will seal his doom. He will fall to my fire just as everybody before him has. I will not spare him, though I will do everything in my power to pry the identity of my crossed star from him before I deliver him unto death.

I slice my blade at the Godslayer. The black flames arc out in its wake like striking serpents searching out their prey.

At the very last moment, the Godslayer raises the rough-hewn hunk of steel that passes as his greatsword in an almost lazy parry.

The weight of his weapon knocks mine off course, taking the fire with it.

The effortlessness of the move is infuriating. Fresh anger flows through me as I realize that my whole court is watching with bated breath. Why has the Godslayer come here? Why has he forced me into this fight?

I lash out again, this time aiming for one of the Godslayer's legs. If I can kneecap my opponent, it won't take long after that to put him out of his misery.

But once again, the blow never lands.

The Godslayer dances back just outside the scope of the swing. He moves so lightly even in that bulky armor, all whilst dragging that greatsword with both hands.

I've always thought of him as a brute that got lucky against my father, not a warrior of any particular skill. It's true that my spies spoke of the Starless hero's exploits throughout Alastria following his victory over the Flaming God. They told me how he felled monsters and rescued damsels, that he never spoke, never ate, and was perhaps something more than just a man. But those stories always sounded like the fairytales my mother used to read to me as a child, impossible and exaggerated.

Now, as the Godslayer sidesteps a third strike, I wonder if perhaps there is some truth to those tales. Is it possible that I have underestimated the Godslayer's skill?

He confirms that notion by making a move. I fully expect him to cleave the greatsword in a downward strike as any average knight would do, but I'm quickly realizing that this man is no normal fighter.

Instead, the swing comes low and horizontal, aiming for my calves. The blow is so quick that I barely have time to react. Unable to do anything else, I jump as high as I can in the air, tucking my knees to my chest in hopes that I've cleared enough ground to avoid the steel.

The crowd gasps as the greatsword misses by mere inches. I feel the rush of the swing, and then my feet hit the earth again. Beneath my ceremonial armor, my heart pounds at the close call. But I cannot let my people see my fear, so I school my features into a cool, emotionless mask.

That control allows me to see my next opening. The force of the Godslayer's swing has turned him around in almost a full circle. He's still carried by the momentum, and any movement with the heavy greatsword will take him just a bit longer than usual.

I jab the end of my sword toward him, willing the flames to lick at him as he pivots. In his heavy armor, he can't bend to avoid the jab, nor can he parry in time.

But he slides out of range once more, this time by rag dolling down and letting the end of his swing carry him in a roll. He stands again seamlessly, as though he had pulled that gimmick a hundred times before.

Who *is* this man? How did he learn to fight like this? I've never seen anybody move this way before. Most soldiers, Demigod and Starless alike, are trained in camps. They learn the same techniques and fighting styles, but the Godslayer seems to use none of them. I don't even recognize any foreign influence. It's as though his combat technique is his own, innate rather than learned.

This only deepens the hate I feel for him. As the crown prince of the Celestial Court, I was trained practically from birth. I studied warfare with the best generals in the kingdom and fought alongside the fiercest warriors. There are few in Alastria who can match me in skill and knowledge.

I will not allow some Starless heathen who fights like a beast to defeat me now.

A growl rips from my throat as I lunge at the Godslayer. Before, we were just poking and jabbing at one another, getting a sense for how the other might react. Now, the fight begins in earnest.

I wield my sword in one hand and my black flame in the other. The Godslayer throws up his greatsword, deflecting both blows simultaneously. I expect him to push back with the blade almost like one might do with a shield, but he instead kicks out at me with one foot, catching me in the shin.

The assembled Demigods murmur as I stumble back with a curse dripping from my lips. The strike doesn't hurt much, though I'm sure it left an angry bruise. But the fact that the Godslayer pulled such a dirty little move is unforgivable. I glare at the Starless hero, who says nothing to goad or distract me. He's simply silent beneath the blank face of my father's helm. Is he laughing? Or does he feel nothing at all?

Enraged by either prospect, I charge again. The Godslayer meets my blade in another lazy parry and then twists behind the greatsword, dancing out of the path of a slash of black flame I send his way. Using the weight of his weapon as leverage, he swings us around and releases my blade, causing my wrist to buckle slightly. I meet this strategy with another burst of fire, this time aiming for his helm in hopes of blinding him. He staggers back, and I take the opportunity to slice at him, though my sword whistles only through air as he once again dodges out of reach.

The game continues for a long time, neither of us giving any ground. Sweat drips down my forehead. The tunic I wear beneath my armor clings to my back. My mouth tastes of ash, not victory. I am tiring, but I will not give in.

I see signs of fatigue from the Godslayer, too. He's swinging his greatsword less, instead favoring low shots and blows with feet or fists.

One of us is going to have to give—and soon.

The opportunity comes when he risks a hit with his colossal blade. He swoops the steel in a downward arc toward me, aiming to lob off an arm. Usually, I'd parry the blow over my head and force the weapon to the side, but something tells me to wait to move until the greatsword has nearly hit its mark.

At the last second, I duck out from beneath the swing and lash out with my flaming sword. The jab catches the Godslayer by surprise. Clearly, he wasn't expecting me to use one of his own tactics against him.

The fire-clad blade strikes him low on the rib cage. The air sizzles with the scent of burning leather and flesh as it sinks through the layers of his armor and bites into his skin.

He stumbles back even as I pull the blade away. I catch sight of singed dragonhide and white fabric underneath before the blood comes. The heat would normally have cauterized the wound, but the poison, inherited from my mother's venomous gifts, halts the progress in its tracks.

The assembled Demigods jeer as the Godslayer goes down on one knee. A touch of the black flame is, I'm told, agonizingly painful. I've never seen a man stand after receiving such a blow.

And yet, my eyes widen as the Starless wretch struggles back to his feet. The courtiers fall silent.

The Godslayer takes one step toward me and then another.

Then a shudder runs through him, and he falls to his knees.

Triumph thrills through my veins as I stride forward and kick the greatsword out of his hands. It clangs haplessly onto the ground, out of his reach. A second swift strike of my boot throws the man onto his back. He hits the stairs leading up to the dais, propping him up on an incline. An audible rush of breath sounds from beneath my father's stolen helm as the air is knocked out of his lungs.

Drunk on victory, I loom over him. "You disappoint me, Godslayer," I sneer. My voice is steady, but underneath, I'm feeling almost rabid from the thrill of this conquest. "The famous hero, the light of the Starless..."

I wait for him to reply, to beg for mercy or death, but he says absolutely nothing. I can't even see his eyes behind the helm. He's simply anonymous.

In that moment, I realize that the Godslayer really is more than just a Starless soldier who got lucky. He's a story, a legend whispered in the dark, more myth than man. Suddenly, the urge to see the face of the knight who killed my father and fought so brashly is overwhelming.

I need to unmask him.

I need to see his face.

Brandishing my sword, now devoid of the black flame, I swipe it under the Godslayer's neck. He flinches, unaware that this attack is not one meant to wound. Instead, the blade slices cleanly through the leather strap that secures the golden helm.

I step forward until I'm close enough to reach out and touch him. Then, I turn to the Demigods who surround me. They're eager to see how I'll finish off the Godslayer, and I certainly will not keep them from what they so wholly desire.

More to the crowd than to the Godslayer, I demand, "What coward are you, who hides beneath my father's helm?"

And then I grasp the edge of the golden helm and pull, revealing the face of the Godslayer once and for all.

CHAPTER 11

Lyanndra

A gasp ripples through the crowd as the crown prince pulls the helm roughly from my head. The leather tie that holds my braid in place snags on the metal and snaps. The simple plait comes free, unraveling quickly so that my long honeyed hair cascades around my shoulders.

Squinting against the sudden unfiltered sunlight, I brush my fingers against the wound at my ribs and wince. My blood is hot, too hot, against my skin. I half expect the Lord of the Midnight Flame to swing his sword and finish me off before my eyes can adjust, but no such blow arrives. Instead, I only sense the murmurs that whip through the surrounding courtiers in a frenzied tornado of spec-ulation.

As the world swims into focus, I can feel the incredulous stares of the assembled Demigods fixed upon me, but the crown prince's gaze is the only one that matters.

His face is frozen in a pale mask of shock, his green eyes locked on mine.

Triumph bubbles up through the pain. Even though the blow he dealt me shouldn't be fatal, I know that something is grievously wrong. It's as if the black fire that coated his blade is now coursing through my blood, burning a raging path through my body and wracking my nerves with agony. The flames are consuming me from the inside out.

I will not survive this.

It's a shame, in a way. The crown prince fought well. The way he wielded his midnight flame was truly frightening to behold. Several times throughout the fight, he almost struck me down in spite of my best efforts to evade him, but it wouldn't have served my ultimate purpose to allow myself to die so early in combat. I wanted him to believe that he could best me.

But the truth is that for every blow he nearly landed upon me, I could have dealt him two in turn. I fought just hard enough to fool him into thinking that I was really trying to beat him but not enough for me to win. He needed to believe that I was there to best him, or he would have gotten suspicious of my true intentions. He fell for it completely.

And when I let him strike me, he didn't suspect a thing.

Now, I lay here, dying. Even the will of the stars wasn't enough to stop me. All that's left for me to do is reveal my plan. I want to see the crown prince's face twist in realization at my words before I go. I want to hold close the satisfaction that I have driven him to madness as the heavens finally take me.

I don't have much time left. Pain wracks my body as the infernal poison spreads. The stairs to the dais dig into my spine in spite of the protection of my armor, but I don't move. Instead, I try to focus on that sensation to distract from the burning that creeps unrelentingly through my flesh. I can't let myself succumb quite yet. There's still one more thing I have to do.

"What... what is this?" the crown prince demands, finally finding his voice. His eyes bore into mine, begging me for answers.

The Demigods around him seem to share his confusion. Their comments flutter restlessly in the air like a flock of birds with nowhere to roost, untethered and relentless. I catch snippets of their desperate words, and I can't help but feel grim satisfaction at their attempts to digest the situation.

"A woman? The Godslayer is a *woman*?"

"This can't be! Women can't be knights!"

"A woman killed the king?"

A strange sense of pride wells up in my chest at their collective disbelief. I know that the people of Alastria, Starless and Demigod alike, tell stories about me. They speak of how I defeated the Flaming God and ended the great war, of how I helped countless Starless find safety and justice.

But they always assumed me to be a man. Certainly, nobody ever theorized otherwise.

What stories will they tell of me now that they know I'm a woman? Even among the Starless, where females work in the fields and as midwives, girls do not grow up to be knights. The Demigods are no better. They expect their ladies to dress in fine clothes and jewels, to be gentle and soft and no more useful than a pretty painting or a fleeting symphony.

Will they speak of me with disdain, even after everything the Godslayer has done for them? Will they praise me for rising above the life that had been prescribed to me as a girl, for showing that a woman can wield a sword as truly as any man?

What will they say of a woman who killed a god and sacrificed herself to doom another?

The crown prince speaks again, jolting me from my thoughts. "Why have you come here?" he demands. "What have you done to my crossed star?"

I glare up at the crown prince. His neat features are creased with open confusion. It's clear to me that he still doesn't understand who I am, not fully.

It's time he knows the truth.

"I came here to die," I spit. The wound at my ribs throbs jaggedly with every word. I move my right hand to cover it. Feverish blood slicks my dragonhide glove as I press against the torn skin in a weak attempt to staunch the flow and stabilize the muscles. It won't keep me alive, but it will buy me some time.

A flash of rage crosses the Demigod's face at my impudence. "And die you will," he snarls. "But even with death closing in on you, you *will* bring me news of my crossed star."

I marvel at the intensity of his anger. I assumed that he fought me because I'm the Godslayer, and he wanted revenge against the Starless knight that killed his father. Is it possible that the crown prince actually took up my challenge thinking that I had harmed his crossed star?

Was he trying to protect her?

Was he trying to protect *me*?

I push that thought aside. No Demigod is capable of that sort of devotion, certainly not the son of the Flaming God. He probably sees his crossed star as little more than a weakness, as something to lock away and covet for his safety, not hers.

Disgusted by the crown prince's machinations, I bare my teeth in a silent growl. I know I must look a sight, bloodied and half-wild with my hair streaming loose over my blackened armor. Just like all Demigods, he probably thinks I'm just a Starless animal, so I will show him what he wants to see.

"My death will bring you nothing but madness, Demigod," I sneer.

I watch his face carefully for any sign of realization, but the hot anger and confusion still remain. Does he still not understand who I am and why I am here?

It seems I'll have to show him.

Not daring to lift my right hand from where I'm applying pressure to the wound, I raise my left gauntlet to my mouth. The crown prince observes with that same puzzled agitation as I catch the metal in my teeth and pull the piece of armor off. I toss it to the side with a jerk of my head and then repeat the process with the dragonhide glove beneath.

Once my hand is bare, I hold it up to reveal my secret.

"No!" The Crown prince gasps. The color drains from his face as horror floods his features. Behind him, several Demigods shout in surprise and protest.

I elevate my hand higher, forcing him to imbibe the sight. The gold band on my finger flashes in the sunlight. The black onyx, carved with the serpentine symbol of the royal line, is unmistakable.

My eyes flicker down to the crown prince's left hand. He wears golden ceremonial gloves, but I know that if I were to remove them, his ring would match my own.

"This cannot be!" he exclaims. He can't seem to look away from the band that glitters on my finger like a flame in the dark.

Before he can say anything else, a spasm of pain, as lithe as a serpent's tongue, arches through my body. I gasp, and then as my lungs begin to burn, the sound morphs into a weak cough. My left hand instinctively drops to join its twin, and I cough again as the wound flares with jagged embers.

The movement breaks the crown prince's concentration. His green eyes fly to the wound and widen as he seems to realize what he's done. When he meets my gaze a moment later, there's something new written across his features.

Fear.

A fierce, bloody grin spreads across my face. "Our stars are crossed; our souls bound." I hiss, speaking aloud the horrible truth. "They call you Lord of the Midnight Flame? May you rule over a kingdom of *ash.*"

Any response he's planning to muster is cut short as agony clutches at me with hungry talons. Black spots scatter across my vision like insects. Death calls to me, and I now know that I can go to that dark place willingly. The crown prince reaches for me with golden gloves as his eyes brim with desperate horror.

I bark out a wheezing laugh at the absurdity of it all.

And then the pain overtakes me, dragging me toward the rushing darkness.

Toward peace.

Toward the end.

CHAPTER 12

Syran

This cannot be.

The thought rings through my head over and over again as my mind struggles to catch up to the nightmare playing out before me.

The Godslayer–*my crossed star*–is sprawled on the steps of the dais. Blonde hair the color of summer honey fans across the ground, cushioning her head against the rough stone surface. Her features, far from the delicate and predictable beauty of the Demigod ladies of the Celestial Court, are striking. Her mouth is full, her nose slightly aquiline. Hazel eyes brimming with hatred and pain burn up at me as she utters the final words of her terrible retribution.

She is *stunning*.

And she is going to die.

My eyes flicker down to where she clutches her ribs. Blood seeps from between her fingers and rolls down her armor in hot tears of red. The wound is bad, but it is not what is killing her.

No, the deathblow came when I struck her with my fiery sword, imbuing her flesh with the poison of my midnight flame. Her face is livid with agony as the creeping venom claws its way deeper into her body, inch by excruciating inch. It won't stop until it's consumed her completely.

Guilt and regret curdle together in my gut. My horror only grows as those expressive hazel eyes roll back, and her eyelids start to flutter wildly.

I can't let her, my crossed star, die, not when I've just found her.

Panic spurs me forward. I lunge toward her, closing the distance between us in less than a second. At the same time, I bellow, "Torran!"

I fall to my knees beside the Godslayer's prone body. Years of battle-honed instinct kick in as I reach for the wound. My healing abilities are no rival to Torran's, but like any good soldier, I know the basics. I push my crossed star's hands away from the tear at her ribs and replace them with my own. She offers no resistance, and I'm speared by a strike of fear when she doesn't make any effort to fight back.

Am I too late?

But the blood still pulses with the dwindling beat of her heart. Beneath my gauntlets, I can feel the stuttering rise and fall of her chest as she struggles to breathe. When I push hard against the ragged gash, a pained moan is forced from her throat. These are all signs of life, though they're fading fast–too fast.

In my peripheral vision, I see Torran pushing his way through the tense front line of the crowd. His face is calm, but his eyes belay the turmoil that simmers beneath. He carries a battered leather satchel, the kind that healers use in combat when they have to treat their patients in the midst of active battle.

"Move," he commands as he sinks down beside me. Under normal circumstances, I would have the head of anybody who would presume to order me around like that, but in this instant, I simply do as he says.

I peel one palm back from the wound, just enough to give the old Demigod a clear view of the injury. The slice is clean, splitting the blackened chest plate in a melted line. The dragonhide leathers below, impervious to most attacks, are singed and mottled by the sheer heat of my black flame. And then there's the flayed skin beneath, barely visible under all of the blood.

Torran shakes his head in dismay at the sight. "This is bad," he mutters under his breath. "Very bad."

"Will she make it?" I demand. The question should have been strong, but instead my voice wavers with fear.

The old Demigod spares me a glance. "Perhaps," he admits. "Perhaps not. I will do what I can." He opens the leather satchel and peers into it, searching for something. "Keep your hand there to slow the bleeding," he advises me. "And try to wake her up."

I oblige. I lean my weight into my palm at her ribs. With the other hand, I cup her cheek. I can't feel her skin against the golden gauntlet, but I'm sure it's hot with the blazing effects of the poison.

"Open your eyes," I urge, my tone low and pleading. "Please, just open your eyes."

The Godslayer's lashes stutter once, twice, and then fall still again.

"Keep trying," Torran presses. He plucks a small, round bottle from his satchel and holds it up to the light, examining its contents carefully. The liquid that swirls within is a pale, opalescent white that seems to emanate a preternatural glow.

Before I can ask him what it is, Kartas strides into view. He's breathing hard, and his face is grim. "I've had the guards secure the crowd," he explains as he drops down on the other side of the Godslayer's ailing form. His expression hardens further as he takes in the grim reality of my crossed star's condition.

"Is she...?" he breathes. His voice trails off into nothing, as though he doesn't dare utter the possibility of what I fear most.

"Not yet," Torran tells him. "But she won't last much longer unless we can get her to drink this." He gestures to the bottle, which glints strangely in the afternoon sunlight.

Kartas' face crumples in confusion. "What is it?"

"An antidote," Torran replies. I open my mouth to argue that my midnight flame has no counter, but the older Demigod holds up a hand to preemptively silence me. "I brewed this long ago for your mother. She was always afraid that her gift to produce such a toxic substance would one day harm one she loved." He shoots me a pointed look before he continues. "You are her blood, Syran. Her poison worked much the way yours does. This antidote might not be perfect, but it may just save your crossed star."

"It could also make it worse," Kartas counters as he eyes the effervescent substance with unguarded suspicion.

"She will die if we don't try it," Torran says coolly. "Though she may well die if we do." He turns to me then, his blue eyes alight. "The choice is yours, Syran."

My response is instant and sure. "Do it."

Torran nods, and I feel that I've earned his approval. "Very well. But first we need her conscious. I won't be able to do anything to stop the bleeding until the poison is neutralized."

This task proves to be difficult. Keeping pressure on the wound with one hand, I gently pat her cheek with the other. "Come on," I insist through gritted teeth.

Every second that passes by means that she slips just a little bit further out of reach. I know she won't survive much longer. Desperation drives me toward anger, and I channel all of those emotions toward her.

"You won't escape me that easily," I growl, willing her to wake up. "Not now. Not when I've just found you."

Her eyelids flutter. I expect her to sink back into unconsciousness, but instead, her eyes open to unfocused slits.

Torran seizes this opportunity. Uncorking the bottle, he stoops over her and holds the rim to her lips. "Drink, girl," he urges.

The Godslayer slams her mouth shut.

Her hazel eyes swim from side to side until her gaze lands on mine. Though her lips are still pressed shut in a tight seam, I have a terrible suspicion that I know why she's doing this.

She wants to die.

And if she dies, I lose her.

If she dies, I lose my mind.

Kartas seems to have reached the same awful conclusion. Without asking for approval, he darts his hands out toward the Godslayer's face. He grips her lower jaw tightly, working a gloved finger between her lips to leverage them open. As soon as he forces a gap, Torran seizes the opportunity and pours the potion into her mouth. She manages to spit out a few drops before Kartas clamps his hand down over her lower face, sealing the liquid inside. His palm also covers her nose, cutting off her air supply.

Her reaction is immediate and violent. Her body thrashes against his grip, but she's no match for him in her weakened state. She grasps at his arms with bloodied hands as she claws at him, desperate for air, leaving red smears across the glowing gold of his armor.

Instinctually, I lunge forward to stop him, to force him to release my crossed star, but Torran pushes me back. A split second later, I see the Godslayer's throat bob as she swallows down the potion.

Kartas quickly draws his hands away and holds them up to me in surrender. Part of me wants to tear him limb for limb for daring to touch my crossed star, but the rational side of me understands that he was doing what was necessary to save her life. Even so, I shoot him a piercing glare before turning my gaze back to the Godslayer.

To my immense relief, she sucks in a rattling breath, then another. As her chest continues to rise and fall in a settling rhythm, her body starts to relax. Her eyes falter shut again, and her face goes slack. The flush of the poison beneath her skin is already clearing, though her cheeks are worryingly pale beneath the ruddiness.

"I think it worked," Torran murmurs. "But she isn't on steady ground quite yet. She's lost too much blood." Once again, he rummages within his leather satchel. I hear the clinking of glass and metal as he searches for something else. "Ah, here it is," he says triumphantly as he resurfaces a moment later with a slim waxed paper packet.

Both Kartas and I have no trouble recognizing this particular bit of medicine. The packet contains a fine rust-colored powder that can help slow or stop bleeding even from the most horrific of wounds. It's a common item for soldiers to carry on the battlefield, though it is not a permanent solution. Eventually, the bleeding will restart unless the injury is treated.

Torran tears the edge off the packet and motions for me to remove my hand from the wound. I do as he instructs. As soon as my fingers are lifted, he pours the reddish brown powder into the cut at the Godslayer's ribs. It foams up slightly before it settles, and I'm relieved to see that the bleeding has slowed once the reaction clears.

The old Demigod sits back on his heels and sighs. "She's strong," he tells me. "I think there's a good chance she'll survive now."

Though his words don't fully vanquish the fear and panic that still writhe around my heart, they do bring me a sense of release. My crossed star has made it through this initial danger. I say a silent prayer to the stars in hopes that the worst has passed.

"What now?" Kartas asks. He's barely looked away from the Godslayer since he forced her to drink the antidote.

"The wound will need my attention," Torran replies. "And there may be further injuries we are not yet aware of. I'll need to take her to the infirmary."

Kartas turns his incredulous stare upon the old Demigod. "The infirmary?" he repeats. "You want to take *the Godslayer* into the palace? You know, the place with all of the Demigods, the people she slaughters for fun?"

"She is in no fit state to raise a sword against a fly, let alone a Demigod," Torran scoffs. "Besides, where else would we bring her?"

"To the dungeons! We should drag her down there and throw her in a cell!" my cousin argues.

"Enough!" I cut in forcefully. "She may be the Godslayer, but she is also my crossed star. She will be treated with the same respect we would afford any lady of the Celestial Court. Do I make myself clear?"

I meet Kartas' stare, daring him to defy me, but he drops his gaze in deference.

When I continue, I will myself to keep my voice strong and filled with authority. "Torran, prepare the royal suite in the infirmary. I will follow shortly."

The old Demigod nods, grabs his satchel, and hurries away.

I turn to Kartas. "I want a rotation of guards at the infirmary. Nobody goes in or out without my approval."

My cousin tips his head in acknowledgement. "If that's what you want, I'll see to it," he promises. "But I do think she'd be safer in the dungeons. Not every Demigod will be glad to have her in our midst."

With that, he turns and strides off to round up his Celestial Knights and assign them their new duties.

Acutely aware that time still is not on our side, I stoop down and work my arms beneath the Godslayer's still form. She doesn't stir as I lift her and gather her to my chest. And while I carry her toward the palace in Torran's wake, I can't help but think about Kartas' words.

I will not toss her in the dungeon, not for her safety or mine. Even if she is my sworn enemy, the Godslayer is my crossed star.

I'm not going to lock her away, not when I've finally found her.

CHAPTER 13

Lyanndra

Consciousness comes floating back to me first, and pain follows quickly on its feather-light heels.

My whole body hurts. A swollen ache throbs in my temples. Every shallow breath I take sends shudders of burning pain rippling through my torso. My limbs feel leaden and heavy, as though I'd ridden Barra for hours and hours. But the jagged agony tearing at the bottom of my ribcage is by far the worst of it, a deep and rending anger that threatens to launch me back into the soft darkness of sleep.

Snippets of memories float through my mind as I struggle to remember what happened. I recall fighting the crown prince of the Celestial Court, leading him in a deadly dance to secure the fall of the Demigods with my own demise, and the flash of his midnight flame as the sword sliced cleanly through the layers of my armor and the skin beneath.

I have a vague impression of thrashing, of struggling to breathe as liquid was poured down my throat.

I remember staring into those fathomless green eyes.

And then there was nothing.

Fear, sluggish beneath the pain, seeps through me. I'm supposed to be dead, but my aching body betrays the truth: somehow, I survived the crown prince's deadly poison.

This was never part of the plan.

I was never supposed to live.

How long have I been unconscious?

The thought brings with it a fresh round of alarm. I've seen the brutality of the Demigods firsthand on the battlefield. What might they have done to me while I was unresponsive? Have they tossed me in the labyrinthine dungeons that are rumored to sprawl beneath the palace of the Celestial Court?

There's only one way to find the answers I seek.

I open my eyes.

Gentle candlelight illuminates the room in a flickering glow. Shadows slide gracefully across the pale marble walls. Sinuous moonlight cascades through the elegant arch of a window on the far side of the room. It's certainly no dungeon, or else it's the most luxurious cell I've ever seen. In fact, the familiar smell of ointment and herbs hangs heavily in the air, and I realize I must be in some sort of infirmary.

I turn my head slowly to one side. My right arm is stretched out over a luxurious white silk bedspread. The material is nicer than anything I've ever felt before.

But the strangest thing is that my arm is clothed not in tarnished armor or dragonhide leathers, but in the flowing lace sleeve of a nightgown. It's an absurd sight to see such a fine garment against my skin. The novelty quickly wears off as I realize that if I'm dressed in fresh clothes. Somebody must have changed me from my armor and undergarments into this outfit. The thought fills me with dread and a strange sense of embarrassment.

Brimming with this new concern, I look over to the left. My eyes pass over the gold and onyx ring that sits on my finger to fall on a glove that somebody has left on the side of the bed. The golden gauntlet is so close that it's almost touching my skin.

But then that gauntlet moves, and I notice that there is a gold-clad arm attached to the piece of armor, which in turn connects to a breastplate worn by a man with flaming red hair and green eyes…

Panic surges through me as I realize that the crown prince of the Celestial Court is keeping vigil at my bedside. I try to sit up, but the sudden movement sends an electric bolt of excruciating pain resonating through my body. I'm unable to stop myself from crying out.

The crown prince raises his gloved hand and pushes me, gently but firmly, back down. I don't have the energy to fight him. Black splotches throb at the edges of my vision as the pain makes my head swim, but I don't dare take my eyes off him. The pressure of his palm against my shoulder is strong and agonizingly familiar. It's the same touch from that infernal dream, where he ran his hands over my body and did wicked things to me beneath the cool moonlight.

I blush at the recollection even as I try to push the memory back. This man is my mortal enemy, just like his father before him. I can't think of him like that.

But it's hard not to look at him. He's as handsome as I remember, though he's lost that vicious edge I saw in him throughout our raging battle. Now he just looks tired, as though he hasn't slept in several days. He still wears the ceremonial golden armor he fought in. Judging by the ash and blood that's smeared over the gleaming metal, I surmise that he hasn't changed since our battle.

Has he even left my bedside?

It's a foolish thought. He's probably worried that I'd wake up and go on a murderous rampage through the palace, slaying Demigods with wild abandon and dancing in their blood.

But something, some strange feeling that curls deep in my gut, tells me that he isn't here to keep watch over the Godslayer. He's here for his crossed star.

He's here for *me*.

A shudder runs through me at the thought. Memories of the dream, of our bodies intertwined in unspeakable ways, force themselves to the surface. When I think of them now, I know with absolute certainty that the man who rolled his hips into mine has red hair that falls about his shoulders and green eyes that follow the curves of my body with breathtaking reverence.

This Demigod is my crossed star as much as I am his.

I hate him for it.

If the Lord of the Midnight Flame feels the same dangerous attraction to me, he doesn't show it. Though his face is tempered by exhaustion, his expression remains cold and aloof. He regards me carefully before he breaks the tense silence that has built up between us.

"You are badly injured, my lady," he says coolly as he removes his hand from my shoulder. "You need to rest."

Anger seethes through me at his words. After slicing me open like a side of beef, is that the best he can do? Any fear I may have held toward him evaporates like mist in the summer sun. I want to shatter that icy exterior of his, crack him open the same way he ripped through my armor and my flesh. I want to expose him.

So I say the most antagonistic thing I can think of. "I am no lady," I sneer.

The crown prince visibly tenses at the sound of my voice, and I feel some measure of satisfaction at his reaction.

Goading him further, I say, "You should have let me die."

The royal Demigod remains still. I'd been hoping for a flinch or a gasp at my uncouth words, but his façade remains smooth and unflustered. He leans forward, his green eyes shining in the candle-light as he asks earnestly, "Would my madness really be worth the price?"

I flash my teeth at him in a wild snarl. "My death alone would be worth it, if it frees me from you," I utter. My voice is raspy, and my throat burns with every word. The wound near my ribs throbs in time with the frantic beat of my heart as I wait for him to lash out at me.

To my delight, hot fury flares behind his stoic green eyes. Still, his tone remains flat and even as he grits out, "You know nothing of me."

A small part of me admits that he's right. I don't know much at all about the crown prince. I don't even know his name. If he were some Starless traveler I met on the road, or even a Celestial Knight before the war, I would have given him the benefit of the doubt. I would have asked him about his life and his adventures, however mundane.

But this Demigod is no normal man. He is the son of the Flaming God, the heir to a throne steeped in blood and paid for in flesh. There is no story he could tell or name he could give that would change who he is.

So I spit, "I know enough. You are a Demigod, and your kind are all the same."

Anger seethes in his gaze. Though his expression does not appreciably change, I can tell that my remark has wounded him deeply. "Do you really think so little of my people?" he demands in that same measured tone.

"Yes," I say simply, knowing full well that the one word carries just as much venom as the crown prince's midnight flame.

Rage flashes across his face, twisting his handsome features into an echo of our battle. But then he draws in a deep breath, and, when he releases it, he schools his expression back into that controlled mask, and all signs of weakness are once again buried.

"You are wrong," he tells me. "You do not know who I am or what I stand for."

"Who are you, then?" I ask, my tone mocking. In my weakened and disarmed state, my words are my only weapon. Perhaps I can make him so mad he throttles me where I lie. Perhaps I can simply annoy him into finishing the job.

He fixes me with his cool green gaze.

I do not look away.

"Syran," he states. "I am Syran, Crown Prince of the Celestial Court and Lord of the Midnight Flame."

Syran.

Unbidden, my thoughts flit back to the dream. What would it feel like to cry his name in the throes of passion, to beg him to drag me once more to that terrible and delicious brink? The images conjured by such lewd fantasies rob me of any biting retort that I could muster. So I say nothing at all.

The crown prince–Syran–frowns slightly when I don't reply. After a long moment, he asks, "Tell me, my lady, what is your name?"

I stare up at him, hating the expectation written plainly across his face.

Aside from my family, there isn't a soul alive who knows my name. Over the years, I picked up several different monikers, mostly those of characters in stories or of comrades who died on the battlefield. My transient lifestyle always made such evasions possible and sometimes even easy.

But ever since I killed the king, I've gone by only one name.

I offer him the cruelest smile I can muster and answer, "I am the Godslayer."

Syran's eyes flash with anger as his schooled demeanor once again shatters. He jumps to his feet and opens his mouth as if to demand more of me, but he stops himself before he can utter even a single word. After a long moment, his jaw snaps shut, and his mouth curls into a frustrated grimace.

He's barely holding himself back. I expect him to unleash on me, but instead, he spins on his heel and sweeps out of the room. The door slams behind him. A split second later, the distinct click of a lock echoes through the room.

The sound summons a wave of dread that crashes over me in a terrible tide.

The door is locked, and that can only mean one thing.

I'm a prisoner of the Celestial Court.

CHAPTER 14

SYRAN

Even alive, the Godslayer is going to drive me mad.

I fume as I barge out of the infirmary. The two guards standing watch at the door jump as I slam and lock it behind me, but they know better than to speak to me when I'm in such a dire mood.

I storm through the corridors of the palace, glaring down anybody who dares cross my path. I'm furious with my crossed star. Even wounded, unarmed, and at death's door, she wields her tongue as a weapon. The audacity of her impertinence surpasses even Kartas, who seems to make a habit of continuously pushing the limits of my patience.

And yet she's the most striking woman I've ever seen. Everything about her reeks of power. How many Demigods has she slain with those calloused hands, those same hands that clutched at my body as I drove my manhood into her in our dream?

If I stayed in the royal suite with the Godslayer, I would say something I would later regret, either out of anger or lust. So I left her there, though every fiber of my being yearns to go back to where she lies, alone and in pain, in the infirmary.

But I can't go back. Not yet. It's all I can do to force my feet to carry me toward the library and the Demigod I hope to find there.

When I reach my destination, I slip inside the vast double doors with practiced ease. Beyond lies a terraced room of marble. Shelves are carved into the very stone, and all of them are stacked to bursting with a patchwork of tomes. Spindly golden ladders span the three levels of balconies, and the open spaces are dotted with plush velvet furniture and delicate wooden tables. A bank of stained glass windows takes up most of the space on one wall, and the moonlight that spills through them reflects back in wide prisms of ethereal color.

I pause for a moment to take in the sight.

The library is one of my favorite places in the palace. I spent hours in here with my mother as a child, and then later with Torran as I studied to prepare for my ascension to the throne. As much as I'd like to stop here and lose my troubled thoughts in a book, I instead sweep through the room toward a small, shadowed corner tucked away in the back of the sprawling space.

There is a door here concealed in the latticework of darkness. On it sits a plaque, lacquered in gold, proclaiming this place as the Archive Room. Warm light leeches through the crack at the bottom, confirming my suspicions that I'll find Torran inside.

I push the door open to reveal him seated at a plain square table, stooped slightly at the shoulders as he examines the text of the crumbling book that lies open before him. The old Demigod glances up at me as I cross the threshold and fixes me with his knowing blue stare.

"I take it she is awake?" he asks.

"She is," I confirm.

Torran lifts one bushy gray eyebrow. "And?"

I let out a shaky breath before replying, "And she's impossible." My firsts clench by my side as I think back to her words, about how she'd rather die than live as my crossed star. "She wants no part of this. She wants no part of *me*. What am I to do, Torran?"

The elderly man sighs. "I cannot tell you that," he admits. "Only the stars can guide you now."

"It's the stars that have gotten me into this mess!" I snap. Regret instantly claws at me as hurt flashes across Torran's face. I sink down into the chair opposite him and mutter, "I apologize. I shouldn't shout at you when you're only trying to help."

He waves a bony hand. "Think nothing of it." He forgives me. "And while I cannot speak for the stars, I can interpret the secrets they whisper to me."

That piques my interest. I sit up straighter in the chair and ask, "Have you found something?"

"I have," Torran intones. He taps a finger gingerly against the page that's open in front of him. Like that last book he showed me, the text is just a mess of lines and squiggles, indecipherable to me. But the characters seem to pose little challenge to him as his eyes skim over the writing with ease.

"Well?" I prompt. "What does it say?"

"Remember what I told you earlier? About how crossed stars are matched in power?"

I nod, recalling the conversation in the dining room that took place weeks ago.

Torran points to a section of text. "This volume is a diary of a Demigod from almost five hundred years ago. She wrote about how she had no crossed star and that she was sad to see her friends matched with others while she stood perpetually alone. Still, she participated in her own Ceremony as tradition dictated. To her surprise, the ancient rite revealed that she did, in fact, have a crossed star. He was a Starless man, one of their last great kings."

"Starless?" I gasp. The story twines through hundreds of years of history to echo my own.

"Indeed," he says. "She described feeling a pull toward him in her dreams. They eventually met outside the gates of Nexus and consummated their match."

A seed of hope blooms in my chest. "What happened to them?" I ask eagerly. "Did the Starless king accept their union?"

Sadness flickers across the old Demigod's face, and the warm blossom within me puckers and dies. Torran laments, "Alas, he never lived long enough for them to find out. The girl wrote that the Demigod king disapproved of the match, and, disregarding the will of the stars, had the Starless ruler murdered that very night."

I hardly want to know more, and yet I can't help but ask, "What happened to the Demigod woman?"

Torran shakes his head as he explains, "Though they were together for only one night, it was enough for the lady to quicken with child. The baby was taken from her and abandoned beyond the city gates, never to be seen again. Soon after, the woman, driven to madness by the loss of her crossed star and her infant, perished."

A sick feeling lodges in my gut at the grim outcome of the story. I desperately want this account to be false, so I press, "Why have I never heard of this before?"

"Because it is shameful," Torran says simply. "As Demigods, we see ourselves as superior, gifted, divine. To think of a Starless as an equal is akin to blasphemy."

"But how can it be blasphemous when it is the will of the stars?" I push back.

Torran's eyes glint in the low candlelight. "Now you are beginning to ask the right questions," he states. "The heavens have deemed you and that pretty young thing in the infirmary as equals in power. Do you believe that?"

I recall the Godslayer's mighty swings of the huge greatsword. She moved like a fox, using her size to her advantage as she dodged my every strike and flame.

Until the last one.

Choking guilt bubbles up in my throat at the thought, but I swallow it back down before answering, "I do."

"But not everybody will see her that way," Torran reminds me. "Our current understanding of our faith and divinity cannot coexist with a Starless Queen. Some will challenge their beliefs, as we are doing at this very moment. Others will seek only to destroy that which threatens their ignorance."

While I already assumed that some of my fellow Demigods would not take kindly to the pedigree of my crossed star, my introspection had not been so deep. Fresh anxiety rises in me that this cannot work.

But I will not give up, not when this is just the beginning. "She will be safe in the palace," I assure Torran. "And I am grateful for your council. May I ask one more favor of you, old friend?"

He bows his head. "Anything."

"Find me answers," I beg. "Anything about the Godslayer. What makes her so powerful? Who is she? Where did she come from?"

Torran fixes me with an unreadable stare. The look sends a thousand whispers through my mind, scuttling through the shadowy corners of my thoughts like spiders fleeing from the light. It's like he's gazing down into the very heart of me.

Finally, he nods, as though he's seen something invisible inside of me. "It will require travel," he warns.

"I will spare you a horse and supplies, whatever you require."

"And I may be gone for quite some time."

"It will be worth it if you find the knowledge I seek," I assure him.

He stands from his chair, his old limbs creaking as they work. "Very well, Syran. I will do this for you if it brings you peace," he acquiesces. He offers me a small bow before he exits the musty space, leaving me alone with the journal of a damned woman.

The room suddenly feels very small, as if the book on the table is sucking the very air out of the space. Uncomfortable, I slip out the door, leaving the echoes of history behind.

I toy with the idea of visiting the infirmary as I stride through the colored motes of moonlight that waterfall in from the stained glass windows of the library. But as strong as the pull is to see the Godslayer again, I don't know how to approach her. While Torran's discoveries were of great interest, they won't help me bridge the chasm that spans between my crossed star and me.

I decide that it will be far better to let out some of my anger and frustration in a more productive way. By the position of the moon, I estimate that we must be in the early hours of the morning, which means that the training grounds will likely be empty.

After a quick detour to my chambers to change into a pair of leather trousers, a tunic, boots, and a deep black cloak embroidered with the golden serpent of the royal crest, I make my way out of the sleeping palace and into the courtyard.

Remnants of what should have been the previous day's festivities litter the moon-drenched landscape. Black crepe and banners hang like shadows overhead. The raised dais stands empty and abandoned. A splash of red, deceptively dark beneath the wash of the night sky, mars the stone steps where the Godslayer fell.

Guilt wells in my chest as I think of how hungry I was for the Godslayer's demise. I was drunk on victory when I hit her, and yet I've never sobered so quickly as I did when I realized who she was. I picture her armor, which is locked away in a cupboard in my chambers, and the blood that licked the tarnished plate and the strange dragonhide leathers beneath.

My eyes fix on the bloodstain leading up to the dais as the reality of my situation hits me a second time.

I nearly killed the Godslayer.

I nearly killed my crossed star.

Drowning in regret, I force my legs to move. I cross the courtyard and round the side of the palace to where the training grounds lie. As predicted, the open space is unoccupied. Sparring dummies and targets loom in the darkness like ghosts.

I draw my sword in one hand and my midnight flame in the other. The fire sparks to life in my palm, roiling against my skin like a living thing. I run my fingers over the blade of my sword and coat the metal with the spectral blaze.

All of those feelings–guilt, regret, anger–swell in my chest and ignite my blood. A yell rips from my throat as I lunge toward the nearest dummy. I let the emotions flow from me like lifeblood as I rend and strike at the motionless figure, tearing it to pieces.

I only rest when there's nothing left of it to destroy. I extinguish the flame before burying the tip of my sword in the packed dirt of the ground and leaning on the hilt, breathing heavily.

A bolt of electricity sizzles up the metal, zinging me with a mild jolt. Recognizing my cousin's calling card, I turn and glare at him. I want to be alone out here, but Kartas was never one to respect those sorts of boundaries.

"What did that dummy ever do to you?" he jests as he steps up to the smoldering remains of the straw and burlap figure. He knocks at it with the tip of his boot and then leaps back as I conjure a tongue of black flame that licks up at him.

He glances at me and finally seems to pick up on my dark mood. I expect him to joke again, but instead he looks back at the dummy and sends a flash of electricity from his fingers down to the eviscerated figure.

It's a wordless proposal, and I accept by approaching the next dummy in the line. Kartas slips into a fighting stance at my side. Together we hurl our combined powers at the straw form, demolishing it with frightening speed.

It isn't until we've destroyed two more that we take a break. I sit down on the hard ground, and Kartas flops down next to me.

There's a beat of silence before the question just slips out of me. "What do I do?" I ask my cousin.

He glances over at me and shrugs. "I still think we should lock her in the dungeon."

"She's not an animal," I shoot back.

"She acts like one," he spars. But then a contemplative look passes across his face as he suggests, "Maybe she's had a tough life that's made her that way, scrapping for meals like a dog or something. Besides, the Starless teach their kids that us Demigods are evil and bloodthirsty for their kind. She probably despises us because all the others do."

"Maybe." I hate to admit that he's probably got a point. The hardness in the Godslayer's eyes tells that story loud and clear.

"She's certainly not like any of the ladies here at the Celestial Court," he continues.

An image of Ressa flashes through my mind, and I once again concede that Kartas is right.

"The women here are used to being pampered," he says. "Maybe a soft, safe life like that at the palace would mellow her out and convince her that Demigods aren't so bad."

While my cousin's words make sense, they're also too good to be true. Would it really be so easy to tame the Godslayer? Such a wild creature as the Starless hero won't tolerate captivity if I try to keep her in the palace. But how can I possibly let her go?

"A cage is still a cage," I murmur.

Kartas grins at me, his teeth flashing in the dark. When he replies, his words are soft and devious.

"Not if the beast doesn't see the bars."

CHAPTER 15

Lyanndra

Exhaustion sinks its claws deep in my flesh, yanking me relentlessly back from the brink of wakefulness.

I don't even remember falling asleep in the first place, but I must have drifted off sometime in the wee hours of the morning. Now, I squint against the full and luxurious sunlight as I try to figure out what drew me back to consciousness.

Something tugs at my left hand. It takes me a bleary moment to realize that the pressure is coming from the ring. Half-awake and hazy, I drag my gaze to the gold band, which shudders upon my finger as if on its own accord. The onyx stone quakes as though an unseen force has caught it in its grip.

And then a shape–a figure–shifts beside me, and I realize that this stranger is *doing something* to the stone to make it move.

My warrior's instincts kick in. Before my sluggish brain can catch up, I'm already throwing my right fist out at the approximate location of the person's face. My knuckles crunch against what feels like a cheekbone, and the high-pitched, feminine wail that follows provides me with a bit of satisfaction even as my wounded ribs throb from the sudden movement.

Blinking the sleep from my eyes, I focus on the stranger. The woman is perhaps the single most beautiful one I have ever laid eyes upon. Her skin is flawless and impossibly pale, except for the bloom of red where my fist collided with her cheek. Dark hair, a brown so deep it's almost black, curls into an elegant twist at the nape of her neck. Equally fathomless eyes glare at me, dripping venom. She wears a silver dress dewed with intricate beading and swathes of pearls, and precious stones dangle from her ears and throat.

Her mouth opens in a snarl, marring the beautiful mask she wears. She lowers her hands from where they flew up to cup her cheek and holds them out toward me. I feel the pressure on the ring again, and when the stone quakes, I realize that this Demigod is using her powers on me.

When the gold band doesn't budge, the woman takes one menacing step toward me. The power I felt from punching this audacious stranger quickly wears off as I realize that I'm effectively powerless in my wounded state. I have no weapons with which to fight back, and I'm willing to bet this Demigod is not as frail as she looks.

She draws her palms up, and I wait in frozen calculation for her to make her next move, but then the door opens behind her, and she swirls to face the newcomer.

A man, another stranger, pushes his way past her. He does not look happy with her. Panic settles into the woman's face at the sight.

I'm confused, though I try my best to keep my expression neutral. Who are these Demigods? What do they want?

I don't have to wait long to find out. The man glances curiously toward me before settling on the woman's face. His eyes linger on the red mark my knuckles made upon her delicate cheekbone before returning to me. I'm surprised to find some amusement there.

"Making friends, are we, Ressa?" he asks. On the surface, his tone is light and joking, but a vein of something far more threatening lurks beneath.

The woman—Ressa—glares at me. "She struck me, Kartas!" she whines. "She's wild!" Her voice holds a saccharine quality that immediately puts me on edge. This Demigod is dangerous, especially now that I'm in such a compromised state.

The man she called Kartas frowns at her. "You didn't seem to have a problem with it when you slapped the crown prince," he jabs.

My eyebrows shoot up. Kartas catches the change in my expression and flashes me a sly smile, as though we're sharing some sort of inside joke. I don't know what to make of it, but I certainly don't trust it.

"Syran will not stand for her treating me this way!" Ressa rages.

Syran? I glance down at the ring on my finger, the one she tried to remove. Does she want the ring because she wants *him*? If that's true, then she's more than welcome to keep the crown prince.

Kartas rolls his eyes. "Syran told you to leave her be," he retorts. "Why are you here, Ressa?"

As if confirming my suspicions, the woman hisses, "He's *mine*. That ring should be on my finger! We both know that's the truth, Kartas. The stars be damned!"

He holds up his hand in mock defeat. "By all means, go and curse the stars," he says. "But do it somewhere else. Run along now, Ressa."

Anger flushes through her face. "How dare you!"

Clearly annoyed, Kartas snaps, "How dare *you*, Ressa? The crown prince expressly forbade you from coming here, and yet you did so anyway. And what were you going to do if you couldn't pull the ring off her finger with your powers? Cut it off?"

From the look in Ressa's eyes, I have little doubt that she would have stooped to that level of desperation, though I would have welcomed having a digit sawed off if it meant being free from Syran's fiery hold. Still, the woman doesn't answer.

"Leave," he commands her, pointing toward the door. "And if you attempt to enter here again, I'll tell Syran all about this little indiscretion."

It looks like she has a thousand things she wants to say to the other Demigod, but she holds her tongue as she turns on her heel and slinks out the door in a swish of silver skirts.

I keep my eyes locked on Kartas. He's shorter than Syran and stockier. His hair is a nondescript shade of brown that matches his eyes. He's got the look of a commander, of somebody used to ordering others around, though I can't put my finger on why. I don't even attempt to keep the suspicion off my face as I regard him carefully, daring him to make a move.

But instead of advancing on me, he walks over to the chair that Syran occupied the night before, pulls it a bit further from the bed, and flops down into it in a decidedly boneless manner. That formal impression is gone in an instant, lost to boyish charm.

"Good afternoon, my lady," he greets me warmly.

I narrow my eyes at him. I don't trust this Demigod for a second.

When he realizes I'm not going to answer him, he continues, "Please accept my sincerest apologies for Ressa's behavior. She really is very… willful."

He waits again, but still I do not speak.

It seems he's more than content with the sound of his own voice, since he adds, "You must think I'm awfully rude for not introducing myself. I'm Kartas, cousin of the crown prince. Would you do me the honor of giving me your name, my lady?"

I do not, in fact, do him the honor, but he doesn't let that stop him.

"It is a pleasure to meet you, my lady." His eyes flicker down to my torso. The embroidered white blanket is pulled up high over my chest, more to cover the plunging neckline of my nightdress than to hide the wound. But his eyes don't linger in a lecherous way. He seems to be trying to assess the severity of the injury. That theory is only bolstered when he asks, "Are you well? Have you any pain?"

I want to scoff at that. Of course I have pain. How could I not after his lord practically eviscerated me before roasting me with his black flame like a rabbit on a spit? But I'm still unwilling to engage with Kartas, so I keep my mouth shut.

He's too busy to notice. He rises from the chair and makes his way over to a cabinet built into the wall behind him. Rows of phials and bottles line the shelves. Each one is filled with liquid ranging in color from deep black to bone white to clear and everything in between. It's a veritable rainbow.

He pulls out an unremarkable flask filled with purple-tinged syrup. I identify it immediately from sight alone, and the sweet, medicinal smell that flows out when he levers out the cork only confirms it. This is a pain relief draught, one made from the milk of the purple flowers that grow along the western shores of Alastria. Most soldiers carry a flask or two with them in case of an emergency, and I've even known some warriors to drink down the stuff like water.

The male Demigod extends the vessel to me now. "It's for the pain," he explains, as if I don't already know. "This stuff is strong, and it will probably make you very tired, but it will help."

I want to take the flask. The wound is screaming. With every breath I take, I can feel the sharp pain of my broken ribs, crushed by the force of Syran's blade, grinding together and catching on my flesh. It would be so easy to wrap my fingers around the bottle and drink the potion down.

But I don't take it. I don't trust anything that comes from this, or any, Demigod.

Kartas studies me with a sharp eye. "Take it," he urges. "Or do you think it's poisoned?" He flashes me another grin. "I can put some in, if you'd like. I know how badly you want to be rid of Syran, and I can't say I blame you."

Before I can stop it, a single exhale of laughter pushes its way from my throat. It's so absurd to be politely offered poison by a Demigod that I can't help it.

Triumph alights Kartas' face at the sound. "Ah, so you're not just a soulless killing machine after all," he teases as he holds the flask out to me once again. "Don't worry, I won't tell anybody. Your secret is safe with me."

I shouldn't accept the offering, especially now that I've shown weakness to a Demigod who I suspect is quite close to Syran. After all, the comments he made regarding the crown prince would be considered high treason, and yet the way he drops them so lithely in the midst of seemingly pleasant conversation gives me the distinct impression that this behavior is normal for him. Only those close to the Lord of the Midnight Flame would be able to get away with such impertinent language.

But I am in pain. It claws at me, whispering for me to take the potion and drink deep. If I have to live, at least I can allow my body to heal so that I can defend myself from whatever might come next. Nothing good will happen if I let myself waste away.

My resolve crumbles. I reach out and wrap my fingers around the flask, and Kartas grins as he lets go. Before I can change my mind, I chug the entire contents of the bottle in a quick succession of swallows. When I hand the vessel back to the Demigod, he smiles.

The effects of the pain relief draught hit instantly. The soothing warmth spreads through my chest and down my torso. At the same time, my head begins to swim as my thoughts are wrapped in cotton. I still feel the wound, but I simply don't care.

My eyelids are heavy. I don't bother to fight it when they droop and flutter closed. The last thing I'm aware of is Kartas' voice saying, "Sweet dreams, Godslayer."

And then he's gone from the room, the chamber disappears, and then there's only darkness and the sweet embrace of sleep.

CHAPTER 16

I don't know what to do.

My eyes trace the veins in the marble ceiling as I lie in bed, contemplating my crossed star.

According to Kartas, she is not entirely a lost cause. He took it upon himself several days ago to visit her in the infirmary, where he claims he got the Godslayer to laugh–*laugh*! It's an unlikely thing, but Kartas isn't one for dishonesty. Is it possible that there is a softer side to her beneath that brash and deadly exterior?

Do I even want there to be?

I squeeze my eyes shut, but the image of her face is ingrained in the darkness behind my lids. I know I should go see her. I long for a glimpse of her, even if she lashes out at me with that wicked tongue. But I've staunchly avoided the infirmary ever since the night she first woke.

The truth is, I can't bear to be around her when she hates me so. The very embers of my soul yearn to reach out and touch her, taste her, consume her. I want her so badly, and yet how will she ever return that affection?

But she did reciprocate in the dream.

Before she knew who I was, the Godslayer showed me the heart of herself. I picture her as she was then, spread out on the bed beneath me, her angles and curves molded to my body as I sheathed myself again and again inside her wet heat.

Unbidden, a groan spills from my lips. My loose sleeping trousers suddenly feel far too tight as my cock swells at the very thought of her.

I took her right here in this very bed. Even though it was a dream, it was also real. How else would I know the taste of her?

I reach down and loosen the laces of my trousers. The pressure lessens slightly, but it's not enough.

Beads of sweat pearl on my skin. When she thinks of me, does her treacherous body react in the same way? Does her core weep for me in spite of her hatred? Does she touch herself to the memory of the dream we shared?

My fingers curl around my manhood as I picture her down in the infirmary with her hand locked between her thighs. Her imagined moans curl through the air around me as the first swirls of pleasure tighten in my gut.

I can almost smell her now. That battlefield scent has me gasping as the pace of my hand quickens over my shaft. I run my thumb over the head of my cock with every stroke as I keep in time with the Godslayer's imagined rhythm.

What will it feel like to have her small, calloused hand wrapped around me instead of my own? Will I ever feel her hot mouth close over my manhood?

I growl at the thought.

I want that.

I want *her*.

That need pushes me over the edge. My legs shake as I climax and spill my seed across my bare stomach.

For a long moment, I linger there, panting. Blood rushes in my ears, and my heart thunders against my ribs.

But as the thrill wears off, shame quickly trickles in to take its place.

I'm fantasizing over a woman I very nearly killed, who now lays wounded and defenseless in the infirmary. How could I even think for one second that she would want me?

And why, in turn, should I yearn for her so strongly? She killed my father, as wretched as he was, and she would cut me down just the same if I weren't her crossed star.

Why have the stars damned us so?

I wish I could consult Torran, but the old Demigod already left on his journey to root out the answers I seek. He seemed so sure that this match between us is truly the will of the heavens. I cling to that now, that tiny kernel of hope.

And with that sliver of optimism, my resolve hardens. I will go visit the Godslayer today. Nothing will change if I continue to avoid her, but perhaps she may alter her opinion of me if she has the chance to get to know me. Kartas told me that she refuses to speak, but she and I conversed, however angrily, when she first woke. I can only hope that she will talk to me now, or at least do me the courtesy of listening.

I will show her that I am not my father.

After washing up and dressing, I make my way down to the infirmary. I nod at the guards as I enter the royal suite and close the doors behind me.

The Godslayer is asleep. I marvel at her face, where no trace of her past vitriol lingers. Her golden hair fans out across the pillows, and it's all I can do not to reach out and run my fingers through it. The blankets are bunched around her torso to expose the bodice of her lace nightgown and the bulk of the bandages around her ribs. Her hands lay atop the quilt, and the glint of onyx and gold on her left hand catches my attention. A strange satisfaction settles inside me as I admire how prettily the ring sits on her finger.

She looks peaceful in her slumber. I can imagine her in this moment as a lady of the Celestial Court, a fine counter to her wild nature. Will she want that, if I offer it to her?

There's only one way to find out.

I lay my hand on her shoulder.

My crossed star's eyes snap open. For a moment, her gaze is soft and cloudy as she swims toward wakefulness, but then the suspicion and hatred flood in as she catches sight of me by her side.

I draw my hand back as though I've been burned. This is not how I want to start our interaction. It does not bode well for either of us.

The Godslayer regards me carefully, as if assessing me as a threat. I recognize it as a skill honed by years of battle and bloodshed, and I wonder just how much this woman has lived through to mold her instincts in such a cynical way. In line with what Kartas told me, she doesn't say a word, though her mouth curls into a sneer.

I drop into a low bow, one fit for the woman the stars have chosen to be my queen. "Good morning, my lady," I say in my most polite tone.

When I straighten up, the Godslayer's expression has not softened. Instead, she glares at me with open disgust.

What am I doing wrong? Such an action should charm any lady. It certainly worked with Ressa, though my opinion of her refinement is now quite soured.

But the Godslayer is not a noblewoman, I remind myself. Perhaps Starless maidens may dream of being treated as such, but my crossed star is not one of those either. She is a soldier, a warrior. Will she respond to me if I treat her more as a brother in arms?

After struggling for a moment to find the words, I inform her, "The healers say that you are improving quickly. They think you will recover fully, in time. You should have no problem wielding a sword again." It's what I would want to hear if I were to find myself in a similar predicament.

It's hard to tell if the Godslayer appreciates my new approach, but at least her scowl doesn't deepen. On the other hand, she still does not speak.

"Have the guards and healers treated you well?" I inquire. I want to force an answer from her, even if it's a vicious one. "Kartas tells me that your spirits seem to be improving."

The Godslayer scoffs. It's a quiet, wordless sound, but a response all the same, a small but mighty victory.

"I do not wish for you to be uncomfortable," I lay out honestly. "Tell me, please, what I can do to make you happy?"

As I hoped, my provocative words finally goad a verbal response from my crossed star. Her expression twists with malice as she repeats, "Happy?" The sound of her own voice seems to stun her, as though she didn't mean to speak. Still, she continues, "You lock me away and wish for me to be *happy?*"

"Yes," I reply. "You are my crossed star. Do you understand what that means?"

"Your barbaric Demigod rituals mean nothing to me," she spits. "*You* are nothing to me."

I try to ignore the icy spear of pain that lances my heart at her words. "Regardless of what either of us believe, our union is written in the stars," I counter, keeping my tone cool. "We can fight it, or we can make peace with it. I, for one, will not rage against fate. Will you?"

Her fiery expression tells me that she will, to her dying breath. "What a cowardly king you will make if you bend the knee so easily to the gods," she sneers. "I have fought against them all my life, and I will not back down now."

Silence builds, tense and heavy, between us. She will not budge. How can I reason with someone so entrenched in their hatred?

I turn away from her and look toward the window, purposely turning my back to her in a universal signal of trust. My eyes stare emptily through the glass as I needle, "Why do you despise me so greatly when you don't even know me?"

The Godslayer snorts. It's not the delicate, tinkling laughter I'm used to hearing from the ladies who wander the halls of the Celestial Court, and it takes me by surprise. "You are your father's son," she shoots back. "What more do I need to know?"

Anger flares in my chest, but I tamp it down as I turn back to face her. "I am nothing like my father."

"You are just like him and all the other Demigods," she hisses. "I faced him on the battlefield after watching him and his brethren deci-mate my battalion—*my friends*—for the simple crime of being Starless.

You ask me to believe that you would not do the same given the chance?"

"I would not," I insist, but I can see that the Godslayer doesn't believe me, not for a second. She doesn't know that, while I've been completing my duties to ascend to the throne, I've also been plotting. The Demigods and the Starless have been at odds for far too long. Wouldn't an alliance between the two peoples be better for everyone? It will not be a popular sentiment, but I have plans that would ease the union in such a way that neither group will notice until it's too late to pull back.

"You were prepared to kill me on sight," she spits, drawing my focus back to her.

"As were you," I counter. "What was I to do? If I had not fought you, my people would have thought me weak. Your challenge left me no choice. Under other circumstances, perhaps we could have passed one another in peace."

Once again, disbelief wars with anger on the Godslayer's face. "Peace? Do you really think me so foolish? The only peace either of us will ever achieve is through death."

Her disdain brims over, filling the room and threatening to drown me. The worst part is that I can't blame her for feeling that way, even as my rage rises to match hers.

I hate her.

I want her.

"What will it take for you to trust me?" I grit out. "Name it, and I shall do it for you."

Her hazel eyes flash, and I instantly regret asking as she utters the only two things I cannot–*will not*–do.

"Set me free," she demands, "or kill me."

It seems I have made a promise that I cannot keep.

CHAPTER 17

Lyanndra

I am haunted by wicked dreams.

The first occurred the night I killed the wyrm, the night that the stars forever crossed me with Syran. The weeks between granted me some reprieve, but shortly after my arrival at the palace, the visions returned in force.

I blush as I recall the one I had the morning the crown prince visited me with his empty promise in an attempt to buy my trust. My sleeping mind conjured images of his fingers between my thighs, teasing my core as I moaned and panted at his intimate touch. His talented digits coaxed me to the height of pleasure right before he woke me to reality.

Similar dreams have plagued me in the week that's passed since then—Syran's red hair bobbing between my legs as his tongue does unspeakable things to me, his hands roaming my body, his cock pushing between my folds as I writhe beneath him.

Now, I start awake from a fresh fantasy of my sleeping mind. My heart beats against my ribs like a caged bird. Phantom swirls of pleasure tease the place where my thighs meet. I glance around, half expecting the Lord of the Midnight Flame to be standing at my bedside, but the room is empty even as his presence lingers.

I let out a shaky breath and sit up. It's a slow and painful process, but I push through it. After Syran stormed out after denying my request for freedom, I decided that if he won't willingly release me, I will have to pursue my freedom through other avenues. That means gathering my strength and doing everything I can to regain my health.

My efforts have paid off. Wincing, I gingerly swing my legs off the side of the bed and plant my bare feet on the marble floor. The stone is pleasantly cool against my skin. I shift my weight forward and slowly stand. My wounded ribs protest, but I grit my teeth and ride it out. After a few seconds, I'm able to take a few shuffling steps toward the window.

Sunlight streams in through the cut glass. Outside, I can only see the side of the palace grounds that house the stables and the long, low buildings that I guess to be the barracks of the Celestial Knights. A sliver of the city of Nexus is visible on the other side of the golden gates that encompass the palace grounds. It's a gorgeous scene, but even a pretty view cannot disguise the fact that I'm a prisoner.

Behind me, the doors creak open, distracting me from my ruminations. I turn to catch sight of Kartas, who seems surprised to find me out of bed. He's carrying a bundle of fragrant flowers in vibrant shades of red and yellow, their stems bound together with a red silk bow.

I raise an eyebrow at the Demigod who, in turn, offers me a sheepish shrug. "I keep telling Syran you won't accept his gifts, but he insisted," Kartas explains as he sets the flowers down on the small table beside the bed. There are several bouquets already there, all in varying states of wilting decay. If the crown prince thinks he can win me over with fancy flowers, he's sorely mistaken.

Once his task is completed, Kartas leans casually against the wall. This isn't the first time he's come to visit me since Syran's weak attempt to gain my trust. While I certainly don't trust the crown prince's cousin, or any other Demigod for that matter, I have to admit that he makes for easy company. He never presses me to speak. In fact, he seems to prefer the sound of his own voice given the way he prattles on about nonsense like what he ate for breakfast, who won a sparring match, or which knight fell off their horse during training.

"You look well," he comments, clearly alluding to the fact that this is, to his knowledge, the first time I've gotten out of bed since the battle. I prefer it that way. None of the Demigods need to know that I first pushed myself to my feet only minutes after my last encounter with Syran. Let them think I'm weaker than I am. It will only make my eventual escape that much easier.

Kartas nods to the window. "Surveying your future kingdom?" he asks lightly.

I roll my eyes. It hasn't escaped me that by being Syran's crossed star, I'm expected to wed him and become his queen when he ascends the throne. While others might jump at the chance to wield such power, I suspect that the job of a royal woman amounts to little more than looking beautiful and planning balls. I would just be trading one prison for another.

The Demigod pushes off the wall and steps up to join me at the window. I bristle at his proximity, but he either doesn't notice or pretends not to.

"You know, it really is a beautiful day," he muses. His eyes, sharp as a general's, survey me quickly. "You seem steady on your feet. Would you like to accompany me out for a stroll in the courtyard? It's not far, and the fresh air will probably do you some good."

I draw in a breath. I haven't been outside in weeks, not since the battle. Even the window in here is locked, preventing the flow of fresh air. The prospect of feeling the sun on my skin is tempting.

What harm could a little walk do? I can test my physical limits to see how much strength I've really gained back. At the same time, I can survey the route between the infirmary and the palace doors. That will be important information to have for my inevitable escape.

So I nod once as I try not to appear overly enthusiastic.

Kartas' face lights up, and he claps. "Wonderful!" he exclaims.

"Let's get you some shoes. And a robe. Syran will have my head if I let you wander around while you're dressed so scandalously."

He disappears out the doors, which he locks behind him, undercutting his seemingly kind behavior. I remain by the window as the minutes tick by. Is he going to come back at all? Or is this just some cruel Demigod trick meant to twist my mind?

But then Kartas bursts back in the room, his arms laden with fabric. He hands me the bundle first, which I shake out to reveal a flowing robe sewn from fine black velvet. I run my fingers over the plush material and marvel at how unbelievably soft it is. Swirls of golden embroidery decorate the garment, coalescing together into the lunging serpent of the royal seal on the back.

"It's Syran's. I doubt he'll be upset that you've borrowed it," Kartas explains as I pull the robe slowly over my arms and shoulders. He knows better than to try to assist me as I adjust the sides before looping the sash into a knot at my waist. The sleeves and hem are far too long for me, but at least the garment covers the plunging neckline of the nightdress.

Next, the Demigod passes me a pair of flat slippers dripping with ribbons and gemstones. I step into them quickly. He must have gotten them from one of the ladies of the Celestial Court. Nastily, I hope he swiped them from Ressa.

I feel silly adorned with such fine clothes. No Starless, not even the ancient kings of yore, would dress in such opulent garments, let alone a soldier such as myself. I'm much more suited to armor or leathers, though I can't deny how luxurious the exotic fabrics feel against my skin.

Satisfied that I won't cause too much of an uproar in the halls of the Celestial Court, Kartas steps forward and crooks his arm toward me.

He grins as I regard his proffered limb with suspicion. He wiggles his elbow and assures me, "I don't bite, Godslayer. Not as hard as you probably do, anyway."

I roll my eyes again, but his humor is enough to convince me to loop my arm through his. Truthfully, I'm grateful for the support, though I would never tell him. I haven't walked any significant distance in quite some time, and I'm already feeling a bit wobbly. At least this way, I won't present as an easy target to any Demigods we might pass.

Kartas leads me across the threshold. I diligently note the two guards that stand outside. They gawk at me as we pass between them, but they do not speak. I keep my head facing forward, my chin up in a proud façade. We march through the adjoining room, which seems to be the main infirmary, and then out through another set of doors into a high-ceilinged corridor.

My heartbeat quickens as I scan the hallway and realize there are several more Demigods here. Kartas doesn't hesitate to guide me to the right where a group of immaculately groomed women in grand dresses passes from the other direction. Their gazes are cold and furious as they regard me. Even though I expected nothing less than disdain from them, I still feel a spike of anxiety at the ferocity with which they stare.

"Ignore them," Kartas whispers as we sweep past. "They're just jealous of you. Any of those women would sell their souls to be Syran's crossed star. He'll have their heads if they harm you."

I picture Ressa's face in my mind's eye, and I silently agree with him.

We encounter even more Demigods as Kartas weaves me through the corridors of the palace. They all stare, some with a mix of curiosity and fear, others with unbridled hatred. A second group of women snickers behind dainty hands, and several men mutter between themselves as I pass.

I killed your king, I think to myself. *You are no better than me.*

Finally, Kartas steers us toward two tall, arched doors. They stand open, allowing the sunlight to tumble in. It creates the illusion that the marble walls and floor are glowing from within. I step into the unfettered light and sigh as it hits my face.

"This way," Kartas murmurs after a long moment. I allow him to lead me out into the courtyard. Even though the golden gates are securely shut, I still feel his arm tighten around mine as though he's afraid I'll make a mad dash for them. Demigods mill around, strolling through the sunny morning with parasols held high. My gaze flickers to the dais and then down to the stairs leading up to it where my life nearly ended on the cold, hard stone. There's a dark stain there. Blood.

My blood.

I swallow and look away.

I'm relieved when Kartas avoids the dais altogether, instead guiding me around to the side of the palace that I can't see from my window. Here, the worn cobblestones and luscious greenery give way to a huge rectangle of hard packed earth. Straw dummies and red targets painted on white squares of wood lean against several outbuildings. This must be the training ground, I realize.

"I thought you'd find this interesting," Kartas says.

Several soldiers are sparring in the middle of the field. Syran's red hair, pulled back in a ponytail, flashes in the sunlight like a beacon as he swings a staff at three Demigods dressed in what I assume to be the training garb of the Celestial Knights. The crown prince himself is decidedly less clothed. He wears black leather trousers and boots, but his chest is bare. He's well-muscled with powerful, broad shoulders. I recall how I ran my hands greedily over that firm chest in my dreams, how he pinned me down with those strong arms as he thrust into me again and again. A shiver wracks my body.

"Are you cold?" Kartas asks.

I ignore him in favor of watching Syran take down one opponent and then a second. He looks vicious. Arousal thrums low in my gut as I observe him, and I hate that I'm attracted to him. The Lord of the Midnight Flame turns and sidesteps an attack by the last soldier. As he moves, his green eyes catch mine.

His gaze is scalding.

I still feel the ghost of it as he swirls and jabs at his last remaining opponent with the butt of his staff. I don't wait for him to turn back to me. I don't want to see what's written on his face.

Instead, I tug at Kartas' arm. "Tired?" he asks.

I nod.

He doesn't argue at my silent request to leave. He simply leads me back the way we came, past the whispering Demigods and into the cool shadows of the palace. My prison beckons with open arms, and I return to it demurely, knowing all the while that my escape is imminent.

But the whole walk back, I can't get Syran's eyes out of my head. And as my strength wanes, and I begin to lean heavily on Kartas' arm, I can't help but wish that it was the crown prince at my side instead of his cousin.

I can't deny my attraction any longer.

All I can hope is that I can flee this place before I give into it completely.

CHAPTER 18

I can't get the Godslayer out of my mind.

She's always there whenever I close my eyes, teasing me with her beauty and hot fury. It was bad enough when she was confined to the infirmary, but my heart nearly stopped the first time Kartas escorted her out of the palace to observe the exercises on the training grounds. I didn't expect her to be there when I turned around, her gaze surveying and appreciative rather than loathing. I bathed in freezing water after that particular encounter, though it didn't do much to quell the blaze of lust I felt for her in that moment.

After my failed promise and the reaction she dragged from me on the training ground, I don't dare make the journey down to the infirmary. I want to shout at her. I want to kiss her. I want to claim her. And I can't risk doing any of those things.

So Kartas is now my eyes and ears. The Godslayer still will not say much, if anything, to him. I recall the stories that circulated through my spies of how she didn't speak or eat. Neither of those things is true. I've heard her voice firsthand, and while I have yet to take a meal with her, the kitchens report that she consumes more than two guards combined, though where all that food goes is a sheer mystery when looking at her slim, muscled form.

But perhaps she simply does not have a lot to say, or she's gone so long living a solitary life beneath my father's golden helm that she's forsaken the art of conversation. Either way, she's clearly not a social creature.

That much is made even clearer by her habits. Now, as Kartas and I pick at plates of thinly sliced meats and a selection of fragrant cheeses in the dining room, he fills me in on her progress since he first took her out on the grounds a week prior.

"She's stronger," he informs me through a mouth full of gammon. "She's been spending more time on her feet. The guards tell me that they hear her pacing quite often."

"Pacing?" I repeat. It makes her sound like an animal trapped in a cage, plotting to find a way out to freedom. Guiltily, I realize that that's exactly what she is. Even the occasional stroll through the courtyard or the gardens isn't enough. "Surely there's something within the palace that can keep her occupied?"

Kartas nods thoughtfully. "I've allowed the guards to accompany her to the library. It gets her out of the infirmary for a short time, and she takes books back with her." He plucks a chunk of cheese from one of the plates and pops it into his mouth. He chews for a moment before he ponders, "Did you know the Starless can read? My parents always told me that they were illiterate."

It's the same thing my father taught me. "Well, clearly we were mistaken. What kind of books does she prefer?"

Kartas looks at me like I've asked the stupidest question in the world, but he answers anyway. "History and politics, mostly. Some titles are war strategy and geography, but the vast majority are about relations between the Demigods and the Starless."

"Interesting," I muse. I wonder if her instinct is the same as mine, if she's searching for other cases of crossed stars between Demigods and Starless. Has she found anything? I doubt she could stumble across something that Torran missed, but it doesn't hurt to have more eyes searching.

My cousin doesn't seem to share my sentiment. "Imagine having access to the biggest library in all of Alastria, and you pick out some dusty old textbook over an exciting novel. How sad."

I shake my head. I can't imagine how bored the Godslayer must be. If she's feeling better, perhaps I can allow her to wander throughout more of the palace, as long as the guards escort her. It's possible she'll enjoy digging in the greenhouses, cooking in the kitchens, or gazing up at the stars in Torran's observatory. While none of those activities are typically considered fit for a future queen, I will grant her access to anything that will bring her more happiness.

The only thing I can't do is let her go.

Seemingly oblivious to my introspection, Kartas continues to ramble, "Yesterday, the guards complained about carrying books for her, but I told them off. She's doing better, but the healers advised that she shouldn't try to lift anything heavy for a while longer. I warned them that if they gripe about it again today, I'll switch them to cleaning the latrines instead. That seemed to shut them up."

"Today?" I ask, picking the word out of Kartas' diatribe. "You mean she's going to the library today?"

"She's probably there now," he confirms.

I know it's a bad idea, but still I proclaim, "I shall join her."

Kartas furrows his brow. "Do you think she'll be glad to see you?"

I don't dignify that question with a response. Instead, I stand from my chair and move toward the door.

"Syran," my cousin calls before I can cross the threshold. "Before you go to her, you should know that the Demigods are getting restless now that she's moving around the palace. Just... be careful. You don't want to set her off when everybody's already on edge."

This time, I offer him a curt nod of acknowledgement. I don't particularly like his words, but he does have a point. I can't have the Godslayer lashing out now that she's back on her feet. If she harms a single Demigod, all hell will break loose. I'll have to tread carefully.

My journey to the library is swift. There are two guards stationed outside the open double doors. They bow their heads as I approach.

"You are dismissed," I order. They glance at one another but comply, marching in synchronicity down the corridor away from me.

Another pair of Celestial Knights waits inside by the windows. Aware of how voices echo in the space, I silently gesture for them to leave, and they too do as I command.

The Godslayer seems none the wiser. She stalks the shelves on the ground floor like an animal tracking its prey. Every so often, she pulls out a book and examines it. Most of them go back to whence they came, but a handful of titles join an ever-growing pile on the floor beside a plush armchair nearby. I scan the bindings, noting that Kartas' assessment was correct. They're all political histories about the relations between Demigods and the Starless going back to antiquity.

At first I simply admire her from a distance. She's wearing a black velvet robe—*my robe*, I realize with a stir of arousal—over a white lace nightdress. I don't allow myself to picture what lies beneath. Her honeyed hair is tied up in a loose bun with a strip of leather, though several strands have escaped to frame her face. She looks healthier than the last time I saw her, more robust.

I approach her quietly, not wanting to spook her. She's lost in her element, her eyes sharp and intelligent as she seeks out her next target. Her gaze lands on a brown leather-bound volume emblazoned with gold gilt writing that sits on one of the top shelves. She reaches up for it, but even on the balls of her feet, her fingers just barely brush the book's spine.

The urge to be close to her is overwhelming. I feel untethered as I step up behind her. She doesn't even realize I'm there until my chest is inches from her back, and by that time, it's too late. I plant one hand on the shelf beside her, cutting off her point of exit. With the other, I grab the book she's reaching for.

The Godslayer spins in the cage of my body until her chest is near flush against mine. She glares up at me, defiant as always.

"Your book, my lady," I breathe as I draw the tome down into the sliver of space that remains between us.

She snatches it out of my hands without so much as a word of appreciation. Her face is flushed with anger and... arousal? The sight shocks me in the best way. Is it possible that she, too, feels the connection that grows between us? Does she crave the carnal pleasure of my body the same way I hunger for hers?

When she speaks, her voice is low and husky with the turmoil that roils behind her hazel eyes. "What do you want from me?" she hisses.

I answer without hesitation. "You."

And then I lose control.

My lips crash down over hers. She tastes as I remember, unique and irresistible. And though she smells of the flowered soap and herbs of the infirmary, underneath I can still catch that battlefield scent, all raw power and aggression. Some animal part of me growls in appreciation.

At first, the Godslayer freezes beneath me. She tenses, caught up in a fight or flight instinct. But then she melts against me as she gives in to the bond of our desire.

Her mouth molds to mine as she follows my lead. When I tease the seam of her lips with my tongue, they open easily in silent permission. The kiss deepens and so does my arousal as my cock twitches in my trousers, as drawn to her as I am. She can surely feel my hardening length against her stomach, but she continues to drink from me like a woman dying of thirst.

It's only when I roll my hips into hers that I realize I've gone too far.

She arches back, drawing her mouth away from mine. Her lips are bruised, her face flushed. She glares at me with fresh anger, and I know instantly that I have pushed her too much, too soon.

I open my mouth to soothe her, but she doesn't give me the chance.

She brings the book up between us and smacks me squarely in the chest.

I stumble back from the force of it, bringing a hand up to rub at the spot where she hit me. Surprise spills through my body in a frigid wave as she fumes up at me.

"Make no mistake, Demigod," she snarls as she throws the book down between us. The thump reverberates through the open space. "Our stars may be crossed, but our hearts will never be one."

She glares at me for a moment longer before fleeing from the library, leaving me alone in the colorful shadows of the stained glass windows.

My heart thrums in my chest as my mind wars between following her and letting her go. I desperately want to go after her even as I recognize that perhaps we both need space.

Because under all the anger and disbelief that she assaulted me in such an uncouth manner, I'm hurt.

My crossed star has rejected me yet again.

I can't let that stand.

CHAPTER 19

Lyanndra

I have to get out of here.

The thought loops through my mind on repeat as I pace back and forth in my room in the infirmary. Though Syran didn't follow me from the library after I ran, his guards did. They quickly caught up with me in the hallway as soon as I passed through the open double doors. It seems like an entire battalion was present to escort me back to my gilded prison, where they locked me in without a single word.

Emotions swirl through me with intense ferocity. My anger hasn't subsided since the crown prince kissed me. Worse, I'm brimming with fear and shame that I returned the intimate act, if only for a moment.

And I *liked* it.

The admission makes me feel sick to my stomach, like the walls are closing in. Tendrils of smoke, a memory of the battlefield, curl through my mind, tightening around me until I feel like I'll suffocate if I can't get free.

I have to leave. I need to get out of this palace before the magnetic pull that drags me relentlessly toward Syran causes me to do something worse than just kiss him.

This is the moment I planned for. I have two points of egress in this room. The most obvious is through the door. I memorized the twists and turns of the Celestial Court's maze of corridors, or at least the ones I've seen so far. Navigating to the front doors will be easy enough, but it's the guards and other Demigods that I'm worried about. There's zero chance I'll be able to slip past the pair at my door, even if I am able to unlock it. Beyond them, the halls are practically crawling with courtiers. Somebody will try to stop me, perhaps Kartas or even Syran.

The thought fills me with dread. I don't want to see the crown prince's face again. I'm afraid that, if I do, the spell the stars have cast upon us will be too powerful to resist.

That leaves the second option: the window. Like the door, it's locked. An iron latch holds it shut, and I have no clue where to find the key that fits in the tiny hole of the lock. Luckily, I swiped a fork from one of my meal trays more than a week ago for this very purpose. I should be able to trip the mechanism with little trouble.

After that, my path is relatively painless. I'm much stronger than the Demigods realize. Though my wound still bothers me, I've been pretending to be less functional than I am for weeks, lulling them into a false sense of security. The gamble paid off, since the crown prince and his cousin never thought to post guards outside my window. From there, the drop to the ground from the sill is only a few feet. I can cut straight to the stables, steal a horse, and be on my way.

I retrieve the fork from where I've stowed it beneath the mattress. I spear one prong on the bedside table and lever my weight down on it, bending it to a right angle. The dainty piece of silver gives easily. It should be thin enough to work the lock.

I'm just about to try out my makeshift skeleton key when the lock on the door clicks. I turn just as it swings open, expecting to see the seething face of Syran or even Kartas.

However, it's only a pair of guards, though they aren't ones I recognize. I narrow my eyes at them as I discreetly move the fork behind the folds of my nightdress. I wait for them to address me in that obnoxious formal manner common with the Celestial Knights, but they don't.

The lack of greeting immediately puts me on edge. Something is very wrong here.

"So this is the great Godslayer," one of them jeers to the other, confirming my suspicions. My hackles rise immediately at his tone. The other Demigod, the bigger of the two, leers at me. The look in his eyes is unmistakable and sends shivers of primal fear crawling across my skin.

Recognizing that this situation is about to turn ugly, I carefully shift my weight into a fighting stance.

"She's a witch, that's what she is," the second man sneers. He turns to me now, his eyes hungry. "You deceived our lord, you Starless slut. You've bewitched him, haven't you?"

The first guard draws a dagger from a sheath at his hip. "Answer him, Godslayer, or I'll cut that tongue from your pretty little mouth," he threatens.

I bare my teeth at them as I snarl, "Do you really think I want to be here, that I want to be bound to the crown prince?"

But my words fall on deaf ears. Both men step further into the room. Every nerve ending in my body screams that I'm in danger, but I hold my ground. They think I'm wounded and unable to fight back. Let them assume what they will until it's too late.

"I'm going to make you beg for me," the larger man taunts sinisterly.

"You can't kill me," I retort in an attempt to buy a little more time. My palm is sweaty against the handle of the bent fork I still grip, out of sight. "Not unless you want your lord to go mad."

The men glance at each other before flashing me a matching pair of sickening grins. "Who said anything about killing you?" the second Demigod asks, his tone mocking. "When we're done with you, you'll wish you were dead. You'll be so broken, the crown prince will have no choice but to toss you aside."

Dread explodes through me at his words. In all my time as the Godslayer, I was always able to use my identity as a man to avoid some of the more horrific atrocities of war. In fact, I killed several soldiers, enemies and allies alike, who I caught participating in such vile acts. I was always the savior in those situations.

But now it is me who faces this timeless horror, and there is nobody here to save me.

I guess I'll just have to do it myself.

The bigger guard is the first to move. He lunges forward, grabbing at my arms. I dart back just before his hands can close around me. Instead of my biceps, he catches the fabric of my nightdress' sleeves, which rip away in his grasp.

While that Demigod stumbles into the far wall, I throw myself toward his companion. I raise the fork and manage to gouge it into the soft flesh of the guard's exposed neck just above the top of his mail. Blood showers from the wound as I pull the fork back and go in for a second strike. He howls and thrashes, not realizing that all the movement will only hasten his demise.

I'm aiming for a third attack to his jugular when the other guard grabs me from behind, his arms snaking around my torso and pulling me away from the bloodied Demigod. He tears at the bodice of my dress, shredding the thin lace. I kick back against him in a wild frenzy. When that doesn't work, I toss an elbow back into his face.

My joint impacts his nose with a robust crack. He immediately pitches me forward and away from him, howling. I take the opportunity to scramble to his companion. The bleeding guard is on his back, unmoving. His eyes are open, but they do not move or blink, and his chest is still.

He's dead.

I reach down to retrieve the fork from his neck when the remaining guard comes at me again. He checks me with his shoulder, sending me careening off to the side.

I hit the ground hard. Air whooshes from my lungs as I struggle to catch my breath. The wound at my ribs screams from the sudden shock, which is only made worse when the Demigod rolls on top of me, using his weight to pin me down. Blood spatters down from his broken nose onto my face, but I don't turn away.

"You bitch!" he snarls as he reaches for my wrists in an attempt to subdue me completely. I can't let that happen. I hook my legs around his and use all my strength to roll. The momentum carries us together in a tangle of limbs until I'm on top of him, reversing our position.

Unfortunately for me, the Demigod has the weight advantage in this situation. He's twice my size, and pushes me off him easily. I scramble to my feet as he does the same.

We regard one another for a long moment. We're both panting. Blood smears down his face like grotesque war paint. My wound throbs in time with the beating of my heart, and I can only hope that the stitches there haven't opened.

Then he reaches down to his belt where he draws a knife from its sheath. The blade glitters cruelly in the receding light of dusk.

"Your time is up, Godslayer," he menaces as he brandishes the weapon. I'm at a disadvantage, and we both know it. He stands between me and the open door, which is now my only realistic means of escape. The body of his dead companion is behind him, too, along with the knife still clutched in the corpse's hand and the fork sticking out of his throat. I have no weapons other than my body and mind, and neither of those are any sure match in a knife fight.

With no warning, the guard charges toward me. He slams me back against the wall, once again robbing the air from my lungs. I will myself not to panic as I clap my hands in front of his face at the same time he drives the knife toward my eye.

The blade, now trapped between both my hands, cuts into the tender skin on my palms. Blood twines between my fingers and trickles down my wrists as I struggle to hold back the man's attack.

But he's stronger than me, especially in this position. The knife slides toward my eye, closer and closer until I know there's no stopping it.

Just as I'm sure that we're past the point of no return, a rush of heat streams over us.

The charcoal stench of burning meat fills my nostrils as smoke puffs up from the guard's back. His face goes slack, and his grip on the weapon loosens. At the same time the blade trapped between my palms flashes to a searing temperature in an instant. I yelp in pain as I yank the knife to the side, out of the Demigod's grasp, and toss it to the floor.

My attacker slumps forward onto me, but he makes no move to harm me further.

I quickly realize that he can't, because like his companion, he's dead.

The only difference is that the weapon that felled him isn't a fork.

It's a bolt of black flame.

CHAPTER 20

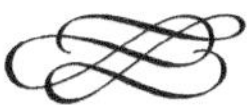

Syran

Ten Minutes Earlier...

"You did what?" Kartas gasps.

"I kissed her," I repeat in exasperation.

Our voices echo through the otherwise empty library. Kartas came rushing in soon after the Godslayer's departure to tell me that the guards intercepted her alone in the hallway and were escorting her back to the infirmary. He stayed with me for several minutes afterward as I attempted to collect myself. Now, as I try to tell him what happened, his constant interruptions are pushing the limits of my patience.

"Why in the stars would you do a thing like that? Didn't I tell you to be careful?" he presses. A playful spark lights in his eyes as he adds, "Was it a good kiss, at least?"

I scowl at my cousin, who only grins.

"It could be worse," he continues. "She could have hurt somebody."

"She did," I growl.

His eyes widen in genuine surprise. "Who?"

"Me." I sweep my cape over my shoulder and pull down the neck of my tunic to show him the rectangular bruise forming on my collar-bone. "She hit me with a book."

Kartas shakes his head. "A book? Really? The kiss was that bad?"

"Shut up," I snap.

Kartas opens his mouth to do the exact opposite, but I raise a hand to stop him. A strange feeling is building in my gut, a sudden surety that something is terribly wrong.

Catching the sudden change in my expression, my cousin asks, "What is it, Syran? What's happening?"

"Nothing good," I murmur. "I think… I think the Godslayer is in trouble. I think she's in danger."

"What do you mean?" he prods. "She's down in the infirmary, perfectly safe. There are guards on her door day and night. Nothing could happen to her down there."

But Kartas' words do little to soothe my growing anxiety. "I need to check on her," I insist, pushing past him toward the door.

"Syran, wait!" he calls over my shoulder, but I don't slow my pace. Instead, I break into a jog and then a run as panic overtakes me.

What is happening? What is this? Is this part of the bond of the crossed stars? I've never heard of anything like this before, but I don't question that it's real. The certainty of it is overwhelming.

The Godslayer is in danger, of that I am sure.

I race through the corridors, pushing past Celestial Knights and courtiers as I go. Most see me coming and have the good sense to jump out of my way. I make it down to my destination in record speed and am surprised to see two Demigods dressed in guards' uniforms standing before the closed door of the infirmary.

Because those two aren't real guards.

They're courtiers, though I can't quite recall with whom they socialize in the Celestial Court. They exchange a terrified look as I advance on them.

"What is the meaning of this?" I bellow. The two Demigods are visibly afraid, but they do not move from in front of the door. "Step aside!" I insist. Still, they refuse to budge.

"We are loyal to you, my Lord. I swear it. We act only in your best interest," one of the pair offers shakily, as if that explains anything. All the while, the feeling of dread within my gut deepens.

That sensation is validated when something crashes beyond the door in the depths of the infirmary. There's no more time to waste. Without hesitation, I surge forward with all the fury I can muster.

First, I dispatch the nearest of the two courtiers with such ferocity that my black flame leaves a scorch mark on the door behind where he stood. The second Demigod attempts to run, but I send out a swath of flame that takes him out at the legs. I don't stop to see if the blow was fatal. If it wasn't, the poison will finish the job soon enough.

I burst through the door into the main room of the infirmary. It stands empty and undisturbed, but the door to the royal suite on the far wall is open and unguarded. The stench of blood in the air is unmistakable, as are the sounds of struggle that emanate from within.

Battlefield fury crashes through my blood as I sprint across the room and over the threshold of the royal suite, where carnage greets me.

The first thing I notice is a male body that lies just inside the door. I barely glance at it. Movement along the far wall quickly steals my attention, and my blood runs cold at what I find.

The Godslayer is backed up against the wall. Her face is twisted with pain and desperation as she clasps the blade of a knife in her hands. A Demigod dressed in guards' clothing–another courtier, I surmise–has her pinned and is slowly driving the weapon toward her face, with less than an inch gap between the knife and her eye.

I don't think. Black flame coalesces in my hand in a sliver of fire. I toss the bolt at the man's back. It hits him squarely with a sizzle of flesh, a death blow. The Godslayer manages to wrest the knife from him and throws it to the side just as the Demigod's body slumps down on top of her.

Charged silence falls in the room in the aftermath of so much violence.

The reality of the situation hits me all at once. Two of my own courtiers lay outside the infirmary, dead or dying by my hand. The body by the door is most likely another one. I raise an eyebrow at the dainty silver fork rising from the man's savaged neck. It's impressive and frightening work. Did the Godslayer do that? Did she provoke them somehow?

The answer lies with the only survivor in the room.

I approach her slowly, concerned that she may lash out if I come too close. But I immediately sense that something is wrong. I'm used to her regarding my every move with open hatred, and yet now, she doesn't even look at me. Her eyes are fixed in front of her on her shaking hands, which are a mess of bloody burns. I can't see the rest of her, not with the bulky body of the courtier in the way.

I use my foot to roll the smoldering body off her. My eyes widen as I take in the blood splashed across her body. Worst of all, the sleeves and front of her nightdress are torn asunder, exposing more of her chest than any lady would ever deem decent. The ruined state of her clothing tells me everything I need to know.

Fresh rage swirls inside of me as I digest what sickening things these Demigods came here to do to my crossed star. I glance over at the body by the door and feel a vicious pang of pride when I realize that she defended herself, and won, with nothing more than a flimsy piece of cutlery.

But any spark of victory is swept away as I turn back to my crossed star. Her gaze hasn't left her quaking hands. The tremors have moved to the rest of her body. I don't know if she's cold, in shock, or both. I whip off my velvet cloak and wrap it tightly around her, covering her exposed skin.

She finally seems to notice me then. Her hazel eyes lock onto mine, sharpening slightly as she returns from the faraway place she was lost in.

"Syran?" she asks hoarsely. She sounds confused, as though she's seeing me from a great distance.

My heart stutters at the sound of my name on her lips. It's the first time she's said it aloud and not just in my dreams. But the sweetness of it is tempered by how small her voice is, how scared. I've never known the Godslayer to be vulnerable, even when wounded. What did these men do to her to drive her to this point?

Now is not the time to find those answers. First, I have to take her somewhere safe and treat her physical wounds. I already know she's bleeding from her hands, but I'll be shocked if the stitches at her ribs haven't popped open as well.

"I'm here," I soothe as I slide my hands beneath her trembling, cloaked form. "I'm here."

"They tried to…" Her voice trails off before she can finish, but I don't need to hear the words to know exactly what they attempted.

"I know," I murmur. "But they're dead, and you're not. You survived."

I gather her up in my arms, cradling her close to me. I worry that she might protest, but she doesn't. Instead, her head lolls against my chest just over my heart as she settles in against me.

I carry her toward the door, intending to take her to the relative safety of my chambers. I'm only halfway across the room when Kartas bursts in with several dozen Celestial Knights on his heels.

He stops short on the threshold, the guards piling up behind him. His eyes flicker between the two bodies on the floor. "By the stars!" he gasps as he catches sight of the Godslayer in my arms. "What happened here?"

I motion for Kartas to enter the room. He does as I ask, stepping over the nearby body with a grimace.

"There were four of them," I say quickly, not wanting to keep my crossed star here any longer than necessary. "Two outside the infirmary and the two in here. They're all courtiers, not guards. Find out who put them up to this. I doubt they're working alone."

Kartas nods down to the body by the door and the fork that protrudes from its neck. "Did she do that?"

"She protected herself," I tell him firmly. "They attacked her first."

He furrows his brow in confusion. "Why would they want to kill her? Her death would drive you mad. What purpose would that serve?"

"They weren't trying to kill her," I growl.

It takes him a moment to understand, but when he does, Kartas' expression darkens. "I'll find who did this," he vows.

"Make sure the guards take care of... this," I order, tipping my head down toward the bodies. I'm very aware of the Godslayer's shivering body in my arms. I don't want to linger any longer. I trust Kartas to clean up here.

"I will," he assures me. "Where are you taking her?"

"My chambers."

He nods. "I'll meet you there when I'm done."

"Thank you, cousin," I say. With that, I step past him, over the body, and out the door. The guards part wordlessly as I carry the Godslayer through the infirmary and out into the hallway. There are more Celestial Knights there, but I pay them no heed as I whisk my crossed star through the corridors toward my chambers.

That's the only place in the palace where I feel I can guarantee her safety.

Because, for the first time, I realize that as much as the Godslayer hates all Demigods, the Demigods hate her more.

CHAPTER 21

Lyanndra

Panic grips me in an iron chokehold.

Thoughts of what those Demigods were prepared to do to me swirl through my mind in a dark tornado. I need to claw my way out of that hole, but I don't know how.

I draw in an unsteady breath as I force myself to take stock of the real and physical sensations that course through my body. My hands sting viciously from clasping the blade between them, and from the radiating heat of Syran's black flame. The wound at my ribs snarls every time I draw air into my lungs. The pain is easy to latch onto, so I cling to it desperately, reminding myself that each throbbing beat is proof that I'm alive.

As the overwhelming fear begins to recede, I start to come back to myself.

The first thing I process is that somebody is carrying me. It takes me a sluggish moment to recall that it was Syran who swept me up in his arms after killing that guard with a bolt of his midnight flame. Now, he holds me close as he navigates the labyrinthine corridors of the Celestial Court.

Normally, I would struggle against such an undignified and

familiar action from anyone, let alone from my sworn enemy. But something inside me whispers that I'm safe here in his arms with his rich velvet cloak swathed around me. I give into that instinct, even as I'm overcome by a wash of shame for finding any comfort in the crown prince's embrace.

I glance up at Syran. His face is hard and unreadable. His eyes remain focused straight ahead, as though locked onto a target I can't see. A fresh surge of anxiety alights through me as I realize that I have no idea where he's taking me. The dungeons, perhaps? He might think that I snapped and provoked those guards, that I'm dangerous. Does he realize I was defending myself, or is he holding me so close because he's worried that I'll cause more carnage if he lets me go?

But any worries I have about being tossed into a cell are extinguished when he carries me easily up a flight of marble stairs, and then another. Even so, I haven't seen this part of the palace before on my excursions with Kartas or my visits to the library. I don't like this unknown element. Where could we possibly be going?

My question is answered moments later as Syran stops in front of a door at the top of the steps. I watch with morbid fascination as he conjures a plume of black fire from midair without even moving his hands. The flame curls into the shape of a key, which fits smoothly into the lock on the door. The mechanism clicks, and then the flame dissipates in a curl of smoke.

The crown prince nudges the door open with his foot and carries me across the threshold.

My heart jumps in my chest as I realize that I recognize this room.

It's the bedchamber from my dream.

Vivid memories of that spectral encounter surge back to me as Syran carries me toward the bed, the same one where he claimed every inch of me in the most carnal of ways. And that means that the dream was *not* a dream at all.

It was *real*.

I shiver in the crown prince's arms. I want to flee from him and this cursed place, from Nexus, from fate, from the stars.

But the part of me that basked in the warmth and safety of those black silk sheets all those weeks ago wants to stay. Because Syran showed me a part of himself that night in the dreamscape, one that felt *right*. When we joined, we were two parts of a whole, equals in power.

Crossed stars.

Before I can decide whether to run or remain, Syran makes the choice for me. He sets me down gently, almost reverently, on the soft sheets of the bed. When he steps back, he looks me directly in the eye for the first time since he picked me up in the infirmary.

His green eyes are alight with anger. I flinch back from him instinctively, expecting him to strike out, but he doesn't. A flash of guilt crosses his face, and he makes a visible effort to soften his expression, though the tense line of his jaw does not relax and the spark of rage never quite leaves his gaze. I can only speculate that the source of his dire mood is that he must think that I attacked his guards like a mindless, rabid animal.

When he speaks, his voice is like a coiled serpent, ready to strike. "Did they hurt you?" he demands.

It's a strange question to ask, given that he probably thinks I picked a fight with two Demigods just for the thrill of it, so I shake my head in spite of my bleeding palms.

Syran studies me for a moment, though I don't know what he could possibly be looking for. Then his eyes flicker down to my chest, where the plush fabric of his cloak still covers the skin exposed by the ripped bodice of my nightdress. And when he repeats, "Did they *hurt* you?" I realize that he understands exactly why I had to kill that guard.

It's not me he's mad at.

I shake my head again. "Not like that," I murmur. Even though they didn't achieve their sick goals, I still feel violated. But those wounds, however deep they run, are internal and unreachable by any bandage or poultice the crown prince could produce.

His eyes linger on mine, and I get the sense that he doesn't quite believe me, but after a long moment, he drops his gaze to my bloody hands. The cuts from the edges of the knife's blade are shallow and angled. They sting terribly, but they'll heal well. It's the burns I'm most worried about. The skin between the lacerations is red and raised with angry blisters.

"Let me see," he requests softly, holding out his hands for mine.

I hesitate for only a moment before placing my hands, palms up, in his.

It's the first time his skin has touched mine in our waking hours. I start at the heat of him. He's like a furnace, radiating soothing warmth into my hands as he inspects the damage. Eventually, he slides his fingers from beneath mine and takes a step back.

"Stay here," he advises as I mourn the loss of contact. "I'll return shortly."

I worry that he's going to leave the room entirely, but he doesn't. He strides across the chamber in the opposite direction from which we entered, where another door stands open. I can just see a raised washbasin and a huge copper tub inside. He disappears for a few moments within, and then reemerges with a small basin of water, which he places on the table beside the bed. He retraces his steps, this time returning with a roll of bandages, several washcloths, and a selection of jars, bottles, and paper packets.

After depositing the items on the bedside table, he kneels and sets the basin of water on the bed between us. His eyes find mine again. "May I?" he asks, nodding to my hands.

I offer them to him once more. He takes my fingers gently and draws them down into the basin. I hiss as the cool water needles the cuts on my palms, but I don't pull away. While there are other ways to clean a wound, I've fought enough dragons in my time to know that this is by far the best way to deal with burns.

As my hands soak, Syran selects a paper packet from the bedside table and tears it open. He pours the contents, a pale yellow powder, into the basin. A floral scent rises as it dissolves into the water, familiar and soothing.

"Chamomile," he explains. "It'll help with the burns."

We sit in precarious silence as my palms soak in the treated liquid. At one point, he dips one of the washcloths in the water and uses it to gently scrub the blood from my wrists and forearms. The sensation is relaxing, almost hypnotic.

Finally, the crown prince gingerly lifts my hands from the solution and blots them dry with another cloth. He then treats the wounds in earnest, smearing fragrant honey over the burns and applying a numbing paste to the lacerations. Once that's done, he winds cotton bandages around each of my hands, lacing the material between my fingers and down to my wrists to ensure that they're secure. His fingers are deft and steady as he works, but I can feel the tension in his actions as the rage still simmers just beneath the surface of his calm demeanor.

Just as he ties off the last bandage, a knock sounds on the door. I jump at the sudden noise, but Syran does not seem perturbed. He stands and answers the summons, revealing a nervous looking maid on the other side of the threshold. She holds a white lace garment in her hands, and I realize that she's come to bring me a new nightdress to replace the torn one I wear.

Syran murmurs words of thanks to her before accepting the dress and closing the door.

He turns to me and says, "I thought you might be more comfortable in fresh clothes."

I nod.

Procuring another nightdress is such a simple gesture and near effortless for the crown prince, but the thoughtfulness of it is profound. I'm used to people doing me favors, but only because I offer them something in return. At this moment, Syran requests nothing of me but my comfort. It's an alien experience that makes me feel both warm and deeply uncomfortable at the same time.

I clutch the cloak tightly around me as I rise carefully from the bed, wincing as the wound at the bottom of my ribs screams in protest. Syran steps forward as though to assist, but I ignore the hand he offers. The gentle help he's already provided is embarrassing enough. I will do this myself.

He hands me the nightdress and then trails behind me as I hobble to the door of the washroom. Luckily, he doesn't try to follow me as I step inside.

I shut the door and lock it for good measure. A quick glance around the space tells me that this room is just as opulent as the rest of the palace. The copper tub I noticed earlier dominates most of the room. An array of bathing oils lines the windowsill behind it. I turn my attention to the raised washbasin, which is full of clear water. A polished mirror is affixed above the pedestal, reflecting my image back to me.

I look like a wild thing. My hair, previously tied up in a haphazard bun, has mostly escaped the confines of the strip of leather I used to tame it. A spattering of blood dots my face from forehead to chin where the guard's broken nose dripped onto me. I let the velvet cloak drop from my shoulders and am immediately overcome with shame at my nakedness. Did Syran see me like this down in the infirmary? He must have, since he covered me so gallantly.

Pushing down the embarrassment, I slip out of the tattered remains of my nightdress. Thankfully, the bandages that cover the wound at my ribs are clean, which means that the pain I feel is likely from the stitches pulling than from the gash reopening. Before I change into the new garment, I grab a washcloth from beside the basin and dip it into the clean water then dab the guard's blood from my face to remove the last traces of the fight from my body.

Only when I'm clean do I pull on the fresh nightdress and exit the washroom.

Syran is waiting for me in the same spot where I left him. His eyes trail up and down my form before he nods. "The dress suits you."

I don't know what to say to that, so I remain silent.

When I don't speak, the crown prince gestures to the bed. "You must be tired," he says. "Rest. You'll be safe here."

I want to believe him, but the defiant part of me that's shaken by his caring behavior blurts out, "Safe? You despise me."

His expression darkens at my harsh outburst. "Do you still think so little of me?"

"I think that anybody in my position would be wary of you," I counter.

"And what position is that?" he demands. "My crossed star? My prisoner?"

"No," I spit. "The Godslayer. The woman who killed your father. Surely, you seek revenge for what I've done?"

Shock flashes across Syran's face. When he speaks, his voice shakes with anger and desperation. "I do not hate you for what you did to my father. I loved him because he was my blood, but that affection cannot erase his terrible deeds. You did what you had to do for yourself and your people. The ugly truth is that I would have done the same. What will it take for you to believe that? To believe *me?*"

My jaw drops in astonishment as I struggle to process the crown prince's words. They go against everything I know, or think I know, about the Demigods and their ruler. And yet, Syran showed me kindness in his own gruff way. I stare up into my crossed star's green eyes, so akin to his father's and so very different at the same time.

If I give him the opportunity, is it possible Syran will really prove to me that he is different?

Only then do I realize that the crown prince seems to take my silence as an answer in itself. Defeat floods his features as he starts to turn away. "Make yourself comfortable," he says flatly. "I'll return in the morning."

I don't think as I reach out and catch one of his large, warm hands between my bandaged ones. He freezes in my grasp, his breath hitching audibly at my touch.

"Stay." It's a plea and a promise, one that I'm not sure he'll accept. It's true I don't trust him, not yet. But the heat of his presence is undeniable, and against all reason, I feel safer with him here beside me.

He turns and fixes me with an incredulous stare. And in that instant, I know that he's as powerless to resist this pull as I am.

The stars may have damned us, but maybe we can pretend for just one night.

CHAPTER 22

SYRAN

I cannot leave her.

Disbelief has stolen my voice. It is all I can do to nod in silent acquiescence, granting her request for me to stay.

We stand for a moment, my hand in both of hers, as the truth settles between us.

And then I say, "Come."

She follows as I lead her toward the bed. Her hazel eyes skim over the black silk sheets, and I notice a small blush start to creep across her face. I wonder if she recognizes this chamber as the place where I took her in our dream and claimed her as my own.

The thought is almost too much to bear, and I forcibly push it down, fearing she'll bolt at the first sign of indecency.

I will my hand to remain steady as I help her slide beneath the sheets. Only then does she let go of me.

I'm hollow at the loss of her touch.

Her eyes find mine once again. "Thank you," she murmurs.

How do I tell her that she doesn't have to thank me, that it is an honor to watch over her? I have no words to offer her, at least none that she will believe, so I simply nod.

She watches me for some time, as though she's afraid that I'll disappear if she looks away. But then her eyes begin to droop, and finally they flutter closed.

A moment later, she's asleep.

I perch gingerly on the edge of the bed and stare down at her.

The stars are so cruel.

For weeks, I prayed to them endlessly to bring my crossed star into my bed. Now, the Godslayer lies beside me, peaceful beneath my silken sheets, yet she remains untouchable.

Still, I consider this a victory. The warmth generated by her request for me to stay hasn't faded, even as her breathing slows, and her limbs relax in sleep.

From where I sit, I'm so close to her that I could reach out and brush the hair from her forehead, but I don't dare do anything that might shatter the tenuous truce that's building between us. Instead, I settle on admiring her from this short distance as she finally rests.

She really is unique. Though she's no traditional beauty like many of the ladies of the Celestial Court, I find her strong features intriguing. Her long golden hair halos out across the pillows, a tantalizing pop of color amidst a sea of black silk. The sheets cover most of her body, but I know from my dreams that underneath all those layers of fabric, she's solid muscle and powerful sinew, deadly and delicious.

It's strange to think that this woman in my bed is the same Starless hero that felled my father and fought me so viciously. Those small hands, now tucked safely away under bandages and blankets, held the greatsword that killed a god. And yet those fingers found mine earlier tonight, grasping at me with a softness that contradicts everything I know about the Godslayer.

Who is she? I wonder. *Where did she come from? What set her on her mysterious path?*

I want to know everything about her, both as the Godslayer and as a woman. I want her ferocity in battle and the gentleness of her hands on mine. I want to hear the noises she'll make when I close my mouth over her core, and when she releases her pleasure on my cock.

I want every facet of her, warrior and all.

My manhood stiffens agonizingly against the seam of my trousers at the mere thought of being inside her. I try not to shift my weight too much on the bed as I adjust myself into a more comfortable position. I don't want to wake her, not when she's finally fallen asleep.

It feels unreal that she trusts me enough to want me by her side while she's at her most vulnerable, especially with what happened in the infirmary.

Though I'm still waiting for Kartas to gather information on the traitorous Demigods, I can't deny that my own courtiers attacked and very nearly overpowered her. How did this happen under my watch?

It's true that I knew from the start that many members of the court would not take kindly to my future queen being Starless. Her identity as the Godslayer doubtlessly turned even more of the Demigods against her. Even Kartas warned me shortly before the skirmish that the rising tensions in Nexus were reaching a boiling point. But how could anybody in the Celestial Court stoop so low as to target her in such a sickening and treasonous manner?

The words of the courtier who spoke to me outside of the infirmary float to the forefront of my mind. He said something about being loyal to me. In some twisted way, did this plot arise out of the idea that I'm just as much a prisoner to this union as the Godslayer is?

I shake my head. I can only speculate until Kartas delivers his report, and I have no way of knowing how long that will take.

A heavy sigh escapes me as I turn my focus back to the Godslayer. She's lucky to be alive and relatively uninjured. Part of that is due to the strange and frightening pull that warned me she was in danger. I still don't know what that was or why it happened, though I'm glad that I didn't ignore it.

If only Torran were here, I'm sure he'd have some answers for me. Perhaps I shouldn't have sent him away so hastily.

A knock on the door of my chambers interrupts my thoughts. I rise carefully from the bed, mindful of the Godslayer's sleeping form. Her brow furrows slightly at the motion, but then softens again a moment later.

Satisfied that she's still deep in slumber, I cross quietly to the door and ease it open. Kartas waits on the other side, his face grim and tired.

I slip across the threshold and close the door behind me. I don't want our voices to wake my crossed star, who surely needs her rest after the ordeal she's been through.

Before Kartas begins his report, his eyes flicker toward my chambers and then back to me. "How is she?" he asks seriously. "Did they harm her?" There's genuine concern in his voice, and I surmise that he's grown attached to the Godslayer after spending so much time with her over the last few weeks.

His shoulders sag in relief as I reply, "She's as well as can be expected. I think she did more damage to them than they did to her."

A grin creeps across his features despite his obvious exhaustion. "That really was a nasty business with the fork. I don't know whether I should congratulate her or be quaking in my boots."

"It was truly a sight to behold," I agree. "Have you made any progress in the investigation?"

"We've identified the courtiers," Kartas informs me. "They're all low-ranking Demigods, which is probably why neither of us knew their names. By all accounts, their gifts were mild and relatively harmless."

This information makes sense when I consider that none of them used their powers on the Godslayer. Some Demigods only possess inconsequential abilities, a shameful characteristic that scholars attribute to weak bloodlines or a lack of piousness. Most of them reside in the outer city of Nexus, though a few still retain positions in the court.

"I think your intuition was correct about somebody else being involved," he continues as I nod for him to go on. "They weren't friends, from what I could dig up. In fact, they barely even knew each other."

"Which means they must have had somebody else in common, somebody who put them up to the attack," I finish. Anger sizzles across my skin at the realization. A Demigod in my own court arranged this act of treason right under my nose. How could I have been so blind to it?

Kartas nods slowly. "I came to the same conclusion."

"And?" I prompt.

"I have no idea who it could be," he sighs. "If anybody knows, they aren't talking. At least, not yet."

Rage broils in my veins, but I don't let it show on my face. I don't want to lash out at Kartas, not when he's only trying to help. I draw in a deep breath to calm my racing heart and then delve into the memory of my encounter with the courtiers outside the infirmary.

They were scared of me, yet they refused to step aside. One of them spoke about their loyalty to me, but it was strange, like he was repeating a line in a play. And all four of them, the two attackers in the royal suite and the pair standing watch outside, were dressed as guards.

"They were dressed as guards," I say aloud.

Kartas regards me with confusion as he replies, "Yes, I know. I thought that was pretty obvious."

"They were *dressed as guards*," I repeat, disregarding his impertinence. "Think, cousin! How did they get those uniforms?"

Understanding dawns on his face at my question. "They could have borrowed or stolen them," he suggests.

"Or perhaps the Demigod behind all of this took care of that part," I offer. It's an intriguing thought, though I have a hard time believing that whoever orchestrated this plot would have been so sloppy.

"I'll look into it," he promises.

"Thank you. And use the messengers to get word to Torran. Tell him it's time to come home," I command.

Kartas bows his head. "Of course." He turns to leave but then stops. "One last thing," he adds. "What do you want me to do with the bodies?"

I consider this carefully. Normally, such a situation would be a stain on my rule, something to be swept away into a dark corner to fade and atrophy until the court forgets it ever happened at all.

However, I cannot let this stand, and I will not allow myself to appear weak in the face of such a treasonous act. After all, any plot against the Godslayer is a plot against my future queen.

I picture the fear on my crossed star's face as she fought the Demigod in the infirmary, and my mind is made up.

"Make an example of them. Take the bodies and display them on the gibbets," I order.

Kartas' face remains hard as he nods. "It shall be done."

"Let the Celestial Court see what happens to traitors who dare defy me," I growl.

Let them see that I will turn anybody who touches my crossed star to ash.

CHAPTER 23

Lyanndra

Voices filter in from behind the closed door, just barely audible from where I lie between the black silk sheets of Syran's bed.

I open my eyes to find the crown prince gone, though the impression of his weight on the mattress is still there beside me. He must have just left, I realize.

I sit up slowly, careful not to make a sound. The luxurious sheets whisper over my skin, and even that seems too loud as I slide out from beneath them. I creep over toward the door just in time to catch a snippet of the muffled conversation that's taking place across the threshold.

"...Your intuition was correct about somebody else being involved." I recognize the speaker as Kartas. From the rest of his comment, I surmise that he thinks the Demigods who attacked me in the infirmary were not acting alone.

Syran's voice chimes in, and it's clear from his words that he agrees with the theory.

Dread churns in my gut as I step back from the door. How many courtiers have glared at me in the halls of the Celestial Court? Too many to count. Any number of them could be behind this, although I can think of only one Demigod who was bolder than all the rest.

Ressa.

I recall how I woke to find her in my room, attempting to remove Syran's ring from my finger. I felt then that she was dangerous. Now, I wonder how she managed to bypass the guards posted outside the royal suite without them stopping her that day. Were they working with her?

Is she more of a threat than I initially thought?

Even as the question rises in my mind, I force it away. It doesn't matter who was behind the attack. Even if Syran finds the Demigod responsible and punishes them, another will just ascend to fill that role.

From what the guards who attacked me said, they think I've bewitched the crown prince. They want revenge for a crime I didn't commit, and no amount of words or violence will be enough to stop them.

If I stay here, it's only a matter of time before one of them succeeds in their twisted plot.

Icy tendrils of fear wrap around my heart and squeeze. The urge to run, to flee to some far corner of Alastria, is overwhelming. But what's worse is the flickering spark deep inside of me that coaxes me to stay.

I squeeze my eyes shut. When did this choice become so difficult to make? It was only this past afternoon that I was ready to make my escape, and I would have succeeded, too, had the guards not intervened.

I don't want to admit what's changed since then. That would mean acknowledging the undeniable connection between Syran and me. I'm losing myself to him, to the blaze of his midnight flame.

In that moment, I realize that the Demigod who attacked me in the infirmary was wrong. I'm not the one bewitching the crown prince. It's him who has cast a wicked spell upon me.

Fresh resolve quickens within me. The pull to Syran is too strong. I have to put some distance between us before I do something I'll regret. My mind turns guiltily to the dream, where he pounded into me as I moaned on the bed beneath him, the same bed that stands before me now.

Something else I'll regret, I amend.

I slink across the length of the chamber toward the washroom. My bare feet make no sound against the cool marble as I duck inside. Syran's velvet cloak is still where I left it, pooled on the floor like liquid darkness. I snatch it up and twirl it around my shoulders before hooking the golden clasp beneath my chin. The material is heavy, but it will cover the glaring white lace of my nightdress.

From there, I return to the main bedchamber. I'm relieved to see that the door is still closed. From the murmur of voices that emanates from the hall, Syran and Kartas still seem deep in conversation.

Knowing that I don't have much time before the crown prince returns, I glance around the room for any potential exits. My eyes fall on a pair of drawn black drapes on the far wall.

Wasn't there a balcony in my dream? Yes, I'm sure there was. I recall looking out on a vast and wonderful garden lit only by the silver glow of the moon.

I approach the drapes cautiously. If I'm wrong, I'll have no means of escape. But it's a risk I have to take, so I reach between the edges of the fabric and feel for anything beyond that might indicate a balcony.

Relief floods through me as my fingers brush glass instead of marble. Lower down, I find a handle. I close my hand over it, ignoring the pain in my bandaged palms, and push it down.

Behind the drapes, the door to the balcony swings open easily in a rush of cool night air.

As stealthily as a thief, I slip between the gap in the drapes and out onto the balcony. The cloying scent of flowers greets me, and I'm certain that this is my way out. I rush to the railing and peer down at the gardens where silent blooms nod lazily in the midnight breeze.

The balcony is higher than I realized.

I frown as I consider the distance. If I were to climb over the railing and jump, I'd probably live, but at the price of a few broken bones or internal injuries. Ruling out the prospect, I turn to inspect the walls on either side.

One side is nothing but smooth, unblemished marble, but a trellis overburdened with creeping ivy is affixed to the other. It doesn't look particularly sturdy, but I don't exactly have many other options.

I draw in a deep breath, summoning my courage. Then I clamber over the railing and reach for the trellis.

For a moment, my hand grips only air, but then my fingers curl around the rough wood of the structure. I ease more weight into that arm, testing the construction. It creaks ominously but holds all the same. I take one foot off the edge of the balcony next, teetering in a precarious balancing act before my toes find purchase amidst the slippery tendrils of ivy.

I wait a few agonizing seconds to see if the wood will collapse beneath me. Luckily, the trellis stands firm, even as I move my remaining hand and foot onto the structure. I'm completely off the balcony now, clinging to the side of the palace like one of the sticky lizards that plague Alastria's southernmost shores.

Syran's velvet cloak swirls around me, shielding me from prying eyes, as I slowly, but surely, begin my descent. I ignore the splinters that poke into my skin and the stinging pain beneath my bandaged palms. The creak of the wood is the only sound as I move down the trellis. When I'm only a few feet off the ground, I risk jumping the rest of the way.

I bend my knees as I land, soaking up as much of the impact as I can while the remaining force jitters up my shins. I spare a quick glance up at the balcony, which still stands dark and empty, before I take stock of my location.

I know from my excursions with Kartas that the courtyard takes up much of the front of the palace grounds. Facing the gates, hanging a right around the side of the vast building would take me to the training grounds and some outbuildings. Going left would lead to the stables and the barracks, as I observed from my room in the infir-mary. That means that this garden must be at the back of the palace, and the stables–where I want to go–should be around the corner to my right.

With my plan figured out, I take off in a run. The wound at my ribs howls in protest, but I grit my teeth and push through it. I fly over grass and dirt, skirting flower beds and shrubs as I make my way to the edge of the garden. I stick close to the palace wall, ducking beneath windows and keeping my swift steps as quiet as possible.

Finally, I round the corner of the palace. A short wrought iron fence separates the garden from the cobblestones of the stable yard beyond. The hem of my dress catches on the metal as I vault over it, nearly pitching me onto my face. I yank at the lace once and then twice before the fabric rips, and I'm free again.

My bare feet slap against the smooth stones that line the yard. The sweet smell of hay and heavy scent of manure grow stronger as I near the long, darkened outline of the stables. I hate being so exposed as I dart through this open space, but soon enough, I'm at the barn doors.

They aren't locked. The Demigods have no reason to steal their own horses, after all. I fling them wide in preparation for my hasty departure, even though I risk somebody from the palace noticing and coming to investigate.

The inside of the stable is comfortingly familiar, even though I have never before set foot in this place. It's something about the universal smell of horses and the soft whickers of breath as the animals swing their heads over their stall doors to peer at me with large, curious eyes.

One beast, a plain brown creature with a white star on its forehead, bobs its head at me, begging for attention. I know immediately that this is the horse that will carry me away from this place. The steed seems to agree, nuzzling at my shoulder as I step forward and unbolt the door of its stall.

I notice a gleaming set of tack hanging from a sturdy rack affixed to the wall nearby. The leatherwork is black, though the cloth beneath the saddle is embroidered with gold. It's a far cry from the chapped leather Barra wears, but it'll do.

There's no time to brush the horse down or check its hooves. I murmur soothing nothings as I throw the cloth over its back and then heft the saddle up on top of it. My new companion nibbles at my hair as I tighten the girth on one side, and then again on the other. I hitch the stirrups up as I go, guessing at their length. Finally, I slide the bridle over the horse's head. To my relief, it takes the bit easily.

I'm just leading the steed out into the aisle when a faint cry rings through the palace grounds. Seconds later, the great clanging of a bell begins to toll, sounding the alarm.

My time is up.

I lodge my foot in the stirrup and use the horn of the saddle to pull myself up onto the horse's back. It tosses its head, spooked by the commotion from the palace. When I gather the reins and urge my mount forward, it surges toward the open door without hesitation, its hooves clattering first against the hard surface of the aisle and then on the smooth cobblestones as we burst out of the stable and into the yard.

A shout arises from nearby as we charge out of the yard and past the barracks. Several groggy-looking Celestial Knights have already emerged, and one even tries to give chase as we thunder by, but we quickly outpace him and leave him behind.

The horse's hooves skid over the cobblestones as we careen around the side of the palace. A handful of Demigods, most in their nightclothes, run frantically about the courtyard. Several dive out of the way as we fly toward the golden gates.

They're closed, which poses a bit of a problem. I glance over my shoulder to see that the guards that are now pouring into the court-yard are too far away to reach me on foot, even if I'm forced to stop and open the gates.

Seconds later, my judgment proves correct. I draw the horse to a halt and kick the gate with one foot until it pops open, freeing up our path.

Before we go, I take one more look back at the palace.

From amidst all the chaos of the assembling knights and courtiers, I catch a flash of red hair.

Syran bursts through the crowd. Panic, anger, and fear war for dominance on his face as his green eyes meet mine.

I don't wait to see if he's willing to use his midnight flame to stop me.

I urge the horse forward, away from the palace of the Celestial Court and into the sleeping streets of Nexus.

Here, the Demigods are much slower to respond to the toll of the alarm bell. I hardly see a soul as we gallop down the hill and past the golden statue of the Flaming God. There's hardly time to process the sight before it's gone, and then we're streaking toward the gates.

Unfortunately, the guards on top of the arch are awake. They're already in the process of lowering the main portcullis. They shout as we approach, warning me to stop and surrender myself.

But I will do no such thing. The guards at the hand crank that controls the gate are working fast.

I'm willing to bet that this horse is faster.

We fly beneath the archway, passing so close to the dropping portcullis that I have to duck low over the horse's neck to avoid the metal, and then we're through.

I'm free.

I urge the horse forward, not even caring where we go from here.

Darkness closes in around us as we gallop into the night, leaving my crossed star behind.

CHAPTER 24

Syran

The Godslayer has betrayed me.

I know it as soon as I catch sight of her. She's on horseback, black cloak billowing out behind her as she kicks at the golden gates that lead out into the city of Nexus.

This cannot be. I can hardly believe the nightmare tableau playing out before me.

When I returned to my chambers minutes ago only to find her missing, I immediately assumed that some rogue Demigod took her. A quick inspection of the room revealed the balcony doors standing ajar behind the velvet drapes, indicating her point of egress. The discovery only strengthened my fear that she was abducted. After all, I never imagined that she would be able to scale down to the gardens in her wounded state, or that she would even want to, not after she finally acknowledged the fated bond between us.

And yet here she is, alone and unharmed.

Fleeing.

The gate pops open beneath her bare foot with a sharp clang. I expect her to immediately urge her stolen horse forward, but instead, she glances over her shoulder back toward the palace.

Her eyes lock onto mine.

Fury burns through me as I meet her wild hazel gaze. I can feel the anger calling to my flames, the embers flaring in my chest. How dare she leave me like this?

Something new flashes across her face, and I realize a moment too late that it's fear. And then she takes off, cloak flying, into the darkened streets of the city.

The Godslayer is gone.

But that frightened look remains seared into my mind, and I realize that she's scared of *me*. Did she think I would hurt her? That I would slash at her with my black flame in an attempt to stop her?

She has reason to be wary of me, I admit guiltily as I recall the vicious wound my blazing sword left upon her ribs. The crippling shame is enough to give me pause, which in turn gifts my crossed star a few more precious seconds of lead in her escape.

"Syran!" Kartas skids to a halt beside me. He's breathing hard, and his face is ruddy, as though he ran the length of the palace to find me. "Is it true?" he demands. "The guards are saying she's left!"

I finally pull my gaze from the gates, which hang open at a crooked angle. "Lower the portcullis," I order sharply, raising my voice to be heard above the tolling of the bell. "We cannot let her cross the city limits."

Stepping seamlessly into the role of general, Kartas nods and then barks the command to a nearby group of guards. When he turns back to me, he asks "Who took her?"

A fresh wave of incredulous anger surges through me as I hiss, "Nobody. She's on her own."

Kartas' mouth falls open in shock. For once, words escape him.

I take the opportunity of his silence to study the chaos that surrounds us. Guards, some in their golden armor and others in their nightclothes, bolt around the courtyard and into emergency formations. Courtiers, draped in lace robes and delicate shawls, huddle near the palace walls, murmuring amongst themselves. As frenetic as everybody is, nobody seems to be moving fast enough.

If I want to catch up with the Godslayer, I'm going to have to do it myself.

I snag a passing Celestial Knight by the arm, interrupting his mad dash toward his regimen. "Soldier, ready a horse and pack for me," I command. The Demigod blinks as though he can't believe that I've spoken to him directly and then offers a hasty bow.

"Yes, my Lord," he acquiesces. He turns on his heel and scurries back in the direction of the stables.

"A horse?" Kartas gasps. "You can't possibly be thinking of following her!"

"What am I supposed to do?" I counter, irate. "I can't just let her go! She's got a target on her back out there alone!"

It's simply not an option. I want her here with me. I *need* her.

Kartas shakes his head. "She's in just as much danger here at the palace than anywhere else," he argues. "I know you must be furious with her, Syran, but listen to me! You have to think this through."

Guilt blossoms in my gut once again at his words, warring with the anger that threatens to consume me. Can I really blame her for wanting to get away from this place? From me? I failed her once by nearly killing her with my black flame and then again by allowing my own people to attack her in the infirmary.

"This is my fault," I utter hopelessly. "I should have protected her. I should have done more to get her to trust me." I turn to my cousin, whose face is heavy with pity. "What am I to do?"

"I can't tell you that," he says, "but I can help you decide. You want to follow her. What about the throne? What happens to the kingdom if you leave?"

"I will not be gone forever," I reply. "Only as long as it takes to find her and bring her back. During his rule, my father would leave the Celestial Court for months at a time. Nexus persevered, and it will remain standing for me too."

"And what if she doesn't want to return with you?" It's a cold, but necessary, challenge.

My answer is just as cruel. "I will not give her a choice. If she dies,

I go mad, and the throne is lost. I will protect her at all costs, for my own benefit if not for hers."

Kartas regards me for a long moment. I know that, as Crown Prince, I don't need my cousin's permission to leave. However, I value his council, even when I do not wish to hear it, and I can think of no better person to act as my proxy while I'm gone.

Finally, he sighs. "Go, then, if you must. I'll see to it that the palace walls don't crumble until you get back."

"You'll be my voice while I'm away," I direct.

"I'll look after the kingdom," he promises. "And you look after the Godslayer. Now that everyone knows she's your crossed star, they'll go after her as a means to harm you. Watch your back—and hers."

It's an easy vow to take.

"I'll see you off," he finishes, nodding in the direction of the stables.

We waste no time weaving through the growing crowd. The activity thins as we round the corner of the palace and pass the barracks. As we jog across the smooth cobblestones, I can't help but admire the fact that the Godslayer was able to scale the balcony, cross the grounds, and steal a horse all within a matter of minutes. It's an impressive feat, though I resent her for it.

By the time we arrive at the stables, the Celestial Knight already has a horse waiting in the aisle. The mount he's chosen for me is a large, athletic beast that tosses its head as I draw closer, indicating a fiery personality to match my own.

Several saddlebags are strapped to its tack. "Food, water, gold, and medicine, my Lord," the guard informs me. "There's a bedroll too."

"Very good," I tell him. I'll also need traveling clothes if I'm gone for long, but I can find those easily enough outside of the city.

I take the reins from the Celestial Knight and lead the horse toward the stable doors. Kartas walks by my side, inspecting the girth and stirrups as we go. But when we get to the yard, we find our path blocked by Ressa.

She's the last Demigod I want to see.

"Syran!" she calls as she rushes toward us, daintily lifting the hem of her silver nightdress so as not to trip on the trailing fabric. A steel-gray shawl curls over her shoulders to protect her from the chill of the night, and her dark hair, usually pulled back with a comb or ribbon, tumbles lithely down her back. Her pale face is beautiful in the moonlight, yet my heart feels nothing but disdain for her as she approaches.

"Not now," I snap, holding up an arm to stop her.

She ignores the directive. Instead, she reaches for me, clutching at my hands. Her long fingers are tipped with nails painted the color of rain clouds, and her palms are soft and unblemished against my own, so different from the scarred and calloused skin of the Godslayer.

I try to shake her off, but she only grips me tighter. "Don't go after her," Ressa pleads. Tears pool in her dark eyes as she presses herself into me.

While I typically would never lay a hand upon a lady, I push my former betrothed away harshly. I can't stand her touch, not after holding the Godslayer in my arms. "Step aside," I command.

She reaches for me again and wails, "Why would you chase after that Starless enchantress? She's forsaken you! She despises you! Why go when you could stay here with me? I'd never leave you, Syran. Never!"

My body trembles from the force it takes me to hold in the hot rage that rushes forth at her words. Flames lick my palms, eager to strike out with poisonous tongues. But I will not lose control, not if it means that the Godslayer can cover that much more ground.

Picking up on my struggle to suppress my anger, Kartas steps between Ressa and me.

"Get out of the way!" the lady howls, but my cousin stands firm and catches her by the shoulders, forcing more space between them.

"Ressa, you need to calm down," Kartas says seriously.

"I will not let him leave!" she snarls.

He shakes his head. "What are you going to do, skip rocks at him? You can't stop him, and he'll cut you down if you try," he counters. "Let him go."

I don't wait to hear how she responds. Kartas has given me

enough room to step into the stirrup and swing my leg up and over the horse. Now astride my mount, there's little Ressa can do. Still, she lunges at me as I guide the steed past. It's only my cousin's quick reflexes that allow him to catch her and pull her back before she can lay a hand on me.

"Please!" she begs.

I grimace at her indignity.

Before I go, I glance at Kartas and offer him a curt nod, and then I click my tongue, urging the horse forward.

We trace the Godslayer's path through the courtyard, beyond the gates, and into the waking streets of Nexus. Once I reach the portcullis and learn of my crossed star's narrow escape, I start off in the direction the guards say she chose.

While she has a substantial head start, it's only a matter of time before I find her.

I won't let her get away.

Not this time.

CHAPTER 25

Lyanndra

I can't go on for much longer.

Wind whips at my hair and snatches at my cloak as the horse carries me farther north into the forest. The night air, sharpened with the promise of autumn, snaps at my bare feet. The cold steel of the stirrups digs into my arches. My hands are numb beneath the soiled layer of bandages as I grip the leather reins between sore and blistered fingers.

Two full days have passed since I escaped the palace. I rode my stolen steed at a breakneck pace, barely stopping to rest or drink from rushing streams. The horse at least managed to graze during our few stops by the riverbeds, but I found only water and a handful of foraged berries to fill my hollow stomach. Hunger gnaws at me now, quaking through my muscles and feasting on what little remains of my strength.

The deep ache of the wound at my ribs plagues me, too. Every stride my mount takes sends waves of agony crashing through my body. To make matters worse, the ground here in the woods is rocky and uneven, but it's the price I pay for keeping away from the main roads. I chose instead to guide the horse down lesser-known tracks and even some game trails in hopes that I'll avoid any Demigods who might pursue me.

Because I'm certain at least one is after me.

I have no words to describe how I know, and yet the surety is strong and unyielding that Syran is looking for me, longing for me. So I continue to run, heading steadily north toward the mountains that cut over the horizon in the distance, where the Starless hold a particular dislike for Demigods.

But I have to survive to make it there, and my odds are dwindling. If I don't find real food, clothes, and shelter soon, I won't be able to face the freezing temperatures of the northern snowfields or the ice-capped peaks beyond. I need to get to civilization-and fast.

There has to be a village around here somewhere. For the last hour, we've been following a dusty track that weaves through the huge, shadowy trunks of the surrounding pines. The narrow road is rutted beneath a layer of dry needles, which tells me that somebody is in the habit of driving a small wagon down this path, probably as a shortcut to get to a main thoroughfare.

As we continue farther along the darkened track, the scent of woodsmoke begins to filter through the fragrant air. The smell brings me close to tears as relief wells in my chest.

It's a sign of people, of food, warmth, and rest.

Over the course of the next several minutes, the trees thin and eventually give way to cleared swathes of farmland. It feels strange to be out in the open after traveling for so long under the cover of the forest, but I quickly realize that there's nobody out here to see me.

Moonlight splays over still fields and empty paddocks. When we finally pass by the first stone house, there are no lights in the windows, though a curl of smoke rises from the chimney to diffuse in the night sky.

I slow the horse to a walk. I don't want the sound of galloping hooves to wake any of the people here. While this is a Starless settlement, I have nothing that identifies me as the Godslayer other than my word. Dressed as I am in my fine lace nightgown and Syran's velvet cloak, they could easily assume that I'm a Demigod and resort to extreme measures to be rid of me.

Stealth is my mistress as I guide the horse past several more homes and barns. The signs of life grow more frequent as we approach the heart of the village. Woodsmoke hangs in a comforting haze in the chilly night air. An orange cat sits in the window of one house, its tail twitching and its yellow eyes following along as we pass. An unseen horse in a nearby paddock whickers softly. It's all such a far cry from the glowing marble and golden perfection of the Celestial Court, one that I didn't realize I missed until this very moment.

Where the narrow track meets the wider street in the center of town, I finally find what I'm looking for. A tavern, silent and dark in the early hours of the morning, stands at the crossroads. A wooden sign painted with a flaming pine tree creaks gently overhead as we pass beneath it toward the attached stable.

I'll leave this horse here. The noble creature has done well to bring me so far, but I can tell it's just as exhausted as I am. In its place, I'll steal a fresh mount for the next leg of my journey, though I hope the villagers see it more as trading than thievery.

With any luck, some stable hand or barkeep will have left some spare clothes or boots in the barn, or perhaps I'll come across some food. And even if a horse is all I can procure, at least I'll be able to bask in the warmth of the building for a few minutes.

I slide off the horse in the shadow of the sign and then lead it by the reins into the stable. Darkness blots out the fine details of the space, but there's just enough moonlight for me to make out five stalls inside. A mule dozes inside one, and a sturdy white pony watches curiously from another. The remaining three are empty, and I guide my companion into the nearest of them.

I slip the bridle off first. Removing the saddle takes a bit longer, as my stiff fingers don't want to cooperate with the buckles of the girth, but I finally manage. When I'm done, I balance the tack atop the stall door. The fine leather will fetch a handsome price for the villagers, far more than the cost of the horse I'm about to steal.

Before I enact that part of my plan, however, I decide to explore the rest of the stable. While I don't find any clothes or boots, I do come across a sickle. It's certainly no comparison to my greatsword, which I assume is stashed away somewhere at the Celestial Court, but it's better than nothing. I carry it with me as I poke around in the shadows, searching for food.

But there's not much else to find. Stacks of baled hay dominate the majority of the space, and the rest of the clutter is mostly tack and tools. Dejected and starving, I break off a handful of straw and toss it into the stall of the horse that carried me here. At least one of us can eat.

Perhaps it's worth trying the door of the tavern? It's a big risk, especially without my armor and the golden helm, but I don't have much of a choice. I need to eat. After all, why should I even bother stealing a horse if I'll only die of hunger a day later?

That grim thought makes it easy to decide. I slip out of the stable into the cool night air, drawing myself into the shadows on the side of the building. It's a short journey to the front door of the tavern. As expected, the latch is locked.

It doesn't pose much of a challenge. I slide the blade of the sickle between the door and the frame, just under the handle. Then I scrape the metal up until it catches on the latch and lift it until it pops free. Holding the weapon in place, I try the handle again, and this time the door opens with no resistance.

Grinning to myself, I step across the threshold.

The inside of the tavern is warm and inviting, even in its empty state. Small, sturdy tables dot the space and a long pine bar runs the length of the room. The hoppy scent of ale hangs in the air, mingling with the comforting aroma of woodsmoke. A single lantern flickers forlornly at the bottom of the staircase beside the bar, which presumably leads up to lodgings occupied by the landlord and any passing travelers.

My first order of business is creeping carefully behind the bar. I hope to find the remnants of a soup or stew cooling on the hearth, but the kettle in the fireplace is empty above the glowing coals. Still, there has to be something to eat somewhere.

I turn to renew my search only to find that I'm no longer alone.

A young man stands at the end of the bar, blocking my only exit. He's little more than a boy, really, barely old enough to shave. He'd be no threat to me, except that he grasps a sword in his shaking hands.

"Stop, thief!" he belts, his voice cracking with fear. He brandishes the blade, and while I can tell he doesn't have much practice with the weapon, I'm well aware that terror can transform an otherwise unremarkable fighter into a vicious opponent.

"Let me pass," I say calmly. I make sure to keep the sickle down by my side, minimizing my threat. Inwardly, I curse as the ceiling creaks above us. Is there somebody else up there? If so, there's no question that the boy's words have woken them.

It's time for me to leave. I take a step toward the young man and am both irritated and impressed when he doesn't move. "Stay where you are!" he warns in a panicked pitch.

I don't have the opportunity to challenge him any further. Two people come barreling down the stairs to flank the boy. One is a woman in a voluminous nightdress and the other is a thick slab of a man who carries a dagger in one hand.

We regard one another in a silent standoff. Confusion and alarm radiate off the man, whose sharp gaze lingers on the delicate lace and plush velvet of my clothes. I know I must look a sight, with wild hair and bloody bandages woven around my palms.

Though I keep my grip on the sickle, I raise my left hand in what I hope is a reassuring gesture. "Please," I implore, "Lower your weapon. I will not cross blades with one of my own."

The man's eyes follow the path of my hand, and then widen as the light of the lantern reflects off the gold band and the onyx that bears the crest of the crown prince.

"By the stars," he breathes.

The woman and the boy glance at him, surprised by his reaction. "What? What is it?" she demands.

The man lowers the dagger. When he speaks, his voice holds a reverence that makes my heart stutter in my chest. "The Godslayer. That's her. Look at the ring!"

Both of his companions instantly seek out the band. I resist the compulsion to pull my hand away from their prying eyes, though I can't stop my fingers from shaking. It never occurred to me that the Starless would be able to recognize me as the Godslayer from Syran's ring, and I'm not going to pass up on this opportunity.

The woman's expression shifts from angry to awestruck in a split second. "We've all heard the talk from the Demigods who pass through," she murmurs. "Oh, the scandal! The Godslayer is a woman, they say, the crown prince's crossed star. He's locked her up in the palace. But how did you get here if you were his prisoner?"

"I escaped," I answer. "I've ridden hard for two days and am in need of food and clothes. I have no coin, but I can offer you a fine horse and tack in exchange for provisions.

The man and woman exchange a glance before the man says, "The Godslayer eats for free."

Relief floods through me at his words. Exhaustion follows quickly on its heels, and it must show on my face because the woman says, "Come. Those clothes are hardly suited for traveling. I'm sure we can find you something sturdier upstairs." She nods to the young man, who I take to be her son. "Stoke the fire and get the kettle on."

Spurred by the promise of food, I allow the woman to lead me up to the second floor where she pulls out an odd selection of leathers, armor, and boots left behind by passing travelers. I manage to cobble together a serviceable outfit and complete it with Syran's velvet cape, telling myself that it's useful and will do well to keep me warm as I continue north. I leave the nightdress with my host, who explains that she's the landlord's wife. I hope that the coin she earns from selling the fancy garment far exceeds the cost of her generosity tonight.

By the time we rejoin her husband and son downstairs, I'm shocked to find the tavern full to bursting. The landlord must have gone door to door and woken the whole town by the looks of it. Silence ripples through the small crowd as I step into the pool of lantern light at the bottom of the stairs.

Then one man raises a mug of ale and toasts, "To the Godslayer!"

The others roar in response. Somebody shoves a cup of alcohol into one of my hands and a bowl of steaming stew into the other. Questions fly at me, but I ignore most of them, preferring instead to wolf down my food in silence. It's the single best thing I've ever eaten, even if it is just identifiable meat and mealy potatoes in watery broth.

I've just finished my second dish when a farmer shoves his way over to me. He drops something down onto the bar in front of me, and I'm stunned to recognize the object as one of my saddlebags. The last time I saw it, it was strapped to Barra while the kelpie fled through the golden gates of the palace.

"This yours?" he asks.

"It is," I confirm. "Where did you find it?"

"Attached to that great awful beast of yours," he replies. "That thing has eaten all my chickens, it has. And the neighbor's cat."

"Barra? She's here?" I gasp.

"Found it chasing sheep out in the fields a month ago. That thing's a right pain in the arse, but we kept it, hoping you'd be back."

It's too good to be true. In fact, I don't believe it until the farmer leads me out of the tavern and to the paddock behind his house.

There, the kelpie stares at me with deep red eyes and whickers softly, the same sound I heard earlier when I rode into town.

My golden helm may be gone, along with my tarnished armor and beloved greatsword. My anonymity is a thing of the past. But as I clamber up onto her back and stroke her sealskin hide, I feel some semblance of normalcy.

No matter what Syran strips from me, he cannot take away who I am.

I am the Godslayer, and I am free.

CHAPTER 26

SYRAN

The Godslayer cannot defy the will of the stars forever, but I am growing weary of this hunt.

I'm drawn to her as the rising moon chases the sun at dusk, forever on her trail but never quite catching up to her. Some days, I feel that she's so close, I could reach out and touch her. Other times, I'm sure I'm pursuing a ghost, misled by clever breadcrumbs and spectral shadows that she conjures in her wake.

Will I ever find her? Or am I doomed to forever seek her light in the dark night of my soul?

Doubt hangs heavy in the air this evening as my horse trudges us through the snow toward yet another Starless town. Up here in the mountains, winter is perpetual. We push through the drifts, some as high as my mount's chest, as I struggle to keep my eye on the beckoning lights of civilization through the swirling blizzard. The heavy traveling cape that I bought in a village some miles back limits the bite of the icy air, and the heat of the black flame that burns inside of me keeps me from succumbing to the cold entirely, but the freezing temperatures still manage to gnaw at my fingers and toes, numbing them.

In the first fortnight of my pursuit of the Godslayer, I couldn't fathom why she would want to flee to such an inhospitable region of Alastria. However, as the weeks stretched toward a month, I realized after I was denied patronage at a tavern based on the quality of my clothes alone that the people in this part of the kingdom hold considerable disdain for Demigods or anybody who may be in league with them.

Since then, I've learned my lesson. I acquired a shoddy wardrobe of garments and made sure to keep my telltale red hair pulled back and covered with the hood of my traveling cloak. This new look allowed me to blend in with the Starless travelers and merchants who wander the northern roads, which, in turn, opened the door to the endless gossip in which the Starless peasants seem to trade.

It's one such rumor that's brought me here to the base of the mountains. One trapper I shared a campfire with told me how he passed the Godslayer on the road several days prior. He described her as riding that great beast of hers in this direction and wearing a mismatched set of armor. When I asked about her golden helm, he said her face was bare and that he recognized her from the black cloak emblazoned with the crown prince's royal seal that she reportedly pillaged from the palace during her daring escape.

It's the best lead I've had in a while, and I can't help but hope that it pays off as a fresh gust of icy air stings my face.

Not long after, we reach the town. It's a surprisingly large settlement. My father would break up any villages that threatened to grow too large or economically powerful, but it seems that his reach didn't extend too far into frigid winter territory of the northern regions. There are several two-story buildings here, a market square, and several shops that are shuttered at this late hour of the night.

So I'm surprised to see that the lights in the tavern still burn brightly when I arrive. Curious, I lead my horse into the nearby stable where an elderly man takes the reins as I slide down from the saddle.

"Busy night?" I ask.

The old Starless man nods. "Everybody wants to catch a glimpse o' the Godslayer," he explains. "Can't say I blame 'em. She's a right pretty lass, she is."

My flaming heart jolts to life at his words. Is she here right now, in this tavern? I struggle to keep my voice from wavering as I ask, "She's here? In town?"

"Aye," he replies. "She's off clearing the nest o' strix from the valley. Folks are a-feared to leave their homes with them swooping about. It'll be a right miracle if she runs 'em off, it will."

Blood thunders in my ears as I process this new information. The Godslayer—my crossed star—is here *right now*. It's the closest I've been to her since her escape from the palace, yet the fact that she's on the hunt for strix chills me more than the freezing night outside.

Strix are foul creatures. They resemble owls, though they're said to hang upside down like great, horrid bats, and they feast indiscriminately on flesh. Traveling in packs, they can easily overwhelm a person, stripping the meat from human bones in mere minutes. I've heard stories of swarms of them plaguing the northern mountains, but I never put much thought into those tales.

Now, I picture the Godslayer, her golden hair swirling, as she fights against hooked talons and vicious beaks.

They'll tear her limb from limb.

Fear clutches my bones as I snatch the reins back from the stable hand whose face scrunches up in confusion.

"What's got into you?" he gasps.

Ignoring his question, I pull my reluctant steed back out into the swirling snow and hoist myself quickly into the saddle. Then we're off, cutting through the drifts in the direction of the valley that sleeps in the shadow of the mountains.

Night closes in around us as we leave the lights of the town behind. I can barely see through the blizzard, and the visibility is only made worse when we enter the forest. Swaying pine branches close in above us, blotting out what little moonlight there is. The snow muffles every sound, even as I strain to hear the telltale screeches of the strix as I imagine them closing in on the Godslayer.

The silence is deeply unnerving. Even my horse seems spooked, though he continues deeper into the trees at my command. And while the darkness is disorienting, at least I know we'll be able to track our own prints in the snow back to town if need be.

And then a shadow swoops soundlessly overhead.

I've never actually seen a strix until this moment, and it's every bit as horrible as the stories describe. The feathers are mottled gray and green, perfect for blending into the branches of the trees they roost in. The talons are curved and wicked, and the open beak shines like a knife's edge in the low light. I catch the gleam of milky white eyes that seem to glow preternaturally in the darkness, and then it's gone again between the rising spears of the pines, lost from sight.

Although it appeared to pay me no mind, I don't believe for a moment that it didn't notice my presence.

Sensing danger, I draw my sword from the scabbard at my waist. In my other hand, I gather a ball of midnight flame in my palm, not a moment too soon.

A screech cuts through the still forest like something out of a nightmare. The horse rears beneath me, wheeling and kicking at the monstrous sound. Though I'm a relatively skilled rider, I'm unable to grab the reins in time to calm him. He bucks, sending me tumbling over his neck and down into the snow.

By some miracle, my sword doesn't hit my mount as I go down. It does, however, slide from between my numb fingers and sail through the air until it disappears into a snowbank in a plume of icy flakes. The flame in my hand extinguishes as I land facedown a few feet from my blade. The impact is softer than I expected, and I'm not even winded as I stagger to my feet and wipe the frost from my eyes.

I can only watch as my horse rears one more time before he gallops away back toward town, leaving me behind with the strix.

As if they sense my sudden disadvantage, a second shriek rings out through the trees. A shadow detaches from a distant branch, and I realize that it's one of the winged creatures. It was there the whole time, watching and waiting. How many more are there?

My question is answered as about a dozen more take flight. They glide soundlessly toward me, bone white eyes fixed upon my form.

Adrenaline pumps through my veins as I dive for my sword. I shove my arm into the drift, feeling for the cold steel as the strix swoop ever closer.

My hand closes over the hilt just as the first of the flying demons reaches me. I jerk my arm up, flaring the sword in a gleaming arc. The blade catches the strix in the wing, sending a shower of black blood steaming through the frigid night air. The creature cries out once and then falls, motionless, onto the snow.

I don't have time to feel any triumph at my kill. One strix alights on the corpse of its fallen kin and tears at its flesh, ignoring me completely in favor of an easy meal. But the others fall upon me, dipping down with outstretched talons and razor beaks and an unquenchable lust for blood.

Moving on reflex, I summon a bolt of black flame and strike out at the nearest strix. Several manage to evade the blaze, but two aren't fast enough. They wheel to the ground in a mess of smoldering feathers. I lash out with my sword next, catching another in midair.

Soon, the stench of burnt feathers and charred flesh fills the air. Black blood splatters the fresh white snow where the corpses have fallen, and yet somehow, more still come, striking out from nearby branches and shrieking through the night sky as I continue to fight them with fire and steel.

There are too many of them. For every one I kill, two more appear. Their attacks are unrelenting even as I slash and sear their ever-growing numbers. They force me to give ground until my back is pressed against the rough bark of a towering pine. I'm breathing heavily, straining from the effort of fending them off as my muscles scream and my heart pounds against my ribs.

And then one manages to slip past a bolt of flame and buffets me right in the chest. Its talons catch in the heavy material of my traveling cloak, giving it the purchase it needs to snap at my unprotected face.

Flailing wildly, I stagger around the trunk of the tree. The strix screeches as it strikes at me and misses once, and then again.

A second sees its opportunity and joins in, its beak sliding harmlessly against the pauldron I wear beneath my cloak.

And then another is upon me, knocking me down onto my back in the snow. The first strix lunges down at me, its beak open and ready to tear at the exposed flesh of my face. I summon my midnight flame, but it dodges the bolt easily.

There's nothing more I can do, I realize with burgeoning horror.

And just as the strix strikes for the last and fatal time, something whizzes through the darkness and hits the monster square in the side. I catch a glimpse of the slim shaft of an arrow before the creature falls.

Seconds later, two more arrows fly from between the trees, taking down the other two strix.

Pushing their dead weight off me, I sit up just in time to watch my savior emerge from the haze of falling snow and smoldering strix, sitting high astride her kelpie with a crossbow on her shoulder.

I breathe her name like a frozen prayer.

"Godslayer."

The hunt is over.

I've finally found her.

CHAPTER 27

Lyanndra

Green eyes.

Red hair.

Unmistakable.

My heart stutters to a halt as I realize that the newcomer I just saved from the strix is no stranger at all.

Syran, Crown Prince of the Celestial Court and Lord of the Midnight Flame, is sprawled on his back in the snow before me, his gaze blazing with triumphant hunger as he stares me down.

Shock swiftly turns to horror, and then to rage. How did he find me? Does he really think that he'll be able to drag me back to the palace so easily? I'll fight him if he tries. The last time we battled, I let him win. He won't be so lucky this round.

But now isn't the time.

A nearby shriek jolts me from my anger. I whip around, readying the crossbow on my shoulder as I catch sight of a strix hurtling through the air directly toward me. With a practiced hand, I grab a bolt from the quiver attached to Barra's saddle and notch it on the tiller. There's little time to spare as the creature approaches. I aim and let loose.

The arrow drives through the strix only inches from my face, sending it plummeting down into the snow in a splash of black blood.

When I turn back to Syran, he's got his sword up and is slicing through several more of the flying beasts. I watch him for a split second as I try desperately to decide what to do.

I could run. I could turn Barra around and gallop out of here. From there, we could go anywhere, as far from the Celestial Court as we can get.

But Syran's already proven that while he fights well, neither of us stands a chance against the strix alone. If I leave him, they'll devour him, and if the Demigod legends about crossed stars are to be believed, his death will only drive me mad.

The choice is an illusion, I realize. There really is only one option if I want to continue my life as the Godslayer.

I urge Barra forward, charging through the cloud of strix that descend upon the crown prince. His eyes meet mine as I approach, and I wonder if he thinks I'm about to run him down.

At the last moment, I stick out my gloved hand.

Surprise passes over his face, and for a second, I'm worried that he may not grab it in time, but then his palm is in mine, his long fingers clasped between my own.

I'm not strong enough to drag him onto Barra myself. Luckily, he's figured out my wordless instruction and launches himself off the ground as I pull. He manages to hoist himself onto the kelpie just behind her withers before he swings a leg over her neck to sit astride her.

But this presents a new problem. I can't see anything past his broad shoulders as he sits in front of me. I make another quick decision and command, "Take the reins. Get us out of the trees."

He doesn't resist as I shove the leather straps in his hands. I don't trust him for a second, but one of us needs to hold the strix off as we ride to open ground. His life depends on this, too.

Keeping the crossbow up on my shoulder, I slide my feet out of the stirrups. I kick my legs over Barra's wide hindquarters and shift in the saddle so that my back is pressed against Syran's for stability.

The crown prince glances back over his shoulder as I notch another arrow in the crossbow. "What are you doing?" he cries over the shrieking of the strix that follow only feet from us. "Are you mad?"

I aim and release the bolt, which finds its home in the wing of one of the pursuant creatures. "Not yet!" I shout back. "You're still breathing, aren't you?"

I load in another arrow and let loose, once again finding my mark. The process is almost hypnotic. Notch. Aim. Release. Notch. Aim. Release. I drop the strix with deadly accuracy even as Barra kicks her way through the snowy drifts.

But it's not enough. The strix have the advantage here in the trees. They blend in so well that it's hard to pick them out amongst the swaying branches of the pines. Their assault comes from every direction, smooth and unpredictable, too many to handle. We need to draw them out in the open, away from the forest.

I grab a fresh bolt from the quiver. There are less than a dozen left, so I'll have to make them all count. Before I notch the arrow on the tiller, I use the fletched end to tap on Syran's shoulder. "I need your fire," I say without looking back at him.

I know he's obliged when I feel the heat of his midnight flame sparking beside me. I glance down to see that he's offered me his hand, where a black fire dances in his palm. It's as eerie and breathtaking as I remember. Hoping that the poison in that miniature blaze works as well on the strix as it did on me, I dip the head of the arrow into the heart of it, setting the wood behind the iron tip alight.

Not wanting the fire to damage the integrity of the bolt, I quickly notch it and let it fly into a group of several strix. As I hoped, the fire flares to several of their feathers, sending them flapping into a shrieking frenzy as the blaze spreads. At the end of its trajectory, the arrow thuds into one near the back of the pack.

Who would have thought that my aim combined with Syran's powers would be so effective?

I have to admit that it feels good to have him at my back, his flame spreading delicious warmth through me as I do what I do best. I still despise him for attempting to hold me in the gilded prison of the palace and for bewitching me with his pretty words and soft touches. But now that he's here, his body solid and real against mine, that spark between us flares, and I once again cannot deny the pull that always seems to drag me back to him.

And I hate him for it, more than ever.

I funnel the wild fury that rises within me toward the task at hand. I drench the tip of each bolt in Syran's black flame before notching and releasing. The rhythm of it once again consumes me as I systematically cut through the strix.

But then I reach for the next arrow, only to find the quiver empty.

A sharp pang of fear presses against the base of my skull. "I'm out!" I holler.

"Almost there!" Syran bellows.

When I glance over my shoulder, I realize he's right. The tree line is right there. And then we're through, breaking through the edge of the forest in a torrent of pine needles and screaming strix.

There's nothing I can do about them now. I toss my legs back over Barra's hindquarters so that I'm once again facing forward. "Turn around!" I order, reaching on either side of Syran's body to grasp the reins.

"What are you doing?" he cries.

"Use your fire!" I shout in return over the cacophony.

I have no idea if he heard my request, but there's no time to change the plan now. I tug Barra's reins sharply as I yield her with my legs. She spins easily to face the forest, where the strix pour out from between the pines and into the night sky in a synchronized swarm.

It's beautiful in an awful sort of way. They spiral down at us, their cloudy eyes gleaming as they dive, talons primed and beaks ready to devour.

And then Syran lifts his arms, and I know he understands what I want him to do.

A surge of black flame pours out of his outstretched hands. At first, it behaves like regular fire, spitting up into the sky in smoking tendrils. But then the tongues of the blaze coalesce into something resembling the head of a great dark serpent, its jaws wide in a silent hiss as it rises up to obscure the strix.

Then those great flaming jaws snap shut, engulfing the swarm in a poisonous inferno.

The sound is dreadful. Squeezing the crossbow between my shoulder and neck, I clap my hands to my ears to block out the worst of it. Syran does the same, and poor Barra shakes her head wildly in an attempt to escape the pained shrieks of the dying creatures.

Then the smell hits, and that's somehow even worse than the deathly cries of the strix. It's burnt meat and feathers, all heavy with a strange iron scent that causes bile to rise in the back of my throat as I do my best not to breathe through my nose.

By the time the flames sizzle out into the frigid night air, there's barely anything left of the strix but a few smoldering corpses that fall heavily into the slushy snow beneath.

We did it.

The strix are dead, and we both made it out alive.

There's no reason to stay any longer, and yet, we linger as Barra paws anxiously underneath us. I'm flush with Syran's back, my arms practically wrapped around him. Every move the kelpie makes presses my hips closer to the crown prince's, evoking the dream where he thrust into me with powerful strokes until I was nothing more than a dripping, panting mess beneath him.

I can't stand it. I kick my leg up and over Barra's hindquarters, dismounting as quickly as possible. I drop down into an icy drift that comes to my knees. Snow forces its way through the gaps in my armor, but even the shocking cold does nothing to diminish the heat that's building inside of me.

Syran watches me from astride Barra, his green eyes unfathomable in the dark, before he, too, slides down from the Kelpie.

I tip my head up to the snowy sky, meeting the crown prince's unwavering gaze. I forgot how tall he is, towering above me by almost a foot. For a moment, we simply stare at each other.

I hate him.

So why do I feel so exhilarated? I want to explain the emotion away as the excitement of such a daring hunt, but it's not just that. We worked together, and we did it well. Have a Demigod and a Starless knight ever done such a thing? And there was something so tantalizing, so unbelievably powerful, about the flaming serpent Syran summoned. What else is coiled in that dark heart, waiting to be unleashed?

And if we were capable of such a wild feat as vanquishing the horde of strix with our combined abilities, what else could the two of us accomplish together?

Some deep part of me wants to know.

So when Syran breaks the stillness to swiftly close the distance between us, I don't back down. When he grabs my waist and pulls me flush against him, I do not push away.

And when he presses his lips against mine, this time, I kiss him back.

CHAPTER 28

SYRAN

Kissing the Godslayer feels like holding the moon in the palm of my hand.

I'm powerless to resist the pull of her, of the very stars that bind us. I close the distance between us, and when my lips crash down over hers, and her body melts against mine, I pour into her everything I feel, all the hatred, the desperation, and the longing.

I expect her to push me away, to smack me with the crossbow she still grips in one hand and pierce me with words sharper than any blade.

Yet, she seems just as bewitched as I am by the spell we've just cast together in the shadow of the snowcapped pines.

Her lips are pliant against mine as I draw her closer to me. There's a muffled thud when she drops the crossbow down into the snow, and then I feel the pressure of her small, gloved hands against my chest. She grips the edges of my traveling cloak in desperate fists, as though she's warring between shoving me away or pulling me even deeper into the kiss.

I don't give her a chance to choose the former. Instead, I catch her bottom lip between my teeth. When she gasps at the unexpected sensation, I tease her with my tongue, promising even more surprises if she stays.

When she still does not break away, I finally allow my hands to explore. I splay one at the small of her back, enjoying how her armored form feels beneath the soft velvet of my stolen cloak. I bring the other to the nape of her neck where my long fingers tangle in her golden locks.

She lets out a breathy moan as I gently tug at her hair. Swallowing up the sound with my hungry mouth, I file the reaction away for later. What will happen when I'm finally inside her and I do the same thing? Will she murmur my name like a prayer while she bucks her hips against mine? The thought has my cock straining against my trousers.

I'd take her right here and now in this freezing tundra if she'd let me. I picture her on her back in the snow, her honeyed hair fanning out beneath her head, her skin rosy in the cold as I worship every inch of her. I imagine the feel of her slick walls gripping my shaft while she wraps her powerful thighs around me and coaxes the very essence from my body.

Would she resist if I tried? Or would she be so lost in this strange magic that she abandons her reservations and allows me to ravage her the way I yearn to do?

But then I remember how I spooked her in the library all those weeks ago at the palace, and I force myself to limit this to only a kiss, nothing more.

As though sensing that we're approaching dangerous territory, the Godslayer pushes gently at my chest. Though I wish this moment could go on forever, I pull away at her wordless request and take a small step back to allow the cold air to rush between us.

My crossed star stares up at me intently, her hazel eyes searching mine. I take the opportunity to study her in turn.

Her lips are bruised from the kiss and the cold, her cheeks pleasantly flushed from the heat of our embrace. She looks well, far better than she did the last time I saw her. Her golden hair, speckled with ice crystals that gleam like diamonds in the moonlight, streams out behind her on the wind. Has her wound healed? I imagine it has by now, given the lithe way she moved during the onslaught of the strix.

I'm struck with a strange pang of satisfaction as I admire how she looks draped in the black velvet of my cloak. Beneath, she wears a set of mismatched armor in a variety of styles. Her breastplate is inlaid with the ethereal feathers and lapis lazuli of the Eastern roosts, while the gauntlets that shield her arms and hands resemble the hammered bronze pieces favored by the Starless of the Southern Caldera. Her greaves, adorned with swirls of writing I do not recognize, are more exotic, possibly from beyond the kingdom altogether.

I feel a sliver of guilt as I picture her favored tarnished armor, the dragonhide leathers, and the scarred golden helm that are still locked away, along with her greatsword, in my quarters at the Celestial Court. Yet even in the ragtag ensemble she currently wears, she looks deadly beneath the silver light of the moon, a vision of danger and resilience.

Even after losing her armor and her identity with it, she found a way to persevere. She's rebuilt herself piece by piece into a living mosaic.

She will not be broken.

She will not be erased.

And it only makes me want her more.

When the Godslayer finally speaks, the hostility in her voice surprises me. It's such a far cry from the heat of her kiss, though I admit that hatred and desire seem to walk a fine line between the two of us.

"Why did you follow me?" she demands.

Because we belong together, I want to say. But I know that she would rather fight against fate rather than accept the inevitable as I have already done, so I reply, "I couldn't leave you out here to fend for yourself."

A flash of irritation passes over her striking features. "I've been fending for myself just fine," she snaps. "Besides, I wasn't the one about to be devoured by some oversized birds."

"And you expect me to believe that you were going to kill the strix all on your own?" It's a low blow but also true. It was foolish for her to attempt to vanquish the nest by herself. Doesn't she understand that?

"I've faced worse," she answers flippantly. "I've faced *you*."

The jab hits home. Fresh anger broils beneath my skin as I hiss, "You didn't face me. You *used* me. You wanted to die that day, all to drive me mad. Did you really think that I'd let you out of my sight and give you the chance to do something else so gloriously stupid when your life is tied to my state of mind?"

"So this is about your sanity?" she growls. She balls her gloved hands into fists at her side, and I eye them warily in case she gets riled up enough to start throwing punches.

"I'd rather not go mad, even if it means that you must live," I snarl.

Even as the words diffuse in the frigid night air, I realize that it's the wrong thing to say. And I don't mean it, not truly. The prospect of her death goes beyond the mere attachment to my state of mind. I recall the horror I felt when my courtiers attacked her, how I longed to rip, tear, and kill if it could save her from the anguish she suffered that night.

But it's too late to say those things out loud.

The Godslayer's expression is darker than my midnight flame. When she springs forward at me, she moves so fast that I almost don't see her coming. Then her fist is in my face and pain explodes through my jaw. I let out an agonized howl as I stagger, falling back into the snow. The metallic tang of blood flows into my mouth, and I surmise that my incisor has torn into the soft flesh inside my cheek.

I wince as my crossed star looms over me, her fist still raised and ready for another strike. Her narrowed eyes brim with hatred and something else–hurt, I realize guiltily.

"Let me be clear," the Godslayer spits. "The only reason that you're alive is by my grace alone. Don't think for a moment that I care more about my sanity than my people. I was prepared to die for them, and I will face madness for them too. If you try to take me back to the Celestial Court, I will slay you where you stand, and you should pray that I will make it as quick as I did when I slid my dagger into your father's black heart."

The blood freezes in my veins, and it has nothing to do with the snow that engulfs my limbs.

Because I believe every word that this wild creature says. I believe that she despises me, and the connection between us, so much that if I really push her, she will sacrifice herself out of sheer spite.

And worst of all, I believe that she sees me as nothing more than my father's son, a monster destined for ruin and flame.

I open my mouth to apologize for my cruel remark, to explain, to utter something–anything–to make this better, but I can't seem to force any sound to come out.

The Godslayer flashes me a dirty look as she shakes her head. Then she turns and begins to walk away, back to where her great, demon-eyed beast stands patiently amidst the swirling snow.

I struggle to my feet in time to see her hoist the crossbow out of a nearby drift. She slings the leather strap over her shoulder, allowing the weapon to cling snugly to her back. She doesn't spare me a single glance as I hurry to catch up to her. My jaw throbs with every step, but I don't slow down.

I reach her just as she swings herself astride the kelpie. Any chance I had to mount the beast is lost when the Godslayer takes off at a brisk trot in the direction of the town. I have to jog behind them just to keep their pace, which is no easy task in the snow.

After a few tense minutes of this absurd chase, the Godslayer halts her steed and twists in the saddle to glare back at me. "Why are you still following me?" she snaps. "Don't you have anything better to do, like run your kingdom into the ground?"

"You'll have to kill me if you want to get rid of me," I counter. I know it's dangerous to call her bluff, but our verbal sparring is the only way I know how to get a response from her.

She bares her teeth at me in a grimace. "Don't tempt me."

"If you let me freeze to death out here, you'll seal your fate as well as mine."

She regards me for another long moment before she once again turns her back to me. But this time, when she urges the kelpie forward, she keeps the pace to a manageable walk.

It's a small concession but a meaningful one. As much as she wishes me dead, she's also not ready to sacrifice herself in the process. That means I still have a chance to get through to her, to convince her of what the stars have already foreseen.

And for that, I will follow her anywhere.

CHAPTER 29

Lyanndra

I will kill him if I have to.

I repeat the grim mantra over and over in my mind as I press Barra ever forward through the snow toward the glimmering lights of town. Even though I'm not quite willing to follow through on my vitriolic threats toward Syran, I tell myself that, when the time comes, I will cut him down.

But didn't he already call my bluff?

His behavior is proof enough of that. He's trailing behind me through the icy drifts like some poor lost puppy, as though I didn't just punch him and threaten his life.

Knowing that he's at my back trudging along in Barra's wake makes me uneasy. I'm vitally aware that he's far too close for comfort, and I'm torn between letting this situation continue and simply galloping off without him.

I hate what he's doing to me. How was I so foolish to kiss him like that? I was so taken in by his pretty words and imploring eyes that I almost forgot that I'm dealing with a Demigod. They're all treacher-ous, manipulative creatures who will say and do anything to get what they want.

Sure enough, he showed me his true face when he revealed that he's more interested in keeping his mind intact than the bond of the crossed stars. All those times he talked about the will of the heavens and the connection between us, he was always more concerned about himself.

It was never about me.

I scowl out into the blizzard. My knuckles ache beneath my gauntlet where my fist connected with Syran's jaw. I don't think I broke it or even did a particularly significant amount of damage, but it still felt good.

How dare he presume to cage me for his own selfish desires?

I will not give him an opportunity to do it again. That, I decide, will be my breaking point. If and when the crown prince attempts to drag me back to the Celestial Court, I will make sure that it's the end of both of us, my last act as the Godslayer, hero of the Starless.

I fume silently as we continue toward civilization, cursing the stars and the infernal bond they've forged between us. It would be so much easier if I could just follow the natural order of things and kill Syran. Yet, even as I feel that way, part of me recoils from the thought of being rid of him.

An echo of my earlier passion rolls stalwartly through my chest as I recall how he conjured the blazing serpent to defeat the remaining strix and the exhilaration I felt as I lit the bolts with his midnight flame before I let them loose on the flying monsters.

As much as I despise him for how he lied to me, I have to admit we fought well together. What would it feel like to do that again, to have a gifted companion at my side in a future skirmish? It isn't like Syran could stab me in the back, even if he wanted to. He's far too pragmatic to kill me, though I suppose he might try to injure or weaken me in order to drag me back to the palace.

I don't trust him. He must have a plan to keep me under his control. Was that the reason he kissed me earlier? Does he think that he can use my undeniable desire for him to sway me?

If he does, he's sorely mistaken. I won't fall for that trick again, no matter how tempting the bait.

Or perhaps he's got other Demigods lying in wait to whisk me away? I can imagine Kartas participating willingly in such a scheme, and the Celestial Knights would have little choice but to obey their lord. But there is no sign of any entourage. Even when Syran was attacked by the strix, no allies revealed themselves, and I highly doubt that his guards would stand by in such a dire situation.

I conclude that the crown prince is likely acting alone. In that case, the only way to find out what he's up to is to keep him nearby, where I can watch him and strike if I need to.

And that means I'll have to tolerate his presence, at least until he makes his move.

Without slowing Barra, I swivel in the saddle to glance at Syran over my shoulder. His green eyes meet mine curiously as he pushes his way through the knee-deep snow. "Have you decided to kill me after all?" he asks dryly.

"It depends on how you answer my questions," I retort. "Are you traveling alone?"

"I am," he confirms.

I scoff at that. "You mean to tell me that you left your lap dog Kartas behind?"

A spark of amusement cuts through the hard set of his eyes as he tosses back, "He would have eaten all my provisions within a fortnight. Besides, somebody had to stay behind to mind the throne."

"What about your knights?"

"What about them?" he quips.

Rolling my eyes, I press, "Where are they?"

"Back at Nexus," he shrugs. "Doing whatever Kartas tells them to do, I suppose."

His face is as flat as his tone. I can't tell if he's lying or just toying with me, so I decide to change my tactics.

"Are you planning on bringing me back to the Celestial Court?" I demand.

He fixes me with an unreadable stare as he says, "I haven't decided yet."

"Decided what, exactly?"

His eyes burn into mine, brimming with that same smoldering intensity that he turned on me earlier before he kissed me as he replies, "Whether I'll drag you there now or if I'll wait until you beg me."

Heat flares in my core at his provocative words and the hungriness of his gaze. Memories of the first dream we shared flicker through my mind, and I feel a flush creeping across my frosted cheeks. Rationally, I know he's trying to get under my skin, but it's hard to push back the echoes of the pleasure he brought me in that spectral encounter.

The struggle must be obvious on my face because he lets out a low chuckle that does absolutely nothing to smother the desire that flickers inside of me.

Thoroughly embarrassed, I turn away from him and squint through the snow. We're almost back in town now. The first buildings are just visible through the blizzard, all with candles or lanterns lit in the windows to guide me back at the end of my task.

I don't even bother trying to figure out where the road is. I simply steer Barra in the straightest path possible toward the tavern, which glows like a beacon in the swirling night. I wonder how long it's been since I left. Hours, probably.

When we arrive outside our destination, I'm not a little bit surprised that nobody rushes out to greet us. It's quite common that Starless townsfolk will vow to stay up until I return from a hunt, only to drink themselves silly once they realize how boring the wait can be. My theory is confirmed when I slide down from Barra's back and lead her into the stable where the elderly man who greeted me earlier snores upon a pile of hay with an empty flagon of ale clutched to his chest.

I see the kelpie into one of the stalls as Syran ducks in out of the snow. He watches quietly as I remove Barra's saddle and bridle, balancing them on the nearby rails fixed to the wall. I sling her saddlebags over my shoulders and then pause to take out a large strip of dried lamb jerky, which I toss toward her. She snaps the morsel out of the air, and I'm pleased to notice the crown prince flinch as she rends it easily between her sharp teeth.

Once I'm sure she's settled, I head back out into the snowy night with Syran at my heels. Now that I'm no longer astride my mount, I realize just how close he really is. I can practically feel the heat of his body and the perpetual flame that burns within on my back as I open the door to the tavern and step inside.

As expected, everybody is out cold. By the amount of empty mugs strewn around the bar and on the tables between the snoring patrons, I think it's safe to say that nobody will be waking up before noon tomorrow. I'm just glad that the landlord already set me up with a room earlier in the evening since I don't fancy shaking him awake out of his current drunken stupor.

Apprehension builds in me as I weave my way through the tables toward the rickety staircase that leads to my lodgings. What am I supposed to do about Syran?

This wouldn't be the first time I've fallen asleep in his presence. There was, of course, the string of days I spent unconscious in the infirmary after he slashed me with his flaming sword. No harm came to me then, not once he knew I was his crossed star. And then I slept in his bed, in the very same sheets where he seduced me in my dreams.

But that feeling of safety and comfort he offered me back in his chambers after the Demigods attacked me in the infirmary is at odds with the biting words he spat at me earlier tonight. I don't know which of those is the real Syran.

I'm still fretting when we arrive at the door to my room. I reach into one of the saddlebags and fish around for a moment before I find the key. By the time I unlock the door and step inside, I still haven't made up my mind.

Before I can decide whether or not to slam the door in the crown prince's face, he slides inside, making the choice for me.

"You won't get rid of me that easily," he warns as I glare at him. "Don't even think about trying to sneak out tonight."

"You're the one who should be worried," I snarl back. "Aren't you afraid I'll slit your throat while you sleep?"

His eyes flash as he answers, "No."

He wanders over to the bed, which takes up the majority of the small room in addition to a small wash basin on a stand and a chamber pot. He runs his hand over the rough quilt, and I sense a wicked plan forming in his mind.

"Which side do you want?" he asks, his voice dripping with false innocence.

I stalk over to him and grab one of the pillows off the bed before he can sit on the mattress. Without taking my eyes off him, I throw the pillow forcibly onto the floor beside the chamber pot.

"You can sleep on the floor," I hiss, "or in the barn for all I care, but you will *never* share my bed."

Syran stares at me for a moment, irritation and grim amusement warring for dominance behind his eyes. Finally, he breaks the standoff by stepping back and sitting down on the floor beside the pillow.

But my triumph is short-lived.

"Oh, I will," he says smugly. "Eventually."

And I hate that, deep in my heart, I think he might be right.

CHAPTER 30

Syran

Sleep will not take me tonight.

I lie awake on the dusty wood floor with only a single pillow beneath my head for comfort. It's frigid down here, but at least my flame keeps me warm. The whole room is awash in moonlight, as it has been since the Godslayer blew out the single lantern hanging from the rafters before she stripped off her armor and climbed into bed still dressed in her leathers.

Her form is barely distinguishable in the darkness. She's huddled on the mattress beneath the thick quilt, her breathing steady as she dozes. She's so close that I could reach out and graze her arm with my fingers, but I don't dare. I have no doubt that even the slightest touch would be met with a flashing dagger or a flying fist.

Because she doesn't trust me, not as she did that night in my chambers when she sought comfort in my presence and asked me to stay. Shame floods through me as I dwell on how much my earlier words have eroded the tenuous balance we forged between us, even as part of me still rages from the betrayal of her flight from the palace.

But what did I expect, trying to tame the Godslayer? The way she fought the strix with such chilling precision while using my flame to her advantage is proof enough of her nature. She's a wild thing, a woman who refuses to be shackled by expectations or fate. To keep her in captivity would strip her of that awful intensity, and I realize now, as I lie beside her in this shabby room, that I have never felt so aroused as I did when I watched her loose her arrows in the snowy woods.

I don't regret coming after her, but I do wish I could take back my cruel comments on how I care more about going mad than craving her company. My subsequent attempts to annoy a response out of her and to rekindle that blazing desire that very nearly peaked back at the palace have fallen flat, too. My inadequate sleeping quarters are evidence enough of that.

How can I reach her now? How can I convince her that I am better than she thinks I am? That I'm worthy of her?

These questions plague me as the darkness melts into the hazy light of dawn. I'm no closer to finding the answers I seek when the Godslayer finally wakes with the sun.

She sits up in her bed, blinking sleep from her eyes. I observe her openly, not even trying to hide the fact that I'm wide awake. When she notices me, her lip curls as though she's smelled something terrible, and then she slides out from under the quilt, almost stepping on me in the process. It doesn't escape my notice that she slept with her boots on, as though she was ready to spring up at a moment's notice.

The normalness of her actions captivates me as she prepares for the day. Is this what life is always like for her? Would she ever share this process willingly with me?

First, she splashes water from the basin on her face. Then she retrieves her armor from where she discarded it on the floor the night before. She pulls on each piece with practiced efficiency, deftly buckling straps and hooking clasps until she's fully outfitted. My eyes catch the glimmer of my gold and onyx ring on her finger before she slides on her gauntlets, hiding the proof of our connection from sight.

When she reaches for my velvet cloak, I finally speak. "That's mine, you know."

Her hand freezes for a moment before she snatches the garment off the floor and swirls it around her shoulders. "Not anymore."

And then she disappears out the door. I would think she's fleeing, but she left her saddlebags up here, and I doubt she would leave without them. I wait until her footsteps retreat down the rickety staircase and melt away into the low murmur of voices in the tavern below before I climb to my feet.

A low ache radiates through my neck and spine from my unsatisfactory accommodations. I roll my shoulders, wincing as my muscles pop, while I toss the threadbare pillow back onto the bed. My routine follows much like the Godslayer's, though I also take a moment to relieve myself in the chamber pot before I finish strapping on my armor.

Satisfied that I haven't left anything behind, I grab the saddlebags from the headboard where my crossed star slung them the night before. They're surprisingly heavy. What is she carrying in here?

Though the urge to snoop is hard to ignore, I decide that I'd rather not be caught rifling through the Godslayer's things. That sounds like a good way to lose a finger if she were to find out.

Instead, I trace her path out of the room, down the stairs, and into the main room of the tavern. As I grow closer, the voices coalesce into heartfelt words of thanks as the townsfolk congratulate the Godslayer on vanquishing the strix from the valley.

But all good humor flies from the room as I emerge at the bottom of the stairs. It seems like the whole village is here, though a handful of drunkards are still snoring away at the bar. The Starless who surround the Godslayer receive me with a mix of shock and horror as they take in my fiery hair and the onyx ring on my exposed finger.

"Demigod!" a man cries, and the shout ignites the room like a spark to kindling. Metal scores in the air as several men draw swords and daggers, their bodies tensing as they face me. The man who originally sounded the alarm rushes forward, his blade flashing in the morning light.

I would prefer not to fight anyone, and I certainly don't want to kill any of these people. The Godslayer would have my head if I did, and something tells me she wouldn't hold back if I unleashed my midnight flame in here.

But I can't just let these Starless townspeople swarm me. I raise a hand, ready to summon a fiery barrier between us, when the Godslayer draws her own sword. She catches the man's blade with her own, stopping him in his tracks.

"Enough," she commands. Her voice is quiet, yet the effect is instant. The Starless pause immediately, though the fear and anger remain livid in their features.

"But that's the crown prince!" the man argues, though he does not attempt to strike at me again.

"I am aware," the Godslayer responds flatly. "He is here with me."

A gasp ripples through the room at this new revelation. If I weren't concerned about a skirmish breaking out, I'd think it comical. As it stands, I can only hope that her power over these people is enough to diffuse the situation.

Before anyone can press her authority further, the Godslayer pulls off her left gauntlet and holds her hand up high. "Do you see this ring?" she asks the crowd. "The same one sits on the crown prince's finger. The stories of the crossed stars are true. We are bound, in life and in death. To kill one is to destroy the other. Anybody who raises a sword against the Lord of the Midnight Flame will find themselves at the end of my blade."

Unease settles across the features of the Starless, and I realize that as much as they're terrified of me, they're afraid for the Godslayer, and maybe even a little *of* her. As far as they know, I nearly killed her with my black flame and imprisoned her in my palace. I can't exactly blame them for their concern or their wariness of a woman who could do the impossible and survive my wrath.

She seems to pick up on the same undercurrent as she turns her back to me in a blatant show of trust and proclaims, "The crown prince cannot harm me without dooming himself. He is no danger to me, nor to any of you as long as he rides at my side. And he has already risked his life for this town by aiding me in eradicating the strix. You owe him your thanks, not your steel."

Fresh murmurs reverberate through the crowd as they process this new information. For a brief moment, I worry that the hatred for me will be too strong and the Starless will turn on their hero, but then the men stand down, sheathing their weapons even as they continue to eye me with wary suspicion.

"We will be on our way," she declares once she seems satisfied that violence has been averted. "I humbly ask for a bedroll and a horse for the crown prince, as it seems he has misplaced his own."

A few of the assembled Starless chuckle at her thinly veiled insult. The reaction irritates me, but I'll put up with it, even at my expense, if it lessens the likelihood of bloodshed.

I'm actually surprised when the people do as the Godslayer asks, however reluctantly. Though the bedroll the landlord provides is threadbare and reeks of mold, it's better than nothing. While my crossed star prepares her kelpie, one farmer brings me a snappish bay mare that observes me with ears pinned flat to her head and her teeth bared. He offers me the reins with a cruel smirk, knowing full well that I'm in no position to refuse.

It takes me several agonizing minutes to climb atop the feisty horse, but I manage it with my dignity mostly intact before the Godslayer leads her own mount from the stables. She barely spares me a glance as she hoists herself into the saddle and urges the kelpie forward. I keep her pace, riding shoulder to shoulder with her as we make our way through the town. The Starless villagers see us off, waving and passing gifts of food and supplies up to their hero as she passes. All I receive are dirty looks and the occasional rude gesture.

We don't speak for a good hour after we leave the town behind. As we trot in the shadow of the mountains, I finally break the silence.

"Why did you stop that man from attacking me?" I ask, genuinely curious.

"Nobody gets to kill you but me," she retorts without even turning to meet my gaze.

For some reason, the vicious comment sends a strange heat rushing through my veins that has nothing to do with the sizzle of my black flame. She says nothing more, and we slowly fall back into our previous quiet as I mull over her words.

Have I made the right choice in abandoning my throne, however temporarily, for this warrior?

There has to be a reason why the stars matched us together, and I'm determined now more than ever to find it.

CHAPTER 31

Lyanndra

"Can I borrow this?"

I glance up from the arrow I'm meticulously fletching to where Syran stands before me, holding my crossbow in one hand.

"Why?" I ask, narrowing my eyes at him in suspicion. It's certainly not the first time I've seen him with a weapon. In fact, he seems to always keep his sword at the ready even when he's asleep in his bedroll. But this is the first time he's asked to use anything of mine, and I'm wary of such a bold request.

"I'm getting tired of living off of jerky and hard cheese," he replies. "I thought I'd go find us something a bit fresher."

The explanation is reasonable enough. It's been a week since we left the deep snow of the mountains and started trekking southeast in search of a more temperate climate, and we've survived that whole time on dried goods and the occasional foraged snack. The thought of meat that isn't salted or tougher than dragonhide is tempting. In fact, the very idea of it makes my mouth water.

Besides, there isn't much trouble he can get into with the weapon. If he's planning on wounding me in order to take me back to the

Celestial Court, he could do it just as easily with his blade or flame as my crossbow.

So I shrug in silent acquiescence, and he grins. "What would you like: fish, fowl, or fur?"

"Surprise me," I say in a tone that implies quite the opposite. Even though the crown prince is adept with his sword, I'm not about to get my hopes up about his aim. I'd rather resign myself to another night of jerky than be disappointed when he returns empty handed.

I toss him the bolt I've just finished, and he catches it easily in his free hand. The rest of the arrows I worked on earlier sit in the quiver by my feet, which I nudge over to him with the tip of my boot. He might as well make some use out of them. Or not, if his aim is as bad as his attitude.

Once he disappears into the surrounding woods, I pick my way over to the creek that runs placidly by our makeshift camp. The water there runs clear and fresh over smooth rocks and the soft green moss that clings to them. Tiny fish dart through the currents, their scales flashing with iridescent rainbows in the light of the setting sun. I wonder what those little creatures must think of me, or if they even comprehend my presence at all.

Is that what we are to the stars, small and glimmering? I ponder the question as I settle in with my back against a tree and my eyes fixed on the life that thrives beneath the surface of the water. The tranquility of it lulls me into a doze that only breaks when the snapping of twigs and rustling of the underbrush in the distance signal Syran's return.

To my surprise, he approaches with the crossbow on one shoulder and a brace of rabbits on the other.

The shock must show on my face because he flashes me a cocky grin and quips, "Did you doubt my superior skills as a hunter?"

I roll my eyes in response before reaching for the rabbits.

He steps back before I can grab them, that same playful light flickering in his gaze. "Now I'm going to have to impress you, since you think so little of me."

Holding my hands up in mock surrender, I decide to take him up on that challenge. I can't imagine this refined Demigod ever skinning, dressing, or cooking a rabbit, not with an entire kitchen staff at his beck and call back at the palace.

Yet, disbelief captures me once more as I watch Syran do just that. Using a paring knife from one of the saddlebags, he deftly prepares our dinner as though he's done it a thousand times before. It's only after the rabbits are crackling away on a spit over one of his strange black fires that I finally find my voice.

"Where did a spoiled prince learn all that?" I question as I stand just inside the shadowy glow of the midnight flame.

He glances up at me from where he kneels beside our dinner, diligently turning the spit, and laughs.

Sparks skitter through my veins at the sound. Have I ever actually heard him laugh before in such a good-natured way? I don't think I have. I definitely would remember the heat the noise evokes in my core.

He doesn't seem to notice how off balance I am as he explains, "This isn't my first time on the road. I traveled a lot before my father..." His words trail off for a moment before he amends, "Before the war."

I wander a bit closer as curiosity takes hold. Back in his chambers in the palace, Syran told me that he didn't agree with his father's treatment of the Starless. Will he say the same now?

When I feel ready to speak, I inquire, "Did you fight in the war?"

His green eyes darken as they meet mine. "No," he says after a moment. "My father wouldn't allow it. He wouldn't risk losing his only heir. But I was there, watching."

There's a challenge in his words, and my stomach sours as I understand the implication. "You were there?" I breathe. For some reason, I never thought that Syran might have witnessed the moment that made me who I am, the moment that took everything from him while gifting him the throne.

He nods once. "I saw my father fall."

"You saw me *kill* him," I correct. For some reason, I feel the need to speak the frank truth. I'm not ashamed of what I did. It was bloody and necessary, as much as it haunts me.

The crown prince's gaze sharpens, and I wait for him to lash out at me, but then he sighs and turns his attention back to the rabbits. After a few tense seconds, he says, "Enough about battles and killing. If I get my way, there will be more peace than war under my rule."

"You can't possibly expect to crush the Starless so completely as to ensure no uprisings," I snap, suddenly angry. Does he really think that I'll allow him to carry out his father's legacy?

Syran's jaw clenches, and his knuckles tighten on the spit. Once again, I'm certain he's going to unleash upon me, but he forces it back. "I have no quarrel with the Starless," he replies quietly, though there's no mistaking the emotion in his voice.

He sounds *hurt*.

"Too many, Starless and Demigod alike, suffered terribly under my father's unjust rule," he continues in that same passionate tone. "Your people were slaughtered. Any Demigod who spoke out against it was put to death on a pyre. I refuse to continue down that path, not when it holds so much death and hopelessness."

Doubt chokes me as I struggle to process this information. It's the same sentiment he shared so desperately in his chambers the night I escaped the Celestial Court. Instinct tells me that the conviction with which he speaks is genuine, yet he's a Demigod. They all lie, especially when they want something.

And I know what Syran wants.

Me.

Still, his words plague me even as silence falls between us. The only sound is the whisper of the flames and the crackling of the rabbits as they cook.

Finally, Syran stops turning the spit and lifts it away from the flames. The smell of crispy skin and juicy meat is enough to entice me closer. When he offers me two of the rabbits, I take them immediately, though I pick a spot on the other side of the campfire to eat them.

I hate to admit that they're cooked to perfection. After a week of salted, dried meat, this is absolute heaven. In a matter of minutes, I devour one rabbit down to the bone. I take more time to savor the second, knowing that fresh game is a rare luxury.

Halfway through the remaining rabbit, Syran surprises me again.

"Why do you hate me so deeply?" he asks.

I nearly choke on a piece of meat at his candid question, but recover quickly enough to sneer, "You deserve it."

He cocks his head. "Why?"

"Your kind kill my people indiscriminately," I growl. "You oppress us, force us into poverty because you think the heavens favor you. Or are those not good enough reasons?"

"That was my father's way," he concedes easily. Too easily. I fix him with a wary glare as he adds, "But it's not mine. Do you know the story of how Demigods got their powers?"

"Of course," I scoff. "The heavens thought your people were so superior that they blessed them with falling stars, granting them divine powers."

The sides of Syran's mouth quirk up in a bitter smile. "That's what the scholars say, at least," he agrees. "But did you know the part about the moon?"

I have no idea what he's talking about, so I stare at him blankly, which is more than enough of a response.

"One of the legends that didn't make it into the canon is about the moon," he explains. "It's said that she disagreed with the other celestial gods about the decision to deliver divinity to the people. She thought it would only cause strife amongst them."

"She was right," I mutter, earning a humorless chuckle from the crown prince.

"She was, but the other gods didn't want to hear it. Instead, they exiled her to walk amongst the Starless she defended, stripping her of her divinity."

I lean forward, transfixed, as the remainder of my rabbit sits forgotten in my hands. I've never heard this story before. It's possible that Syran is just making it up, but something about it, something that takes root in the space behind my heart, rings true to me.

"But they couldn't take away her power, not fully. She used the last of her divinity to curse the other gods and those they chose to favor," he continues.

I can tell he's enjoying my full attention, but I can't stop myself from prompting, "What did she do?"

Now that he knows he's hooked me, Syran grins. There's something feral about his expression in the flickering shadows of his midnight flame that sends a thrill running through me.

"She cursed them with a choice, by way of a prophecy," he spins. "She declared that one day, two twin sisters will be born of her bloodline. One will have the power to destroy the Demigods, the other to save them. When the time comes, the gods will have to choose which sister is which. If they pick the wrong one, the Moon will have her vengeance."

It's a superstitious little tale, especially with its roots in Demigod lore. But in spite of the interest it instills in me, I can't help but to point out the extremely obvious problem with it.

Nodding up at the waning crescent that hangs overhead, I ask, "You do realize that the moon is right there?"

Syran laughs again, teasing out another flood of warmth in my core. "And that's exactly why the scholars rejected it," he notes. "But I always liked the story." His eyes, softened with good humor, find mine. "You remind me of the moon," he adds quietly.

The intensity with which he regards me is breathtaking. It's as though he's memorizing every inch of me, down to my soul. Nobody has ever looked at me like that before. A blush creeps over my cheeks as the heat of his gaze builds in my blood.

"How?" My voice is a whisper, barely audible over the sounds of the fire.

"You did what was right," he murmurs. "You killed my father, even though it came at a cost. You paid it when nobody else would."

His words seep into my skin, and I can hardly believe them even as I breathe, "It had to be done."

"I know." His eyes don't leave mine as he utters his response.

Later, as I lie in my bedroll with my back toward him, those two words haunt me.

I want so desperately for them to be true, but that would shatter everything I know about the Demigods, about Syran.

Could he really be different?

I don't know what to think.

Not anymore.

CHAPTER 32

Syran

Whispers spread along the southern road like wildfire.

The Godslayer and I are certainly not immune to the sparks of rumor that flicker ever brighter with each Starless merchant and traveler we pass. At first, we heard of one or two sightings of Demigods pushing out from Nexus, and we assumed that perhaps Kartas sent out Celestial Knights to make contact with me. But then the stories grew stranger, morphing into claims of courtiers seeking refuge in Starless outposts and begging for asylum.

What is going on in the Celestial Court? Anxiety needles me as I try to parse the situation. Are my people trying to find me? Or is something wrong?

I glance over at my crossed star. She sits astride her great beast, her eyes fixed straight ahead. Concern creases her brow, and, in spite of my own unease, something warm sparks in me at the realization that I'm learning to read her expressions.

Without sparing me a look, she asks, "What?"

"These rumors," I sigh. "I'm worried. Why would so many Demigods be leaving Nexus?"

She shrugs. "Maybe they've grown tired of Kartas' incessant yapping. Or perhaps he's eaten all the rations."

I raise an eyebrow at the casual playfulness in her tone. Even after a fortnight of her softening attitude toward me, it still comes as a surprise whenever she addresses me without vitriol. Ever since I told her the story of the moon, something has shifted between us. Though she still doesn't speak much, our conversations are civil, even enjoyable at times. As I watch her now, I marvel at how different she is out here in the wilderness. How could I have ever wanted to lock her away?

The Godslayer seems to take my extended silence as discomfort and poses, "There's a village a few hours from here. They get a lot of merchant traffic, so they're bound to know something. Do you want to stop there for the night?"

I nod. Even if we don't find out anything new, it's still a good idea. We've been sleeping rough for weeks now, and though my crossed star doesn't seem bothered by resting on the hard ground every night, the knots in my back would welcome a soft mattress and a feather pillow. That alone would be worth seeking civilization.

We fall into a comfortable silence as we follow the road until we reach a crossroad. The Godslayer guides her kelpie to the right, and I follow without hesitation.

It strikes me that, somewhere along the way, I've grown to trust her.

Can she say the same about me?

I'm still pondering the question several hours later when we reach the cultivated fields that mark the outskirts of the village. Though the year approaches the crux of the winter, the midland air is relatively mild and Starless farmers tend to their livestock beneath the late afternoon sun. They look up as we approach. It seems that word of my companionship has reached this place, as nobody tries to threaten or outright attack me. Instead, they staunchly ignore me or glare as they wave to the Godslayer, who raises her hand and nods in return.

By the time we reach the main street of the village, news of our arrival precedes us. A gathered group of Starless, buzzing with excitement, welcomes their acclaimed hero with cheers and gifts.

The Godslayer offers a small smile as she slides down from her beast's back. Following her lead, I do the same.

One woman steps forward and offers my crossed star a deep curtsy. "Welcome to our village, Godslayer," she beams, though her cheery demeanor wavers as her eyes flick over to me. "You've arrived just in time for the Winter Solstice. It would be an honor if you would join us in the festivities tonight."

The Godslayer dips her head in acquiescence, sending up a flurry of excitement in the crowd. I wonder why she prefers to speak with her body rather than her words. I've never actually asked her.

"Come," the woman prompts. "You must be weary from your travels. We've prepared a room at the inn and fresh clothes for you."

The Starless hero follows her wordlessly after handing the kelpie's reins off to a man who promises to house the beast in his barn.

Feeling distinctly out of place, I hold out my reins as he passes. "Good sir, would it be too much trouble for you to take my mount as well?" I ask as politely as I can.

The man eyes me with a combination of suspicion, hatred, and fear. The tension in the air is thick, almost palpable, and sour like the smoke left over after my father's flame. He opens his mouth to spit out a reply, but a different voice cuts him off before he can speak.

"The crown prince is with me," the Godslayer proclaims. The man tenses at the sound, and I'm reminded of that first morning in the inn up north where she came to my defense. I risk a glance over to her.

She is absolutely radiant.

She stands awash in golden sunshine, armor gleaming and eyes hard. Against the matte black background of my midnight cloak, she sparks like an ember in the dark. Every inch of her commands power as she stares the man down, and he seems to shrink beneath her gaze even though she's far shorter than him.

Finally, he ekes out, "As you wish, Godslayer."

With downcast eyes, he reaches for the reins, and I hand them to him. "Thank you," I offer, though he says nothing in return.

Much of the tension in the air departs with him. The Godslayer offers me one last indecipherable look before she turns once again and follows the woman off to our new lodgings.

I want to join them, but I decide against it. These people don't trust me. Why should they? I have given them no reason to do so. But perhaps I can win some of them over. If I can show these Starless that they are not so different from Demigods, is it possible that this could lay the foundation for better relations between our people?

In the spirit of that notion, I turn to the nearest villager and say, "I appreciate your hospitality."

The man spits at my feet, spins on his heel, and stalks off.

Several of the others around us laugh, and I have to school my features into an unbothered mask in order to hide my irritation. As the rest of the crowd disperses in his wake, I wonder what else I can do to bridge this seemingly insurmountable gap.

I glance up and down the muddy main road. The modest buildings are hung with homemade garlands of holly, rosemary, and pine, infusing the air with a festive tang that mingles with the scent of rich cinnamon and anise from a nearby bakery. A small mountain of firewood and kindling is assembled in an adjacent field, and I surmise that there will likely be a bonfire later. But the pile isn't nearly large enough for a satisfying celebration. My assessment is bolstered by the telltale thunk of an axe on wood that echoes rhythmically through the village.

Tracking down the source of the noise isn't hard. I trail along in the direction the Godslayer took moments before and arrive outside the inn. Loud chatter and pipe smoke flow through the open windows, along with the unmistakable bitterness of ale. Instead of going inside, I skirt around the façade of the building and duck around the back.

There, I find an old man chopping wood. His hair is a stark shock of white, and the baggy tunic he wears does nothing to hide his stooped back, which is as twisted and gnarled as an ancient oak. He coughs out a wheezing breath to punctuate each swing of the axe, and it sounds like he's going to collapse at any moment.

I approach him warily. Without the Godslayer beside me, I'm concerned that this Starless elder may strike out at me with the axe, especially if I surprise him. I walk slowly into his line of sight, hoping that he spots me before I get too close.

He straightens up the moment his eye catches me, leaning the axe on the ground like a makeshift cane. Cynical blue eyes that remind me of Torran's study my form with acute precision, as though sizing me up for a fight.

Finally, he grinds out, "Your kind aren't welcome here."

"I go where the Godslayer goes," I answer calmly.

Interest sparks in his eyes at my words. "If she's here, that means you're the king."

"Not quite yet," I correct. "I didn't mean to bother you, sir. I only wanted to offer my assistance with the firewood."

"You?" he spits. "Help? Do you think I'm a fool? Do you think that your father can burn our crops and our brothers and that we would welcome you?"

I shake my head. "My father's sins are his own, but I will pay for them all the same. I wish only to restore what he took from the Starless."

The elder sneers at me. "You Demigods took my sons from me," he snarls. "All three o' my boys were burned to ash. How do you restore my children to me? By chopping wood?"

His anger pours over me in a noxious wave. What can I possibly say to that? I can't deny that my father was responsible for so many needless deaths. I can't change what he did.

The power of the old man's rage topples me to my knees. I stare down at the packed earth beneath me as I utter, "I am truly sorry for what he took from you. The blood he spilled is a travesty. I cannot give you your children back, nor can I bring you justice. But I can vow to you now that I am not my father. There will be no more senseless bloodshed during my rule. I swear it."

When I finally look up, I'm shocked to see tears streaming down the Starless man's face. "What king would bow to a peasant?" he murmurs.

The question hangs in the air between us, unanswerable. Finally, he picks up the axe and tosses it down on the ground before me.

"You're getting your knees dirty," he says gruffly as he runs his sleeve over his face. "Get chopping. We light the bonfire at dusk."

I scramble to my feet and grab the axe by the smooth, worn handle. It's been a long while since I've done anything as mundane as splitting firewood, but the motion comes easily even after all those years. But I forgot how physical the work is, and by the time I get through a dozen logs, I'm dripping with sweat.

I take a quick break to peel off my armor and my tunic beneath, and then I'm back to my task. I fall into an almost hypnotic rhythm and am so consumed by the action that I don't notice anybody sneaking up on me until a voice snarks, "You're rather slow at that, aren't you?"

When I whirl around, I find myself face to face with the Godslayer.

She's wearing a simple dress in a deep shade of forest green. It's a far cry from her usual armor, and it somehow makes her look even more feminine than the gauzy lace nightclothes she wore around the Celestial Court. My blood heats at the sight of her, especially when I realize that she's still wearing my cloak.

She's *beautiful*.

It's not just this version of her. I picture her earlier today, resplendent in her armor while she spoke in my defense. It's the memory of her shooting the strix with deadly accuracy. It's her reaching for a book in the palace library, dodging my strikes in the courtyard, and doing the impossible of cutting down my father on the battlefield in a spray of ash.

Every form of her is striking, and I realize now that I want all facets of her. I want her as a woman, as the Godslayer, as all of the things she is.

She is the moon in my endless night.

I want every part of her.

And I always get what I want.

CHAPTER 33

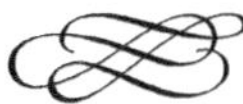

Lyanndra

I cannot suppress the flame that licks at my core, drawing me ever closer to Syran.

When I caught him chopping wood for the old innkeeper in nothing but his trousers, I told myself that it was a natural thing to admire the toned planes of the crown prince's chest and the cords of muscle that roped his arms as he swung the axe. But now, he's once again wearing his tunic, and I still feel that heat inside of me, threatening to ignite my blood and sear my nerves. Every time he looks at me, the blaze only grows.

I can't escape it.

Do I even want to?

My brain and body are at war. I want him. I knew it during that kiss in the snowy field up north, as surely as I know it now. He's shown me that he's different than I thought. The darker side of him is still there, smoldering with rage and stiff anger beneath the surface, but just as a flame can burn, it can also bring warmth. He reveals that side of him with every cocky grin and cheeky comment.

When he saved my life in the infirmary at the Celestial Court, I told myself that he only did it so he wouldn't go mad. But the curse of the crossed stars didn't make him bandage my hands and treat me so tenderly in his chambers that night. It didn't make him follow me and hunt rabbits and crack jokes.

And the bond certainly isn't making him watch me now with eyes as hot as embers.

A blush creeps up my cheeks under his heavy gaze, and I look away quickly to where the men are trying to light the bonfire. But with the steady drizzle that began just before dusk, they're having trouble getting the kindling to take. It's been several long minutes, and the villagers are starting to get restless.

The old innkeeper breaks away from the group and approaches Syran, who stands off to the side. They speak in low voices, too quiet for me to hear over the chatter of the assembled crowd, and then the crown prince nods before following the elder toward the mountain of wood.

A ripple of disquiet echoes through the villagers as the Demigod approaches the pyre. For a moment, there are only speculative whispers, and then a tongue of black flame surges up from the base of the pile. It reaches up to the sky in a towering bonfire, as though snatching at the very stars.

Murmurs and gasps fill the air at the eerie sight. I'm suddenly gripped with fear that the villagers will find Syran's midnight flame to be an affront to their celebration, but then a cheer breaks out, and the merry attitude returns.

I breathe a sigh of relief as several of the men clap the crown prince on the back. I'm about to go join him when the woman who greeted us outside the inn steps in my path.

"We're so glad you're here," she tells me as she loops her arm in mine and steers me toward a group of women standing beside a large table laden with refreshments. Flagons of mead and warm spiced wine take up one side while the other is lined with pastries, hand pies, and other delicacies that make my mouth water.

"It's an honor to celebrate the solstice with you," one of the villagers says. She's a matronly woman with curly brown hair and deep creases around her eyes from smiling.

"The honor is mine," I reply with a quick bow of my head.

"I've never met a female knight before," a young, blonde waif who looks to be in her early teens blurts. Several of the others shush her, but I've grown used to these sorts of comments since Syran pulled off my golden helm.

"Neither have I, besides myself," I reply.

My easy response seems to loosen other tongues, since the matron asks, "How did you learn to fight? Did your father or brothers teach you?"

I shake my head as I push back the memory of my family. It's been a long time since I've pictured them in my mind's eye, and for good reason. Willing my voice not to shake, I explain, "I taught myself. I came from a village like this and bore all the expectations that could be placed upon a woman. But I wanted something different than that life. I disguised myself and joined a band of soldiers passing through when I was still just a girl. I never looked back."

"So I could be like you?" the blonde girl gasps, incredulous. And while some of the other women admonish her, a few simply regard me thoughtfully. Have I just given this child some new option in life? Or have I damned her?

I don't have time to ponder those questions. The matron passes me a flagon of spiced wine and a flaky pastry dusted with fragrant cinnamon. Almost immediately after that, the music starts. Somebody's pulled out a fiddle and is playing a lively tune by the fire, luring people in to dance.

When the other women leave to join the growing circle, I'm left to savor the succulent pastry and sip my wine in peace. The warm alcohol only feeds the fire in me as I watch the revelers. They look ghostly in the black glow of the midnight flame, but the good cheer is undeniable. I find myself smiling and nodding along to the music as I finish my drink.

I'm reaching for another when a hand slides into mine. I turn, hoping to see Syran, but it's just one of the village men. Before I can protest, he leads me into a familiar dance. They're steps I learned in childhood, and though I haven't executed them in quite some time, my feet haven't forgotten the motions.

The man spins me, and I find myself face to face with another of the Starless villagers. I repeat the process again and again, laughing along with the crowd.

It's the lightest I've felt in quite some time. I feel normal. I'm not the Godslayer right now. I'm just myself, some maiden from the Southern Caldera celebrating the Winter Solstice.

I'm free.

And then I'm swept into another dance, and my heart nearly stops as I realize that the arms that hold me now are Syran's. He grins down at me, his red hair swirling around his fine features as he guides us around the fire.

"Having fun?" he purrs.

I can't ignore how his body feels against mine as he presses me closer. The inferno within me rages. Does he feel it too?

"Not anymore," I sass, but there's no real bite to my words. It's all play, and the way his eyes spark tells me he knows it.

"You must be the only woman here that doesn't want to dance with the handsome prince," he jokes. His hands creep around me to splay on my waist, and I shiver. "Did you know that every single man here has his eye on you tonight?"

"Including you?" I challenge.

His eyes darken as he stares down at me, and for a moment, I think I know exactly why the stars crossed us. "Especially me."

I don't know what to say to that. The wild side of me wants to lean in and kiss him, and I think that maybe I'm about to, but then he announces, "I have something for you."

He takes me by the hand and gently pulls me away from the flickering light of the bonfire and into the shadows of the inn. With everybody gathered around the pyre, there isn't anybody nearby to overhear us.

Syran reaches into the pocket of his trousers and pulls out a small, knobby object. When he places it in my hand, I'm surprised at how nervous he looks.

Confused, I examine the gift, and then I gasp. It's a carving, likely fashioned from spare firewood and charred to a gleaming black by Syran's midnight flame. The figure is in the rough shape of a horse, though the comically large teeth jutting awkwardly from its tiny mouth tells me it's Barra.

"I'm not very good at these," he admits as he runs a hand through his hair. The motion is strangely endearing. "I've only made a couple before but I thought you might like it. Don't show Barra, though. She'd probably be offended and eat it."

A laugh bubbles out of me. "You made this?" I ask, astounded. "For me?" I don't think anybody has ever given me a gift before. Of course, the Starless denizens of Alastria offer me food and supplies all the time, but there's always an implicit transaction to those gestures.

Syran made this for *me*.

He isn't asking for anything in return, not my service nor my trust. He crafted it because he thought I might like it. Because he wanted to make me happy.

Stars be damned, I can't stop myself.

I kiss him.

At first, he's frozen in surprise, and I worry that I just made a grave mistake. But then he loops his arms around me, pulling me closer into his chest as he returns the pressure and nips at my bottom lip in a way that makes me gasp. He takes the opportunity to explore me with his tongue, and I melt into him, craving the friction building between us.

After a moment, he draws back, leaving me panting and breathless. His green eyes blaze with hunger as his gaze rakes over me. "I'd take you right here in the shadows if you'd let me," he growls.

The need in his voice makes me bold. Before I can even think about it, I counter, "Why would you do that when we've got a perfectly good bed upstairs?"

For a long moment, Syran just stares at me with that same burning look, and I once again wonder if I was too bold. But then he surges forward, scooping me up into his arms as I squeal in equal parts delight and indignity.

He carries me swiftly inside, through the empty bar, up the stairs, and to our room. After locking the door behind us, he tosses me down on the bed. I expect him to join me, but he doesn't.

"You're beautiful," he murmurs as his eyes skim down my body. "In this dress. In your armor." He flashes me a wicked grin. "In nothing at all."

"And when have you seen me naked?" I ask brashly.

"When we first fucked," he answers.

Wetness pools between my thighs at his brazen words. "And when was that?" I prompt even though I already know the answer, my voice barely above a whisper.

He pulls his tunic over his head and discards it on the floor. As he tugs at the laces of his boots he says, "In the dream. Do you remember when I took you in my bed?"

I swallow thickly as he kicks off his boots and stalks toward me. From where I lie on the bed, I can see the evidence of his arousal straining at the front of his trousers.

He leans forward to cage me in with his arms. His mouth is only inches from mine, his body pressing against my most intimate parts. "Are you sure you want this, Godslayer?"

Am I?

I stare up at him. Those green eyes don't haunt me anymore, not when they're filled with so much passion. No matter how much he looks like his father, Syran has shown me that he's different.

That he's *mine*.

So I give him a gift of my own.

"Lyanndra," I breathe. "My name is Lyanndra."

For a moment, everything freezes.

And when his lips crash down onto mine, the world comes undone. His mouth and hands are everywhere, skimming over my skin and the thick fabric of my dress as I moan beneath him. Time seems to stick as he sits me up and nips at the sensitive spot at the junction of my neck and collarbone while his fingers make quick work of the laces at my back.

Fully loosened, the bodice of my dress sags. I pull my arms out of the sleeves, finally allowing the fabric to pool between us. I push back my embarrassment as Syran drinks in the sight of me.

His molten gaze lingers on my breasts before falling to the puckered scar on my ribs left by his flaming sword. He runs one finger over the jagged memory. "I'm sorry," he whispers as his eyes find mine.

"Show me," I command.

And he does.

His mouth closes over the rosy peak of one of my breasts and I gasp in surprise at this new sensation. It's so overwhelming that I barely notice when he tugs the dress down over my legs and tosses it onto the floor beside his shirt. I wear nothing underneath, which he realizes when his hand brushes the place between my thighs.

"By the stars, you're so wet for me," he growls against my skin. As if to prove it, he teases me once again, feathering his fingers over my heated flesh and sending bursts of pleasure coursing through me.

Then he touches me in earnest, and I'm lost. All I can focus on is the sensation of his skin sliding against me, coaxing ecstasy from my nerves as I moan beneath him. I'm just getting used to this feeling when he pushes one finger inside of me to curl into my sensitive heat.

I grip his arm for dear life as he coaxes me toward that sweet edge. Just as it's building into something uncontrollable, he pulls his hand away with a low chuckle.

"Not yet," he murmurs as he sits up. I watch with bleary eyes as he swiftly loosens the laces of his trousers and kicks them off. The sight of his cock, stiff with need for me, sends a pang of fear through me.

Doing this in a dream was one thing. But in the waking world, I'm still a maiden.

My sudden anxiety must show on my face because he soothes, "If it's too much, we can stop."

I shake my head. I want him more than I can say.

"You're sure?" he asks.

"Yes." More than he could ever know.

His lips capture mine as he presses the tip of his cock against my wet heat. It's heavy with delicious promise, and I can't help but squirm against him in anticipation.

He enters me slowly, allowing me to adjust to his size. The fullness is so foreign that at first, I tense up. Then Syran's voice is in my ear murmuring, "Relax, Lyanndra."

The sound of my name on his lips nearly unravels me. I shudder beneath him, and he lets out a low laugh, which only pushes me closer to the brink. His hips roll into mine, gently at first, but then picking up speed as I move to meet him. Lost in pleasure, I cling to him as he thrusts into me, my blunt nails digging into the skin of his muscled back.

Sinful noises spill from my mouth as he drives me to new heights. He swallows them up eagerly, as though my pleasure only fuels him further. And when he creeps one hand in between us to find the sensitive bundle of nerves just above where our bodies meet, I can't hold on any longer.

I clench around him as spots as dark as his midnight flame burst in my vision. Pleasure like nothing I've felt before thrills through me, consuming me completely in its blazing glory.

Seconds later, Syran drives into me one last time and spills himself inside me with a feral growl.

In that moment, the world seems to tilt. Something clicks inside of me, and I feel something new, something strange and powerful that burns with the force of a black star, and somehow I know that it's Syran.

I *feel* him.

And for the first time, I truly and deeply understand what we are.

Our stars are crossed.

Our souls are bound.

We are one.

CHAPTER 34

Her name is Lyanndra.

I reach out to her sleeping form and brush a stray lock of hair from her face. She doesn't even stir at the gentle movement, and my heart feels like it might burst at that small act of trust. How many times have I seen her spring up from her bedroll at the slightest noise, blade at the ready? But here in bed beside me, it's as though her subconscious knows she's safe.

I can hardly believe it.

In fact, I can hardly believe any of this. It seems impossible that only a few short months ago, we embraced in a clash of steel and blood instead of passion. When the Godslayer first rode into Nexus in her tarnished armor and my father's golden helm, I never thought that she would be my crossed star or that I could ever convince such an untamed spirit to trust me.

Every sneer and every insult were all worth it to get us here. Last night was more powerful than I ever imagined, and somehow, I'm certain that Lyanndra feels it too. She gazed at me after as though she were seeing me for the very first time, like she finally recognized me.

Now, she sighs quietly in her sleep and shifts beneath the quilt. I pull her closer into my warmth and nearly combust when she nuzzles her head into my shoulder. In this tender moment, I marvel that we could have this every day and every night, that we could find this peace within one another in spite of our glaring differences.

But then the reality of our situation hits like a blow from her greatsword.

Lyanndra is the Godslayer. I would be a fool to try to separate those two identities. I learned my lesson when she fled the Celestial Court after I tried to smother her wildness.

And the terrible truth is that the Demigods will never accept a Starless woman, let alone the Godslayer, as their queen. The attack in the infirmary is proof enough of that. They don't understand why she is the way she is, or that her spirit belongs to Alastria. They will never see her the way I do.

Yet, I can't stay out here with her forever. As much as I would like to remain with her on her wanderings, I can't just abandon my crown if I want anything to change. Aside from Kartas and Torran, I simply don't trust anybody else to rule. And with the rumors of Demigods fleeing Nexus that were only reinforced by the mutterings of the villagers last night, I know I'll have to go back to the Celestial Court sooner rather than later to restore order to my people.

I gaze down at my crossed star, who snores lightly into the crook of my neck. Would she come with me if I ask?

Things are different now. Though she'd still be stepping into the viper's pit, she's no longer injured. Instead of pushing back against me, we would be able to present a united front to the Demigods. Even if my people still view her with disdain, they wouldn't see her as a weak and easy target. And no more would she be my prisoner. She could come and go as she pleases, as long as she finds her way back to me eventually.

I'll speak with her in the morning, I decide. For now, I'll let her rest.

Pushing down the fingers of anxiety that prod at my nerves, I press my lips gently to the top of her head. She snuggles even closer to me in response, which in turn reignites the fire in my blood.

Maybe I should wake her up after all. My body answers the thought with enthusiasm, and I'm powerless to resist.

I ghost one hand over her side, admiring the ridges of muscle that line her body. I'm used to the smooth curves and flat planes of the courtiers, who consider it a mortal sin to be anything other than waifishly thin. But there's something so alluring about Lyanndra's form. She's small but dense, a powerful and well-honed weapon. As I trail my fingers over her bicep and shoulder, I recall how she swung that massive greatsword with the entire weight of her body. She's incredible, and I want desperately to show her that.

Dipping my head, I brush my lips against the warm skin of her exposed throat. She sighs again and tips her chin up, granting me access. Her hazel eyes open to bleary slits, and she smiles softly at the sight of me.

Heat surges through me at her placid expression. She's never once looked at me like that, as if she *likes* me. It's enough for me to draw her in for a lazy, yet searing, kiss, which she returns with equal passion.

At the same time, I roll my hips slowly into hers. Neither of us bothered to put on any clothes after last night's encounter, and she moans into my mouth as I press the hot length of my arousal against her bare skin.

"Syran," she breathes.

The sound of my name on her lips drives me insane. I want to taste her while she loses herself in the feeling of me. I want to take her to the brink again and again until she forgets that she ever uttered my title as a curse.

I break away from the kiss to trail my mouth down the smooth column of her neck. Delicious moans flow from her as I nip and lick my way down between her breasts, stopping briefly to attend to each pert nipple before continuing on my journey south.

Confusion flickers in her eyes as I venture lower. She opens her mouth, probably to ask what I'm up to, but any words she might have said turn into a gasp of pleasure as my tongue darts out to explore her slick heat.

She tastes like starlight. I drink from her eagerly while she writhes against my tongue and teeth. Her fingers curl into my hair to pull me closer. Her powerful thighs lock around me, and I couldn't escape even if I wanted to. The control she has over me is thrilling.

Her gasping breaths and low moans come more frequently as I coax her closer and closer to the edge. And when she finally unravels on my face, she cries out my name like a prayer.

It's the best sound I've ever heard.

As she rides out the waves of pleasure, I crawl back up her body to capture her in another kiss. Does she taste herself on my tongue? Does she understand how she's ruined me?

She must because she moves her hand toward my hard cock and brushes her fingers over the velvet skin of my shaft. I shudder at her touch, and she grins against my mouth. Emboldened by my response, she closes her palm over me, and she begins to move. But her actions are timid and unsure, and I realize that this is likely the first time she's ever done this before.

I close my hand over hers, twining my fingers between her own. "Like this," I murmur as I guide her. She's a fast learner. Soon, she's got me coiled like a snake ready to strike. I pant as she swipes her thumb over the head of my cock once and then twice. Pressure builds inside of me, and I'm so close to my release, so close that I'm about to…

A crash and a scream sound from downstairs.

The warrior in Lyanndra overtakes the animal. She springs to her feet instantaneously, her eyes fixed on the closed door of our room. I follow a beat behind, cursing silently to whatever gods might be listening.

People are shouting downstairs in the bar, but I can't make out what they're saying. Lyanndra barely glances at me as she grabs her leathers and pulls them on faster than I've ever seen. I do the same. She trusts me with the tender truth of herself, and I trust her instincts in turn.

We dress quickly, sparing the extra seconds to don our armor and strap on our weapons, and then we rush downstairs.

It takes me a moment to parse the commotion that awaits us in the bar. Several villagers block our view. They're gathered around something–someone?–and they speak in urgent, anxious tones. A robust woman with curly brown hair is barking out orders, and I realize that she must be a healer or something close to one.

"What happened?" Lyanndra asks one of the nearby villagers.

The Starless girl shakes her head. "An outrider spotted him on the road and brought him here. He was asking for you." Her eyes flicker over to me, and she adds, "Both of you."

Lyanndra and I share a glance at this new information before we step forward in tandem.

As we approach, the crowd parts to reveal an old man lying on the floor. One leg of his trousers is shredded, and there's an arrow sticking out of his thigh. The golden fletching used by the Celestial Knights is unmistakable. Dread rises in my throat as I look up at the injured man's face, and my heart stutters to a halt as my green eyes meet a familiar electric blue gaze.

"Torran?" I gasp. I rush forward and fall to my knees at his side. The elderly Demigod smiles thinly up at me.

"Syran," he murmurs. His voice is delicate and papery. I glance again at the arrow in his thigh. Even as the healer tends to he wound, he's losing a lot of blood.

"What happened?" I press.

"Listen to me," Torran implores weakly. "Alastria is in danger."

"Danger? What do you mean?"

He clutches at my hand with one of his. His skin feels alarmingly brittle against mine as he continues, "There's been a coup, Syran."

Panic alights in my chest. How could this be? I think of Kartas and how certain he was that he could keep the kingdom running in my absence. If somebody challenged him, there would be bloodshed. Was he able to get away? Or is he…

I shake my head. I won't even let myself think of it. If Torran was able to escape, I have to believe that my cousin also made it out.

"Who did this?" I demand. "I swear I will strike them down."

I'm surprised to see tears spring up in Torran's eyes as he stares deep within me. "I'm sorry," he whispers.

Horror blossoms within me. Kartas can't be gone. He just can't be.

But then the old man speaks again, and somehow his words are even worse than my wildest fears.

"Kartas is alive," he rasps. "Ressa stands beside him. He's taken over the throne and put a bounty on your head."

The floor beneath me seems to shift. I barely even notice as Lyanndra's hand clamps over my shoulder while I sway beneath the burden of this news.

Kartas, who I love like my own brother, has betrayed me.

And now he will burn for it.

CHAPTER 35

Lyanndra

I'm stunned.

As the healer works on the injured Demigod's leg, I remain focused on Syran. I can practically feel the anger radiating off him as he seethes and paces the length of the bar. I haven't seen him this worked up since my last night at the palace, when he swept me up in his arms and carried me to the safety of his chambers.

How could Kartas do this to him?

Ressa, I can understand. I'm absolutely certain now that she organized the attack on me in the infirmary. From what I can piece together from my limited knowledge of palace affairs, she was once betrothed to Syran and was poised to be queen. It must have come as a terrible shock to her to find out that the man she loved was destined for another. In a way, I feel sorry for her, though her grief does not justify the damage she's done.

But the crown prince's own cousin?

Confusion and anger swirl in me at the betrayal. They were so close, and Syran trusted him both as a friend and a general. I recall my many walks with Kartas and how he cracked jokes so easily as he led me through the halls and grounds of the Celestial Court. I liked him, as much as I allowed myself to. It seems unthinkable that he would do something like this to Syran, his blood.

Yet, the golden fletching on the arrow that pierces the injured newcomer's leg is undeniable proof that he has.

I glance over to the old Demigod and am surprised to see him staring back at me. His eyes are the brightest shade of blue I've ever seen, and they remind me of the effervescent potion I used to freeze the blade of my greatsword in the fight against the wyrm. There's something very familiar about his gaze that makes me inexplicably uneasy, like I'm somehow seeing myself reflected back in him.

He lifts a spindly hand and beckons me toward him.

In spite of my misgivings, I comply with his request and approach. I kneel on the floor beside him, careful to avoid the sticky pool of blood slowly creeping across the wood from his wounded leg. I'm pretty sure I recognize this elderly Demigod. Wasn't he one of my healers at the Celestial Court? I have a vague recollection of those shocking blue eyes assessing me as somebody urged me to drink something.

"It seems we only ever meet in bloodshed," the Demigod rattles, confirming my suspicion. "I am Torran, advisor to the crown prince."

"I am…"

"The Godslayer," he finishes. "Syran's equal in power. I should have suspected it would be you, but alas, I thought you were a man and he saw a woman in his dreams."

I don't even want to think about what my crossed star might have divulged about our nighttime activities, so I change the subject entirely. "What is the state of Nexus?" I pry. I can't imagine the answer will be a palatable one, and unfortunately, his next words prove me correct.

"Death has come to our streets," Torran grits out. "Kartas has turned many of the Demigods against Syran. He claims you have bewitched him. Those loyal to the throne were killed, though some managed to flee from the city before the gates were drawn. Half of the Celestial Knights answer to the usurper now."

"And what is his plan? Surely he has one?"

He grimaces as the healer's hands graze his wound and then replies, "Kartas wants to follow in the footsteps of the Flaming God. Once he's purged Syran's supporters from the Celestial Court, he'll push out to wage war against the Starless. He thinks the Demigods should reclaim all of Alastria, at the price of every soul untouched by divinity."

Torran's eyes flicker to a point over my shoulder, and a quick glance behind me reveals that Syran has ceased his frenetic pacing and has come to join us. His elegant jaw is hard, his green eyes blazing. He's radiant and terrible in his anger.

"Can he be reasoned with?" the crown prince demands.

"No," the old Demigod sighs. "How do you think I got this arrow in my leg? I tried to give him council and nearly paid with my life. It's a small miracle I was able to escape with a few things. I think you'll find them useful." He nods over to the doorway of the inn where a rather large and lumpy sack rests heavily against the wall. "I managed to get a hold of a horse in a nearby village and rode until the beast collapsed then walked the rest of the way. I heard you were close by, and thank the stars that I actually found you."

"You did well," Syran nods.

Torran gestures down to his leg. "I just hope I didn't push myself too hard."

"You'll be okay," Syran assures him, and though I'm no healer, I think he's probably right. Torran has lost a lot of blood, but the wound should heal well once the arrow is removed, as long as infection doesn't set in. I'm more impressed that such an elderly Demigod could make it this far in such a state, especially carrying such a heavy burden as that sack. What could possibly be so important as to lug it all the way here?

While the healer continues her work, Syran and I move toward the doorway. Speaking softly so the villagers won't overhear, I ask, "What do you want to do?"

He fixes me with a pained look. "I have no choice," he sighs after a long moment. "I have to go back to the Celestial Court and put a stop to this."

"How?" I challenge. "You heard the old man. Kartas has an army."

"And so will I," he vows. "It's a fortnight's ride to Nexus. I will gather the Demigods still loyal to me and march on the city."

Fear ripples through me at the thought of him standing alone before the gates of Nexus with only a ragtag group of supporters at his back. The odds are not in his favor.

"What if you didn't go back?" I pose quietly. "Abandon your throne, Syran. Fight with us out here."

I recognize the stubborn set of his jaw and know immediately what his answer will be. It comes as no surprise when he argues, "It's true I can help out here, like you do. But I can do more by claiming the throne. I have to go. I can't let there be another war."

It's not the answer I want to hear, but it's the truth. I will accept it, but he will have to accept mine in turn.

"Then I'll go with you," I proclaim. Syran opens his mouth to reply, but I cut him off. "Maybe this is why the stars have crossed us. Maybe we were meant to put an end to this vicious cycle, to finally unite the Demigods and the Starless. My people will follow me if I ask. We don't need to fight against one another any longer, not when we can march into battle together as one."

The words tumble out to hang heavily in the air between us. For a moment Syran only stares at me, his face unreadable.

Then he closes the distance and sweeps me into a fierce and bruising kiss.

Everything else fades away. The gasps and gossip of the villagers is just noise in the background. Torran's weak laugh barely even registers. All I care about is the heat of Syran's lips on mine as he seals the agreement between us.

We are one, just as the stars intended.

When he pulls away, his expression is hard with resolve. He turns to the villagers, who have largely stopped to watch our open display of affection with unbridled curiosity.

"My cousin wishes to take my throne," he announces tightly. His voice, full with authority, floods the space with electric intensity. "He would march on Alastria to finish my father's bloody work. I will not let him."

From his side, I declare, "The usurper would wage war on our towns. He would destroy what we've worked so hard to build, from our farms to our families. I am the Godslayer. I destroyed the last threat that marched upon us, and I will stand against this one too. Who will join me as we march on Nexus?"

A tense silence falls. Villagers shift anxiously and exchange nervous glances as the seconds tick past. Have I made a grave mistake?

But then a strong voice breaks through the quiet as the innkeeper steps forward. His eyes find mine as he vows, "You killed the monster who took my sons from me. You have my sword."

A younger man pushes through the crowd and shouts, "My blade is yours!"

And then another cry sounds, and another, until two dozen villagers have pledged themselves to our cause.

"We ride with the sunrise!" Syran commands over the sea of voices.

That's only an hour away, and there's much to be done. The Starless disperse swiftly as they scramble to dust off their armor and sharpen their weapons. I doubt that any of them have trained regularly since the war, but I'm hoping that our numbers will outweigh any skill from Kartas' forces.

I'm just about to duck out the door to prepare Barra when Syran catches my shoulder. "The bag," Syran reminds me, nodding to the sack leaning against the wall. "Torran said that whatever's inside could help us."

I don't see what good it'll do, but I have to admit I'm a bit curious. What's so important that he'd risk his life to bring it to us? I can't think of anything, though I suppose rations or other supplies would be helpful.

Syran loosens the knot in the fabric and reaches inside. His eyes light up as he pulls something from the depths, and I recognize the golden gauntlet he holds up as a piece of his ceremonial armor.

And then it's my turn to gasp as he dives in again and this time extracts an unmistakable pile of dragonhide leathers.

I bundle them in my arms and glance inside the sack. It's laden with a mix of our armor.

"How did he manage that?" I murmur. "He's so frail, and this bag must weigh a ton."

"I have no idea," Syran says with a shake of his head. "These were all in my chambers. He shouldn't have even been able to get in there."

I feel around inside the sack and remove several more pieces of armor, both tarnished black and gleaming gold. Even my greatsword is in here, housed neatly in its stiff sheath. Tears prickle at the corners of my eyes as I heft the heavy weapon in my hands again after all this time.

All of my things are here, I realize. My dragonhide leathers and my armor sit in a haphazard pile at my feet. Syran's possessions also look to be in order, down to the midnight mantle he wore the day we fought in the palace courtyard.

But there's something missing.

Syran lifts out the last item and holds it aloft. Candlelight flickers off the golden surface, accentuating the deep scar on its top. The shower of delicate inlaid stars is unmistakable.

It's the helm of the Flaming God.

A wild tangle of emotions claws through me at the sight. That helm was part of me for so long. But it was also a mask, a lie.

It doesn't make me the Godslayer.

I do that on my own.

Syran's green eyes study me as I stare at the helm. "Don't hide behind this anymore," he murmurs as he presses it into my palms. "Wear it because you earned the right to do so."

And when I slide the helm on with shaking hands, I have never felt more free.

CHAPTER 36

The irony of marching into battle with the Godslayer at my side is not lost on me.

She sits high atop her monstrous steed, beautiful and terrible in her tarnished armor and striking gold helm. I'm secretly pleased to notice that she's added my black velvet cloak to her iconic ensemble. Not only does she wear my ring on her finger beneath her gauntlets, but now the insignia of my royal line flashes in gold stitching on her back. The message it sends to the soldiers that march behind us on the road to Nexus is clear.

The Godslayer and the Lord of the Midnight Flame are united.

We had little trouble whipping up an army. We stopped in every Starless settlement on our way toward the Celestial Court, be it a shantytown or a bustling village. Several merchants and pilgrims joined us on the roads, eager to follow their legendary hero into battle.

Word quickly spread to many of the Demigods who fled from Kartas' traitorous purge. Several of them ride with us now, guards and courtiers alike, all dressed in borrowed armor and weapons from their new Starless allies.

They offered us information, too. From what I'm able to weave together from the desperate narratives of my displaced people, my cousin's coup was not as successful as he hoped it would be. Many Celestial Knights turned on him, and some simply left their posts entirely. Lesser Demigods who live outside the palace walls have not been cooperative, oftentimes jumping Kartas' forces in the streets and generally adding to the mayhem.

The thought of those loyal to me standing against the usurper is strangely gratifying. While I would rather that fealty to the throne not be tested in such a sudden and treasonous manner, it sounds like most of the Demigods would prefer my rule over Kartas'. Perhaps more of them would rather extend the last year of peace than lose themselves in another endless war.

Those soldiers stand behind me now, mingled with their Starless brethren. In the fortnight that we've been on the road, I'm repeatedly astonished to see how enmeshed these warriors have become. Perhaps there really is a future for the Demigods and the Starless to unite as one.

I ponder this as the glittering spires of the Celestial Court rise up in the distance. Leading this army, I have never felt so powerful. Though the golden helm hides Lyanndra's face from view, I can tell by her confident posture that she's overcome by the same resolute thrill.

But as we grow closer to the city, I can't push down the shock and grief at the state of the capital. Black plumes of smoke rise from several of the buildings to form noxious columns in the otherwise clear blue sky. The putrid smell that hangs over the road to the main gates, which causes several of the soldiers behind us to gag, is unmistakable.

Death.

I don't allow myself to think about how many souls have already been lost. Instead, I scan the parapets of the gate for any activity. If I were Kartas, I would post archers there to shoot at any sign of opposition. But there's no movement, no flash of golden armor or twang of a longbow.

"It's too quiet," Lyanndra mutters at my shoulder. "Ambush?"

Though her logic is sound, I recall what the displaced Demigods said about the guards defecting and shake my head. "If Kartas can't hold the city, he can't hold the gate either. He'll have reinforced the palace while he tries to regain control of Nexus. But I don't doubt that there are eyes on us right now. I just don't know if they're friendly."

"Only one way to find out," she shrugs. She reaches for the hilt of her greatsword and draws it out in a smooth, practiced motion that makes the weapon appear feather-light. Using both hands, she raises the blade high in the air.

Behind us, the soldiers stop. Feet and hooves shuffle in the dirt as they wait for our command. I wheel my horse around to face our hastily assembled battalion.

"We know not what awaits us beyond the gates," I announce into the crisp winter air. "I am told that usurper's forces are unorganized, but skilled. We will push through them to the palace, but make no mistake–Kartas is mine."

A hail of loyalty rumbles through the amassed soldiers. Guilt pools in my gut as I realize that many of these men will fall. How many more sons, fathers, and brothers will be lost due to Demigod bloodlust?

This ends today.

Gripped with fresh resolve, I turn my horse around. The gates to Nexus hang halfway down at a strange angle, as though somebody tried to hastily lower them but was interrupted. Beyond, the sliver of cobbled road that's visible is smeared with rusty stains and sprawled forms.

Lyanndra is seemingly unmoved by the gruesome sight, which I attribute to her long years on the battlefield. She pushes her greatsword higher into the air, and then points it forward in a word-less command.

The time has come.

The Godslayer leads the charge, and I'm quick to follow as I urge my horse forward. She ducks to the side as she passes under the gates, and I do the same. Fear pounds in my chest as I wait for the whizz of an arrow or a shout from the parapet, but we cross the threshold of Nexus unscathed.

The city we enter is in shambles. A grimy layer of soot coats the once shining marble facades of the building. Rubble is strewn across the ground. Windows are smashed in, and shops are gutted, the interiors blackened with the remnants of fires. Bodies line the streets in varying states of decay, and the air is thick with the stench of rotting flesh.

Pushing back the urge to retch, I force myself not to look at the faces of the dead. There's no time to mourn, not even for those I might recognize.

We make it past the first block of buildings before we're spotted. A cry arises from a nearby alley and a group falls upon us in a flash of golden armor.

Lyanndra's reaction is devastatingly fast. She swings the greatsword in a heavy arc, catching two of the traitorous soldiers in their midsections. The shriek of metal tears through the air as their armor cleaves beneath the power of her strike, and then the sound is quickly drowned out by their rending screams.

I join in the fray, using one bare hand to alight my blade with my midnight flame before I, too, let loose on my disloyal subjects. My first swing misses its mark, but the black fire manages to brush against the mantle of one of the treasonous knights. He howls as the inferno consumes the fabric and licks at his neck, cooking him alive inside his helmet. He staggers, wheeling his arms and howling in pain, and knocks into his final two companions.

My sword connects with one of them as Lyanndra simultaneously cuts down the other. She doesn't break Barra's stride as she barrels over the fallen Demigods and continues ever closer to the palace gates. I follow her as steel clashes behind us, signaling another skirmish.

We work in tandem as we force our way closer to the seat of the Celestial Court. Knights clad in golden armor attack in small groups, but they pose little challenge to our combined skill. Once our loyal soldiers catch up to us, it becomes clear that Kartas' forces are outnumbered. Though several of the traitors use their gifts against us, their powers are weak and ineffective.

But the fighting still takes a toll. Sweat drips down my back as I fling bolts of flame between strikes of my blade. My heart thrums from the exertion, and the blood rushes through my veins on tides of adrenaline. I pull air into my lungs in great, stinging breaths.

Beside me, Lyanndra hasn't slowed. She shows no sign of exhaustion, and I can't help but admire her as she battles her way effortlessly through torrents of Celestial Knights. It strikes me that she could have easily bested me in our duel.

She let me win because she wanted to die.

Now, she fights to live. Between Barra's flying hooves and the long reach of the greatsword, nobody even comes close to landing a blow on her. She dances in and out of each scrimmage like it's second nature, as easy as breathing. Normally, I'd envy such skill, but I only find myself wanting her more as she unleashes upon the Celestial Knights.

Finally, we reach the palace gates. I expect archers here, or at least some defense, but there's only a scattering of guards assembled in front of the last barricade between me and my throne.

"Stand down," I order as Lyanndra and I draw to a halt in front of the gate.

Four knights immediately lower their weapons, but the rest stand their ground.

"I do not wish to kill my own people," I warn, "but I will not tolerate treason. This is your last chance to obey."

Nobody else moves.

"So be it," I sigh.

Channeling the same energy I felt the night we fought the strix, I summon a great burst of black flame. Each tendril of the blaze coalesces into the head of a serpent, striking out at the disloyal guards with alarming accuracy. Fiery fangs sink into armor and skin as the men howl and curse in pain at the venomous attack.

Those that manage to dodge the inferno fall to Lyanndra's blade.

She weaves through the stricken knights and slices wildly until, between our combined efforts, only the four who surrendered remain standing.

We leave them there, stopping only to push open the palace gates. The deserted courtyard stretches beyond in a clear path to the entrance of the Celestial Court.

Both of us slide down from our mounts. Lyanndra steps up to my side, her shoulder brushing my arm. My body aches from the fighting, and I wonder if she's feeling equally battered. I long to reach out and take her gauntleted hand in my own, but I resist the urge. The worst is yet to come, I fear, and we'll need our wits about us.

Unease coils inside of me as we pick our way across the courtyard. Where is everybody? This open area feels like a trap. My eyes dart around the seemingly abandoned place, searching for the slightest sign of life.

As if on cue, a rock hurtles through the air toward us. Just before it hits her, Lyanndra side steps out of the way, and the stone smashes heavily onto the cobblestones where she was just standing.

I turn to confront our attacker, already sure of who it must be.

Ressa.

The Demigod stands up on the dais where I once received my crossed star, her hands outstretched to use her powers once again. My former betrothed looks as unglued as I have ever seen her. Though she wears one of her many fine dresses in an ethereal shade of silver, the fabric is rumpled and torn at the hem. Her hair, usually coiffed to perfection, hangs limply around her face in knotted coils. Madness twists her delicate features as she glares down at us.

"I knew you'd be back," she snarls, "but I hoped you'd leave that Starless whore behind."

Lyanndra tenses beside me, and I sense her coiled rage at the Demigod's snub.

"I'd say it's good to see you, Ressa, but lying isn't very becoming of a king," I retort easily. I know it's probably not the best idea to rile her up, not when her dark eyes shine with that strange and feverish glow, but I won't let her insult stand. "Now step aside, and you have my word that I will let you live."

Instead of heeding my words, the beautiful Demigod sneers. "This has gone on long enough, Syran," she hisses. "You belong with me!"

"I belong with the Godslayer," I declare, and I have never felt that more strongly as Lyanndra shifts her weight beside me. "There is nothing you can do to change that."

Ressa laughs, and I wonder how I ever found that sound to be endearing. "I can kill your precious crossed star. I hoped that my loyal courtiers would take care of her that night in the infirmary, but I guess I'll just have to do the job myself."

Finally, Lyanndra speaks. "If you take my life, you will drive Syran to madness. Is that what you want?" she challenges.

"I'd rather he be mad than be with you," she fumes.

To my surprise, Lyanndra steps in front of me and hefts her greatsword. "So be it," she says simply. "I'll handle Ressa. Go find Kartas, and put a stop to this."

I stare at her for a long moment. I don't want to leave her here, but Ressa is just a well-bred courtier. She's no warrior. Even with her powers, she's no match for Lyanndra.

Confident that my crossed star won't be harmed, I nod.

Because somewhere inside the palace, my cousin sits on the throne.

I will put an end to this bloodshed.

I will take back what's mine.

CHAPTER 37

Lyanndra

What Ressa lacks in skill, she makes up in sheer rage.

While most of the Demigods' gifts have been diluted over the centuries, Syran's former betrothed retains some of the raw power of the stars. She flings a barrage of heavy rocks toward my head, which I deflect with the broad blade of my greatsword. The impacts send shockwaves rolling up my arms and into my shoulders, which ache beneath my dragonhide leathers and tarnished armor. Not for the first time, I'm glad that my golden helm hides the grimace on my face as I brace against the pain.

Ressa doesn't seem to notice my momentary weakness.

"How dare you wear his cloak?" she seethes as she uses her powers to rip several cobblestones up from the ground of the courtyard. Clots of earth rain down in turgid droplets, marking the place where Syran once spilled my blood across the steps of the dais. "How dare you wear his royal sigil?" She sends the second volley of moonstone toward me to punctuate her words.

The rocks hurtle through the air toward me at terrifying speed. I roll out of the way, though one projectile manages to graze my greaves. The hit produces a thick metallic resonance that makes my teeth hurt and my eyes water. I wince, knowing that even that slight impact will probably bruise.

Rising quickly to my feet, I watch Ressa carefully as she tears up another batch of rocks. Each time she uses her gift, I notice that it seems to take a toll on her. Her shoulders are significantly slouched from the effort, and sweat beads on her forehead. Her pale skin is more gray than porcelain, and it strikes me that perhaps I can simply tire her out without ever landing a blow on her.

But part of me itches to swing my greatsword at her. As much as I dislike how she talked about me, I hate the way she's treated Syran. I understand that she must feel swindled out of the throne and his heart, but it wasn't exactly his choice. Why does she still fight for him when he wants no part of her anymore?

One glance at her eyes tells me all I need to know. Her gaze is furious but somehow empty, as though she's lost all reason. When she flings her next onslaught of stones, the force is powerful, but the aim is lackluster, like she's not fully in control.

She's getting tired, and it's making her sloppy.

I once again dart out of the way of the rocks. My boots skid over the smooth cobblestones as I weave closer to her. Less range will make me an easier target for her attacks, but it will also give me a chance to strike.

I'm close enough now. Every instinct in my body screams for me to kill her. But something within me, the burning, coiled thing that awakened the night Syran and I consummated our bond on the Winter Solstice, whispers that I shouldn't.

Because as much as I hate her and as much as she disgusts Syran, he would never forgive me if I did it.

So when I finally strike, I spin my greatsword at the last second so that I slap her in the midsection with the broad side of the blade instead of the sharp and bloody edge.

The impact forces the breath from Ressa's lungs in an audible rush of air. She falls backward, and her head cracks loudly against the marble of the dais. Pain rolls across her face in a worryingly slow wave as her eyelids flutter.

Have I killed her?

But Ressa's dark eyes don't close. She stares up at me, dazed and gasping for air, as I loom over her. I wait for her to raise her hands for another attack, but they remain still at her sides.

"Finish it," she spits.

As tempting as the notion is, I shake my head. I take a risk and pull off my helm, revealing my face to her. "You'll suffer more if you live," I tell her.

"I'll kill you," she threatens, though we both know by now that she doesn't have the strength left to follow through.

"Not today," I quip. "But I'll end you if you harm Syran."

"You don't care about him! You only want the throne!" she snarls.

Anger flares in my chest at her words, and I have to actively resist the urge to strike her down where she lies. Instead, I grit out, "And you *do* care about him? How could you so brazenly hurt the man you claim to love?"

Ressa tries to laugh, but only succeeds in driving herself into a fit of ragged coughs. Did my blow break some of her ribs? It's a distinct possibility, and one I don't feel particularly bad about. "That was never part of the plan," she reveals once she's recovered enough to talk. "After all his other attempts to get rid of you failed, Kartas promised to lock you away so that I would have Syran all to myself. All I had to do was help convince the courtiers to back his bid for the throne. Syran would have gotten over you eventually. I know I could convince him."

My blood freezes at her words. "Other attempts?"

Cruel hunger flashes across her face as she goads, "Kartas despised you from the start. Before you came along, he was content to whisper in Syran's ear and rule from afar. But the second he learned you were Starless, he knew that Syran was a lost cause. At first, he tried to win you over so that you'd fall for him, or at least go to him for counsel. But you didn't, you stubborn bitch. So he tried to influence Syran instead by parading you through the court to anger the other Demigods, but our crown prince was too smitten to throw you in the dungeons. The stars only know what he sees in you." She pauses for a moment to cough again before continuing, "Kartas came up with the idea to disguise some courtiers as guards and have them ambush you in the infirmary. He enlisted me to talk them into it. But somehow Syran figured it out before they could do any real damage. What a shame."

"That was Kartas?" I gasp, shocked by the revelation. I was so sure that Ressa was behind the attack. Kartas played the part of a concerned friend and general so well that he fooled Syran and me with ease. Horror floods through me as I think back to every interaction with the crown prince's cousin. The first time I met him, I thought something was off about him, but I chalked it up to the fact that he's a Demigod.

Now, I know the truth. As deceitful as Ressa is, I don't think she's lying. Kartas was willing to betray his own blood to be rid of me.

He used Syran, but he used Ressa too.

I look down at her and no longer see just a rabid Demigod lost to brokenhearted madness. When I really take the time to study her, I realize that she must be around the same age as me. She's beautiful, yes, but I doubt she has even a fraction of my worldly experience. She's just a young woman who was probably promised to Syran at an early age. That betrothal must have guided and shaped her entire life, and then the stars snatched it all away from her. Now, her heart is twisted with grief and pain at that loss, morphing her into an easy target for manipulation by a powerful man like Kartas.

All of the bloodlust I felt, all of the hot desire to end her life, drains from my body. I'm left with a deep, hollow sadness at the ruin of the woman who lies before me.

I can't kill her.

I lower my greatsword, and her eyes widen. For the first time, I realize that she would actually rather die than be without Syran. That sort of obsession is dangerous, but I just can't do it.

"This is the mercy of the Godslayer," I declare. "I'll let you live so that you might have a chance to be your own woman. I hope it haunts you that a Starless spared your life."

"No!" Ressa howls desperately. "You can't have him!"

I don't reply.

Confident that she's too exhausted and injured to surprise me with an attack, I turn my back on her and start toward the palace doors. She screeches all manner of threats and profanities as I walk away, but I tune them out. Pity settles deep within me as I cross the threshold of the Celestial Court.

The marble halls engulf me into their cool embrace. I'm not sure where I'm supposed to be going, but Syran's left me a helpful path of bodies to follow. I marvel at how silent the corridors are as I follow the morbid trail of breadcrumbs. The last time I was here, the labyrinthine passageways were always bustling with courtiers and guards, and the air was alight with gossip and laughter.

Now, the stench of blood presses in on me as the thick, glowing walls mute the terrible sound of the fighting that still rages out in the streets of Nexus. How many have died? How many more will fall? Bile rises in my throat at the thought, but I swallow it back down. This is a battlefield like any other. I'll have time to mourn once the war is won, but until then, I need to focus on my task.

I have to find Syran.

My heart clenches when I think of him battling his cousin. The truth is that I don't actually know that much about Kartas' abilities. Syran told me on the road to Nexus that the usurper can manifest small bolts of lightning and that he's an adept fighter. But I've never seen his skills myself. If he's as good as Syran says, then I have every reason to worry about my crossed star.

I quicken my pace as I weave through the seemingly endless corridors. There's a strange pressure growing in my chest that whispers that Syran is in danger. Normally, I'd dismiss the feeling as anxiety, but I know intrinsically that it's something more than that. In fact, it reminds me of the certainty that overtook me the night we fought the strix. I was drawn to him then, sure that something terrible was about to happen. Is this part of our connection?

My alarm only grows as the seconds pass by. Fear wells inside of me, creeping through my veins and drowning my nerves as I break out into a full sprint.

Because I *know* that Syran is in trouble.

And I'm not worried about his death causing me to go mad.

I *care* about him.

And maybe, just maybe, it's something more than that.

CHAPTER 38

Syran

"Welcome back, cousin."

Kartas grins lazily down at me from the throne—*my* throne. His legs are sprawled out across one arm of the gilded chair, and he leans back against the other, completely at ease. The sight heats my blood to a fiery boil.

"Kartas," I acknowledge coldly. He doesn't seem at all surprised to see me here in front of him, and his next words only confirm that suspicion.

"You took your time," he says. "I thought for sure you'd come running the second you heard about Demigods fleeing the city, but you never showed."

"I was busy pulling an arrow out of Torran's leg," I parry.

My cousin straightens up on the throne and clicks his tongue. "And here I was assuming that the mad old wretch would bleed out on the road. But none of that matters now that you're here." He peers around me, as though expecting to see Lyanndra at my shoulder. "Where's your little pet?" he asks. "Or did the Godslayer let you come here all alone?"

I don't grace his impertinent question with an answer. He might sit on the throne, but I am still king.

"How could you do this?" I demand instead. "We grew up like brothers. Does blood mean nothing to you?"

"Blood?" Kartas barks out a sardonic laugh as he rises to his feet. "What do you know about blood? Your own father shaped an entire kingdom for you. He did what was needed to bring the Starless to heel, but you would toss that legacy away in a heartbeat."

It's hard to process his words. The Demigod I thought I knew was sharp and quick with his wit, but he was also gregarious and peaceful. But now the mask is peeling off to reveal the ugly truth hiding beneath the smooth veneer. How did I not notice this before?

As though he relishes my shock, Kartas continues, "I should have been the one to ascend to the throne after the king died. You never had the stomach for warfare. You even watched the Godslayer cut down your own father, and you didn't have the gall to go after her. All this talk of peace is just a façade to hide your cowardice."

"The throne is mine," I growl, "and my father deserved what he got. So much blood was spilled under his rule, and for what? For the cycle of death to continue?"

"The Starless are scum!" Kartas snaps. The surety in his voice is horrifying. "They're nothing more than vermin, even your precious Godslayer. Your bleeding heart would stand in the way of the Demigods achieving greater power. How could you crush your own people in order to raise up an inferior race?"

"Justice for the Starless does not take anything away from us!" I counter.

But Kartas is too far gone to listen to reason. It's growing clearer by the second that he holds these beliefs so strongly that the only way to rid him of them is to wrestle them from his cold, dead grasp.

"You could have just done what your father wanted," he rants on. "If you'd just carried on in his footsteps, I would have been content to stand by you and manipulate you from the shadows whenever necessary. But then the Godslayer came along."

"She plays no part in this!"

My cousin shakes his head. "She only drew you farther into this fantasy of peace. I tried to drive a wedge between the two of you from the very start."

The knife of betrayal twists in my gut at his words. I think back to how Kartas initially wanted to throw the Godslayer in the dungeons. He only softened that stance once I made it clear that I wouldn't tolerate such treatment of my crossed star. Then he suggested that I should keep her caged like an animal, taming her with the riches of the Celestial Court.

He tried to set us up to fail, I realize with growing rage. After spending so much time with her, he must have known that such a strategy would only serve to push her farther away from me.

A terrible notion strikes me. "You were behind the attack in the infirmary, weren't you?" I gasp.

Kartas smirks, and I know it's true before he confirms, "Guilty, cousin. Nothing I did seemed to be working. I knew I had to take some more drastic measures, so I had our darling Ressa sweet talk some courtiers into dressing as guards. She promised them higher stations and privileges, and they fell into line just like that. It's a pity they didn't get to do a little more damage before you stepped in. And of course, I underestimated just how much of a brute the Godslayer is. It really was a nasty business with that fork."

I picture the utensil sticking out of the dead Demigod's neck and snarl, "That should have been you."

"But it wasn't," Kartas counters. "When I told you my investigation stalled, you just ate it right up. You didn't suspect a thing. And then when you went in and found the Godslayer gone, it was like the stars just handed me the throne."

Fury builds inside of me as I begin to understand the extent to which my cousin deceived me, stoking the midnight flame that roars through my veins. "You tried to talk me into staying," I argue as I try to make sense of the terrible truth.

"Only because I knew that you'd go anyway," he replies. "And when you chased after her and left me to rule in your stead, I knew it was my only chance. Now, I will finish what your father started."

"You've already failed," I growl. "As we speak, my army is taking back the city. Those loyal to you are dead or dying. You've lost your brother and your kingdom. You have nothing, Kartas."

He smirks again. "I have everything, as long as I hold the throne."

"Then I shall take that from you, too."

I draw my blade. Black flames ripple up the steel, called forth by my power. I've clashed swords with Kartas more times than I care to count, but those have always been sparring sessions, not true duels to the death.

Now, when he raises his weapon, the stakes couldn't be clearer.

Only one of us can sit on the throne.

The other has to die.

A howling war cry rips from my chest as I charge. He meets my blade with his and then quickly sidesteps a subsequent strike of my flames. As he meets each of my attacks with equal ferocity, I catch a telltale whiff of ozone. Seconds later, Kartas' sword crackles with electricity.

I know from experience that the sizzling bolt of energy will transfer into me if he lands a blow on my weapon or my golden armor. I've seen the destruction Kartas has wrought both on the training grounds and on the battlefield, and I certainly have no plans to be on the receiving end of his powers, so I twist out of range as he swings his blade down.

The sword crashes into the gleaming marble floor with a momentous boom. The stone splits into a shower of shimmering fragments, sending a small plume of iridescent dust glittering up in the air between us.

Ignoring the ringing in my ears, I take the opportunity to lash out with my midnight flame. But Kartas knows this trick all too well. He darts off to the side as he brings up his blade to deflect the searing tongues of fire that reach for him.

"Is that the best you can do?" he goads as he slices at me once again.

I parry the cut and spin away, my black mantle swirling at my shoulders. "We're just getting started," I promise him.

The dance continues through the throne room. My flame snatches at him mercilessly but only manages to catch one of the grand tapestries that hang on the wall behind the throne, rendering it to a pile of ash in mere seconds. Electricity snarls off Kartas in snapping arcs, blowing divots in the marble floors as I continuously dodge his strikes. In between, our swords clash in a tangle of steel and sparks, but neither of us seems to be able to land a blow on the other.

We're too well matched, and we know each other's fighting styles far too intimately. If I'm going to get the upper hand in this battle, I'm going to have to change things up.

What would the Godslayer do? I think back to when we clashed in the courtyard all those months ago. She didn't just use her blade against me. She used her body, too. In fact, the ugly purple bruise she left from kicking me on the shin lingered for weeks after our fight.

That's the kind of unpredictability I need now. So when Kartas rushes me, I push down the instinct to meet his blade with mine. Instead, I duck beneath the trajectory of his sword and stick out my foot. The result is immediate. Already off balance from the missed swing, he stumbles right into my outstretched leg and plummets face-first toward the marble floor.

I'm on him in a flash. He just barely has enough time to roll out of the way as I unleash a deluge of poisoned flame at the spot where he fell. Then he's on his feet again, panting and unsure.

"That's new," he muses cautiously as we circle one another again. "Did your Starless bitch teach you that?"

Fresh anger flares in my gut at his words. How dare he speak of Lyanndra that way? "She could destroy you without breaking a sweat," I snarl.

Realizing he's hit a nerve, Kartas offers me a cruel smirk. "Maybe," he admits. "But she's not here, is she?"

I desperately want to goad him that by now, she's probably dealt with Ressa and is already in the palace. The same tugging feeling that drove me into a frenzy when she was attacked in the infirmary pulses in my chest now, whispering that she's on her way to me. But Kartas doesn't need to know that. Let him think that our fight is equally matched. Perhaps his hubris will be the death of him.

To distract him from any thoughts of my crossed star, I lunge at him with my blade held high. He doesn't seem to expect the attack and hesitates just a moment too long before he moves. But where I expect him to sidestep or parry, he simply raises a hand and presses it out against my golden chest plate directly over my heart.

Electricity sears through my armor in an agonizing jolt. My jaw locks, and I taste blood in my mouth as my vision flashes white hot from the shock. The explosive force blasts me away from Kartas' outstretched arm, sending me flying limply through the air. I hit the ground hard on my back, the impact knocking the air from my lungs as I slide the last couple of feet until I slam into the base of the throne.

I gasp for breath and blink the flash from my eyes. My limbs are leaden and tingling with the vestiges of the shock, and my dazed horror only mounts as I realize that I'm no longer holding my sword. Somewhere behind the ringing in my ears and the pain that courses through my body, I register that Kartas is moving toward me, but it isn't until he looms directly above me that I realize just how dire the situation is.

I have no weapon. I can't move. My fire flickers weakly in my hands as my body struggles to recover from the electricity coursing through my armor. When Kartas raises his blade to deal the death-blow, there's nothing left for me to do.

The sword swings down, flashing in the dying light of my midnight flame.

I let out one more breath, sure it will be my last.

But then a second blade flashes into view, heavy and sure. It knocks Kartas' weapon off course, the force shoving him back and away from where I lie.

A swirl of black velvet, embroidered with gold, blots out my view as somebody new steps in front of me to face my cousin.

The Godslayer has joined the fight.

Kartas doesn't stand a chance.

CHAPTER 39

Lyanndra

Syran is still alive.

Relief floods me as I resist the desperate urge to go to him. He's sprawled out on his back at the foot of the throne, his cape charred, and his armor steaming. His red hair is spread out in a wild tangle beneath him, and his face is slack with pain. Tendrils of black flame flicker between his outstretched palms.

What has Kartas done to him?

Judging by the sharp odor of ozone that simmers in the air, I'd wager he used his electricity against Syran. The shock wasn't enough to kill him, but it looks like it came disturbingly close.

"Godslayer," Kartas greets me with a farcical bow, dragging my attention away from my crossed star. "How lovely to see you again. I was worried you'd let my cousin come alone."

I remain silent. Kartas isn't worth the breath it would take to reply.

"I see you're still your same chatty self," he mocks as he adjusts the grip on his sword. "It's a pity that you're Starless. If you were a Demigod, I think we could have been friends."

But I know how Kartas treats those who he claims as his allies. He betrayed Syran in the worst way. He tried to manipulate me and succeeded in stringing Ressa along like a desperate puppy. Even if he were Starless, I would want nothing to do with such a despicable man.

"Now that you're here," Kartas continues, "we may as well finish this." His eyes flicker over to wear Syran lies, groaning, on the chipped marble floor. "Though it looks like I might have already succeeded where my cousin is concerned."

Rage and fear twine through my veins in a ferocious tandem at the thought of losing Syran. Now that I've admitted to myself that my feelings for my crossed star have grown into something warm and unexpected, I know in my heart that I want him here with me. And if he does die, I'd rather go mad. At least that way, I won't be haunted by the memory of him.

Beneath my golden helm, I bare my teeth at Kartas in a feral snarl. This isn't about the throne anymore, or war, or even the fate of Alastria.

He isn't going to take Syran from me.

I surge toward him as he opens his mouth to continue his one-sided conversation. He barely registers my movements until I'm nearly on top of him, my greatsword already screaming through the air in a wide, heavy arc.

Kartas drops to the ground beneath my blade, which whistles harmless over his head. In a blur, he's back on his feet, his sword ready and dancing with sparks of electricity.

"Have you ever been struck by lightning, Godslayer?" he asks. "I'm told it's not a very pleasant experience by those who survive."

I say nothing as I track his stance. He's using his words to distract me from the subtle shift of weight between his feet, but it's not going to work. Tuning out his prattling voice, I instead focus on his actions.

The strategy pays off. He cuts out at me mid-sentence, jabbing toward my armor with the tip of his charged blade. If I had listened to him, I probably wouldn't have seen it coming, but since I was paying attention, I manage to dance away easily as his weapon slices only air.

My nimble dodge seems to anger him. He swings again, this time in a horizontal cut toward my shoulders. Normally, I'd bring my blade up to push his back, but the lightning that crackles over the steel gives me pause.

I don't know very much about electricity, but I do know from experience that lightning and thunder are lovers, and bolts tend to strike tall things, water, and metal. I've seen wildfires start from a single shock, and once I watched from the cover of the trees as one flash kicked up the water in a nearby lake. Seconds later, dead fish bubbled to the surface, fried by the energy.

I would rather not float belly up, I decide. So I notch the tip of my greatsword into one of the cracks in the marble floor and push off with my feet, using the momentum to duck and spin my body at an almost horizontal angle. My boots slide easily against the stone as I loop around the blade in a semicircle.

Kartas doesn't have time to get out of the way. My feet slam into his knees, throwing him off balance. He pitches to the side and lands hard on his shoulder with an audible crunch.

"You bitch!" he howls as he clutches at the joint. Even hidden beneath layers of armor, I'm pretty sure it's broken, or at least dislocated. But the luckiest thing is that it's his combat arm. There's no way he'll be able to swing a sword now.

I'm not going to give him the chance to regroup. I yank my greatsword free of the crack and bring it down hard toward him. To my dismay, he scrambles over just before the blade chops down onto the marble where he was just sprawled, leaving less than an inch between his side and my weapon.

In the time it takes me to ready myself for another strike, Kartas is back on his feet. His right arm hangs limply at his side, useless, and his sword rests on the ground where he dropped it.

But he's not giving up. Even without a weapon, Kartas still has his lightning. He cringes through the pain as electricity roars over his skin and ripples across his armor in a shower of skittering sparks. The stench of ozone bites the air, causing my head to swim and my stomach to churn.

I had no idea he could manifest his gift without using his sword as a medium. His desperation must have unlocked some well of power within him, and it flares up now with frightening intensity.

"I'm going to destroy you," Kartas snarls as he staggers toward me with his good arm outstretched. "And then I'm going to kill Syran."

I can't escape. My tarnished armor is no help here. It'll only serve to roast me alive. Even a fatal blow of my greatsword will result in my death. The reality is that I'm covered in metal, and that makes me a walking target.

Kartas seems to know that too. He flashes me a humorless grin as he says, "Goodbye, Godslayer."

I ready myself for the inevitable shock he's about to throw at me, but a voice cries out from behind him, high and clear.

"No!"

Something whistles through the air and clips Kartas on the back of the head. He stumbles but doesn't fall. I look down at the projectile and realize that it's a piece of marble, the milky white stone now smeared with red.

I retrace the rock's trajectory and my eyes widen with shock as I realize who's come to join the fray.

Ressa sways in the doorway, her dark gaze wild. Blood trickles down the delicate column of her neck, presumably from where her skull cracked into the dais in the courtyard during our skirmish. Her hands, pale and shaking, are outstretched before her, evidence that she used her powers.

Kartas spins to face her. "Ressa?" he gasps incredulously. "What are you doing?"

Unhinged rage surges through her features. "You were going to kill Syran!" she hisses through bloodied teeth. "That wasn't part of the deal!"

"No. No, I wasn't," he insists, his tone suddenly gentle. "I just... I got carried away. But I'm not going to kill him. I promised you, didn't I?"

I see an opportunity, and I take it. "He's lying, Ressa," I call. "Think about it. He promised fealty to Syran and friendship to me, and he betrayed us both. What makes you think he won't turn on you too?"

Confusion flickers across the female Demigod's face as her gaze darts between Kartas and me and then over to where Syran struggles to his feet by the throne.

"She's right," Syran coughs. His voice is weak, but his words are strong. "I know you must hate me, and you have every reason to do so. But Kartas is using you. Don't you see that?"

"Enough!" Kartas bellows. Small bursts of lightning arc off him as his temper flares, and Ressa winces at the violent show of force. He doesn't even bother to tamp down the fury on his face as he turns on her and snaps, "Syran betrayed you first. He broke your heart and tossed you aside like you were nothing! And yet you grovel at the feet of a man who doesn't even want you? You're pathetic, Ressa!"

A new wave of potent anger seizes her features. "Pathetic?" she snarls. Her eyes land on Syran once again before she turns her attention back to Kartas. "You actually were going to kill him, weren't you?"

The usurper sneers at her. "Were you really stupid enough to believe that I wouldn't? If I let him live, he would never rest until he took back the throne. Syran has to die." His words are resolute and leave no room for argument.

But they're also not what Ressa wants to hear.

She lifts her hands up high, calling on her powers. Several large chunks of rubble, far bigger than the cobblestones she flung at me out in the courtyard, rise into the air before her.

Kartas' expression darkens with anger, but there's fear there, too. "Don't do it, Ressa," he menaces.

"May the stars damn you!" she shrieks in a high and terrible voice. Guided by her pale hands, the rubble hurtles forward, each piece aimed squarely at Kartas.

There's nothing else he can do if he wants to survive the onslaught. Lightning crackles over his skin as it coalesces into his palms, and then he flings it at Ressa with a pained cry.

The energy surges into her, and she lets out a horrible wail. Her dark hair stands on end and starts to sizzle, as does the gauzy fabric of her silver dress. And then she collapses, her limbs twitching as she writhes and finally stills, her body steaming on the cold marble floor.

At the same time, the rubble falls harmlessly to the ground a few feet away, no longer controlled by her powers. Safe for the moment, Kartas sways where he stands, visibly exhausted from the effort it took to manifest his gift. The lightning has dissipated, but it's only a matter of time before he regains his strength.

I may not get another chance.

I dash toward him and strike out with my greatsword, aiming to slice him cleanly beneath the ribs. As my weapon arcs through the air, Syran catches my eye from across the room. He leans against the wall, clearly depleted, but the hard look in his gaze tells me he has enough energy left for one more attack.

He lifts his hands and unleashes a stream of midnight flame. The blaze coalesces around my blade, sending up a shower of dark embers as I complete the swing.

Kartas turns to face me just as the fiery greatsword cleaves into his side.

His eyes bulge in shock as the weapon sinks deeper. His astonished gaze meets mine while blood pours out of the wound and spills onto the marble floor in a crimson pool. His jaw works once and then twice, but the only sound that bubbles from his mouth is a low, pained whine.

And then his eyes dim, and his face goes slack. His body collapses, peeling away from the blade of my greatsword with a terrible sloughing sound that makes me want to vomit through the visor of my golden helm.

Kartas falls to the floor, lifeless.

The usurper is dead.

CHAPTER 40

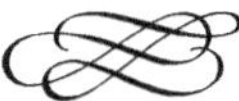

SYRAN

Everything is quiet.

Afternoon sunlight filters in serenely through the vaulted windows, illuminating the aftermath of the failed coup. The marble floor of the throne room, previously unblemished, is a scarred and sooty mess. Chunks of rubble and debris are scattered across the large, open space, and columns of dust and ash drift in great motes through the air. Tapestries hang, torn and singed, at odd angles. The only thing still untouched is the throne itself, which glints innocently as though it didn't just almost cause a war.

Ressa, too, is still. From where I stand, I can't tell if she's even breathing. A pang of guilt cuts through my heart as I realize how terribly I treated her. I should never have promised myself to her, not when I knew in my soul that I didn't belong with her. And she did save us in the end, even if her logic was twisted.

But we can deal with her later.

I turn my attention to Kartas, whose lifeless form lies mangled upon the destroyed marble. His brown eyes stare blankly back at me. Blood claws its way across the stone with crimson fingers, reaching desperately for Lyanndra's boots.

She does not cower from it. Instead, she stands preternaturally still, as though transfixed by the sight of him. Turgid droplets of vitality and gore drip steadily down from the blade of her greatsword and burst upon the marble floor, the only sound in the aftermath of so much carnage.

I've seen this before, I realize with a twist of unease. When I watched her strike down my father, she froze in the same way she does now. At the time, I assumed she was gloating beneath her helm at her unholy victory, but I know her better now. Though death is her trade, she doesn't take any sick joy in it. This is something else, something that overrides my tangled emotions and jolts me into action.

"Lyanndra." I call her name softly, breaking the sacred hush that's fallen over the throne room in the wake of Kartas' death.

She doesn't react.

Disquieted by her lack of response, I approach her cautiously. Numbness still grips my body, but the strange static caused by Kartas' lightning has receded enough for me to feel the deep ache in my legs that radiates with every step I take. My head pounds, but the white spots that danced in front of my eyes are thankfully gone, along with the infernal ringing in my ears.

I keep my eyes on her golden helm as I move in front of her, blocking Kartas from her view. Standing this close to her, I can hear her breaths coming in short, panting gasps through her visor.

"Lyanndra?" I repeat. With the helm covering her face, I can't tell if she's looking at me or not. Taking a risk, I reach out with unsteady hands to brush the clasp at her neck that secures the piece of armor to her head. I'm acutely aware of the bloody blade of the greatsword in my peripheral, though I know she would never purposely hurt me. Careful not to startle her, I run over the lumpy stitching at the point where I sliced through the leather strap all those months ago until I find the metal latch that holds it in place. It takes me a moment to work it free, and then I gently pull the helm off her.

Her hazel eyes, wide and panicked, are fixed straight ahead. Sweat slicks her skin. Her face is unusually pale, as though she's going to be sick, and her striking features are twisted with a strange mix of guilt, rage, and fear.

Was this what she went through when she was standing over my father's corpse?

My heart shatters for her at the thought. The Godslayer's triumph over the Flaming God was written into legend as a bloodthirsty act of victory. Even I misread her actions as I watched her hold my father's golden helm high on the smoky battlefield.

But this is what I saw on her face when I killed the courtier attacking her in the infirmary. Is this what she's so desperate to hide beneath her golden helm? A conscious?

"Lyanndra," I say again, and this time she snaps out of it.

"Syran?" she murmurs. Her eyes drift into focus and then trail up to meet mine. I notice that she's trembling, and I don't think about what I do next.

I step forward and wrap my arms around her, pulling her close.

"I'm here," I soothe, my breath ruffling her hair. "I'll always be here."

A shaky sound, half sigh and half sob, escapes her. The greatsword slides from her hands, clattering to the ground beside us. My heart swells as she twines her arms around my torso and leans her head against my golden chest plate.

I hold her tightly, savoring the feel of her armored body against mine. We stand there for quite some time until the tremors run their course, and her breathing returns to normal. Only then does she pull away from the safe haven of my arms to regard me with worry in her hazel eyes.

"Are you injured?" she asks as her gaze slides over my limbs, searching for wounds. "When I saw you lying there, I thought…"

"Only my pride," I assure her. Though Kartas' lightning attack stunned me, I'm quickly recovering. Now that the feeling is returning to my extremities, I'm certain that the growling ache in my bones is the only real damage I've sustained today.

But I can't say the same for my cousin.

I swallow thickly as I turn to survey Kartas' corpse. He betrayed me. I should be glad that he's dead, but all I feel is hollow grief.

"I considered him a brother," I whisper.

"I'm sorry," Lyanndra says sadly. "But it had to be done."

"I know."

Tears well in my eyes as I stare down at the Demigod who lied to me so effortlessly. Why did it have to come to this?

Lyanndra steps up beside me and slides her gauntlet into my hand. I squeeze my palm against hers, and she returns the pressure.

"We should go," I state after a few agonizing seconds. I can mourn for my cousin later, after we put an end to the fighting in the streets of Nexus. Too many have already died for Kartas' needless power grab, and every moment I waste in my grief puts other lives at risk.

I stoop down and haul my cousin's body over my shoulder. Ignoring how his blood, still warm, seeps onto the exposed skin of my neck, I straighten up with grim determination and turn to face my crossed star.

She pulls on the golden helm, taking a moment to latch it before she retrieves her greatsword and replaces it in its sheath on her back. Then she pulls Kartas' sword from where it lies amongst the rubble, a symbol of his demise. I follow her as she steps over Ressa's unmoving form and out into the corridor.

We make a morbid pair as we wend our way out of the palace. My shoulders and arms scream from the exertion of carrying Kartas' armored body, but it's a necessary pain. His men won't stop fighting until they see for themselves that the usurper is dead. Most victors would have saved themselves the trouble of carrying their fallen foe and simply taken the head as proof, but I can't bring myself to desecrate my cousin's body in such a way. So I bear this terrible burden until, at last, we step out into the courtyard.

The battle has reached the palace. Skirmishes boil through the grounds. Screams and war cries rend the air as steel crashes and sparks fly. Demigods wield their power with wild abandon, sending up flares of dust and water, and the stench of blood hangs heavily over the scene as soldiers fall by the dozens. Everyone is so caught up in combat that nobody seems to notice as we climb atop the dais.

There's only one way I can put a stop to this carnage.

I lift one hand to the sky and call my flame.

A torrent of black fire hisses forth from my outstretched palm. The blaze coalesces into the maw of a great dark serpent that thrashes and roars in a rain of embers.

Silence falls as Demigods and Starless alike turn to behold this terrible wonder. The faces of those closest to us twist into masks of awe and fear at the sight. There's no question that if I choose to do so, I can unleash this viper and turn the whole city into ash.

But I hold back the dreadful serpent, taming it into my hand as quickly as I summoned it.

Satisfied that I have everybody's attention, I shift Kartas' body off my shoulders and set it on the hard stone of the dais. Gasps and whispers ripple through the amassed soldiers as my cousin's lifeless eyes gaze out onto what once was his home.

"The usurper is dead!" I bellow. My voice rings out over the court-yard in the wake of my midnight flame. "There will be no more bloodshed in Nexus this day!"

A cheer rises through the city at my words, followed quickly by the clatter of metal as Kartas' remaining forces drop their weapons on the cobblestones. In time, I'll deal with those traitors, but for now, I pay them little mind.

From where she stands beside me on the dais, Lyanndra holds my cousin's sword aloft in a symbol of victory. "The days of war between the Demigods and the Starless are over!" she cries. "Behold the start of a new era when the Starless and the Demigods will rule as one!"

The crowd roars, but I barely hear them. Her words play over again in my mind. Does she understand what she's saying? Does she really mean to rule by my side as my queen?

And when she whips off her golden helm, the fire in her eyes tells me that she understands the implications of her announcement perfectly. We regard one another for a long moment, drowning in the cheers of our people, and then she closes the distance between us.

Her mouth slams into mine with the ferocity of a clashing blade. All her passion and need pour into me as I gather her in my arms, pressing her armored form firmly against mine. She holds me like she never wants to let go, and I give her everything I have, down to the very embers of my soul.

Because this kiss is a promise of our future.

Lyanndra is finally mine.

CHAPTER 41

Lyanndra

"What should we do with the traitor, my Lord?"

At the healer's words, Syran frowns down at the pale form stretched out on the makeshift cot at his feet.

We're in the infirmary, which is full to bursting with the wounded and dying. The smell is horrendous, the air rife with groans, screams, and sobs, but it's important for us to be here. War doesn't end on the battlefield. It dies here amidst the blood and the bandages as lives fade and soldiers mourn. It's our dark duty to be here for our people in this time of loss.

Ressa is just another casualty in this sea of bodies. Her chest rises and falls in a shallow rhythm, but she remains otherwise still. A strange pattern of burns, red and creeping like the vines of some unholy plant, crawl up over the delicate skin of her bosom to lick her slender neck. If she's in distress, she shows no sign of it. Instead, she looks oddly peaceful, as if she's only sleeping.

The healer's question hangs in the air like a curse as Syran stares down at his former betrothed.

We all know that treason is punishable by death.

Understanding that this is not an easy decision for my crossed star to make, I instruct the healer, "Leave us for a moment. I'm sure there are others who need your attention more."

The Demigod hesitates, as though he's unsure if he should truly heed my words, and I'm worried that he won't listen to me, but then he bows his head respectfully and slips away.

Syran turns to me then, conflict raging behind his green eyes. "Ressa should die for her crimes," he mutters in a voice low enough that we won't be overheard even in such tight quarters.

"She should," I agree. "But was she not a victim, in a way?"

"Of Kartas or of me?" he challenges.

"Both," I answer honestly. As painful as the truth is, I'm not going to lie to him. "You made her a promise you couldn't keep, but what Kartas did was far worse. I do not think she would have stood against you without his influence."

Agony flickers across Syran's proud features as he processes my words. "I cannot put her to death for something that I drove her toward," he confesses after a long moment. "It would be wrong of me. But if I don't punish her, I'll appear to be a weak king before my rule even begins."

"Then let her live," I suggest. "Banish her to the dungeons."

He fixes me with a puzzled look. "Why would you show her mercy?"

How do I explain that I see a piece of myself in the broken young woman who lies before us? She is the person I could have been, a small spirit relegated to a small life. While death might be a release for her, I don't think she deserves it.

And I don't want Syran to make a choice that he'll later regret. Ressa can't do any harm locked away in the dungeons, but she will have the option to regain her sanity and become better than what she is. If he kills her, she'll just be gone, along with all of her potential futures.

"Death is final," I say after a thoughtful pause. "Life, even an imprisoned one, is not."

Syran seems to understand because he motions for the healer to return. "You may treat her wounds, and then have the guards take her to the dungeon," he orders.

"Yes, my Lord." The healer obeys with a bow.

With the terrible choice made, we don't linger over the cot any longer. Syran takes my hand in his, his long fingers twining over my gauntlets as he tugs me gently in the direction of the door. I follow him out into the corridor, which is bustling with activity.

I draw in a deep lungful of clean air. I'm glad to be out of the infirmary. I spent far too long in there recovering from my wounds months ago, and now the overwhelming stench of blood and death is taking a toll on me. As we weave through the corridors along a familiar path, I'm relieved to find that we pass fewer and fewer people. By the time we reach the staircase leading up to Syran's chambers, we're entirely alone.

Here with my crossed star, there's no more need to keep up my act of resilience. He's seen me at my weakest and fought by my side at my peak, so I'm blissfully free of shame when I allow my body to sag against his as we make our way up the steps.

He unlocks the door at the top with his fiery black key, and then we're finally in his haven, safe and hidden from prying eyes.

Wordlessly, Syran begins to undress me. He starts with my gauntlets, sliding each one off with heated reverence. His lithe fingers make quick work of the rest of the buckles and straps of my armor, and I feel a little freer as each piece drops to the ground at our feet. Next come my dragonhide leathers, which take a little more effort to peel off, and finally, my stolen velvet cloak. Syran tosses that onto the bed before he returns to stand before me.

I'm almost entirely naked now, with only my smallclothes and my chest wrap shielding my most intimate parts from his view. Though my skin is grimy with dried sweat, blood, and ash, he stares at me like I'm the most wondrous thing he's ever seen.

He holds my gaze as he begins the same process on himself. I watch, transfixed, as he sheds the shell of his golden armor and then his leathers. Wetness pools between my thighs as I realize that he wears absolutely nothing underneath. The way his cock stands to attention at the mere sight of me stokes the heat that rushes through my exhausted body. We haven't explored our passion since the night of the Winter Solstice, and those long two weeks of nothing more than a stolen kiss or caress only makes me want him more.

Fully bare, Syran stalks toward me like a beast gone wild. His eyes flare with need as he growls, "Do you regret lying with me, Lyanndra?"

"No," I breathe without hesitation.

"Then prove it," he challenges.

So I do.

I reach out and pull him close, my nails digging into his skin as I claim his lips with mine. He meets me with fierce enthusiasm. He snakes his arms around me, gripping me like a serpent holds its prey. With a deep roll of his hips, he presses his heavy cock against my stomach, mere inches away from the part of me that throbs with need for him. A low whine escapes me as I rub against him, eager for that devastating friction.

Syran chuckles against my swollen lips and then pulls away. "Soon," he promises with a teasing grin.

I scowl at him, but I still allow him to lead me by the hand to the washroom. When we enter, I'm astonished to find the huge copper tub full to the brim with fresh, clear water. The maids and servants can't even get into this room, so who drew this bath?

Noticing my silent surprise, Syran smirks and points to the ornate tap. "Aqueducts," he explains. "They run underneath the city, and there are several pipes that bring the water to the palace. We call it plumbing."

As I muse this new wonder, he summons a shock of black flame in his palm and holds it up to the side of the copper tub. Within seconds, the water inside is steaming. Then he turns back to me, his eyes once again brimming with hunger.

"Strip," he commands.

A bolt of need strikes my core at his blunt order. Ever a good soldier, I lift my shaking hands to my chest wrap and begin to unwind the cotton strips. Syran's eyes widen as my breasts are revealed to him once again, and then he looks like he's going to faint when I step out of my smallclothes. Finally, I pull the leather tie from my hair and comb out my braid with my fingers.

Once I'm finished, he offers me his hand, and I take it, allowing him to steady me as I step over the high edge of the bath and into the water. A thrill runs through me at the sudden heat and I shiver.

And then Syran joins me in the huge tub, and the fresh wave of fire that spreads through my veins has nothing to do with the temperature of the water.

He rests his long form against the edge of the bath and then pulls me to his chest so that my back is flush against him. I can feel the hard weight of his cock behind me as I settle between his legs. The steaming water laps at my breasts, and I sigh at the relaxing heat that leaches into my sore muscles.

"Lean back," he instructs. His hand on my shoulder guides me as I dip my head back and dunk my hair into the water.

I watch through slitted eyes as Syran reaches over to the collection of oils and soaps on the nearby windowsill and selects a slender bottle filled with pale green liquid. When he pours some into his palm, the scent of fresh mint stings my nose. He lathers the soap into my hair, massaging my scalp with deft fingers. I melt beneath his ministrations and nearly moan as his lips ghost over my neck while he washes the ash and marble dust from my roots.

How long has it been since I've actually cleaned my hair? And with soap, too? I can't even remember. I lose myself in Syran's gentle touch as he rinses the lather from me with tender hands.

"Your turn," I declare once he's finished. He quirks an eyebrow and smirks but doesn't resist as he wets his hair. Using the same soap, I run my fingers through his red tresses and enjoy the sigh he releases when I tug through a particularly messy knot. The process is over far too soon, and Syran doesn't waste any time in pulling me back against him once I'm done.

The water, frothing with minty bubbles, suds around us as he growls, "Enough."

I don't get a chance to ask what he means before his lips find mine, snatching my attention with desperate hunger. He splays his fingers across my ribs, his thumbs just brushing over the livid scar he left there during our first encounter.

After what feels like an eternity, his hands finally move. One shifts up to cup my breast and circle my nipple while the other travels down toward my core. I gasp into his mouth as he teases the tender skin of my thighs and belly but never quite touches me where I want him the most.

"Syran, please," I beg.

His breath fans the shell of my ear as he murmurs, "Tell me what you want."

"Touch me," I breathe.

My words shatter whatever boundary that's held him back thus far. His hand grazes my core, and his fingers trail over me. I shudder at his touch as ripples of pleasure flow through my body. Encouraged by my reaction, Syran slides one digit into my slick heat.

But it's not enough. Even as he works a second finger inside of me, I want more.

I *need* more.

"Syran," I moan.

His fingers slide out of me, and I huff in frustration. But my displeasure quickly transforms into fresh desire as he shifts me into his lap and drags the tip of his cock against my dripping entrance.

"I need to hear you say it," he growls. "I need you to tell me you're mine."

"I'm yours," I promise as he slides his length over my heated core.

"If you run from me again, I'll hunt you down," he threatens with a vicious roll of his hips.

I turn my head to meet his blazing green gaze. "Chase me to the ends of Alastria. Never stop. Swear it to me."

"I will follow you until the stars fall," he vows.

And then he's inside me, driving me to the heavens themselves.

CHAPTER 42

SYRAN

I have waited my whole life for this day.

Beyond the closed double doors to the throne room, I can hear the excited drone of my people–*our* people–as Demigods and Starless alike gather to celebrate my coronation. Black and gold bunting drapes every inch of the palace, including the antechamber in which we wait, and I can already smell the feast the cooks are preparing in the kitchens down below.

Even though I have dreamed of this moment for years, anxiety grips my nerves now.

"What if I'm a terrible king?" I pose for what has to be the hundredth time today.

Lyanndra, whose small, calloused hand rests in the crook of my arm, rolls her eyes. "You cannot be any worse than your father."

She's right, if not a little crude. I grin down at her, hoping she doesn't catch how nervous I really am. My heart flares when she offers me a rare smile. It lends her face an effervescent glow and emphasizes how radiant she looks in the candlelight.

Traditionally, as my crossed star, she should be wearing some sort of rich, luxurious gown. However, Lyanndra is no lady of the Celestial Court, and I will never again force her to be anybody but herself. Instead of gauzy fabric and shiny baubles, she wears her tarnished armor, which is now inlaid with swirling gold patterns redolent of a serpent's scales. Her golden helm is tucked in the crook of her other arm, and my black velvet cape swirls around her in a midnight cascade.

It brings me immeasurable satisfaction to see her wearing my sigil on her back as well as on her exposed finger. Her ring glints in the low light, matching the one that sits on my left hand in a perfect pair. I'm dressed in my ceremonial armor, but before we enter the throne room, I have one more piece to don, which is currently folded neatly over my free arm.

Breaking away from my crossed star, I turn away from her. "Would you do me the honor of removing my mantle?" I request.

"You want me to undress you here?" she jests. "By the stars, you're insatiable."

I let out a snort of laughter as her nimble fingers make quick work of the clasps that hold the mantle at my shoulders. The fabric falls free and ripples down my armor to pool at my feet in a midnight shroud.

Facing Lyanndra again, I shake out my new garment from where it hangs over my arm and hold it up for her to see. Confusion ripples over her features as she asks, "A cape?"

"Indeed," I confirm with a smirk. "I needed a new one because some horrible little thief stole mine."

"How dreadful for you," she deadpans.

I sweep the cape over my shoulders and fasten the clasp at my collarbone. The velvet is liquid soft beneath my hands as I brush out any stray wrinkles.

"How do I look?" I ask.

"Dashing," she observes. "Like a proper king."

I turn around, showing her the gold embroidery at my back, and she gasps. It's the reaction that I wanted, and I can't suppress the boyish grin that spreads across my face as she runs a hand over the detailed stitching.

Unlike the snake that graces the back of her pilfered cloak, the embroidery on mine depicts a greatsword standing upright with her golden helm balanced on the hilt. A monstrous, fiery serpent wraps around the blade, entwining the two in a deadly embrace.

"It's us," she breathes reverently.

"Do you approve?" I prompt.

She nods and then further confirms it by stretching up to plant a quick kiss on the corner of my mouth. That small act of affection and her acceptance of the new royal seal give me courage for what's to come later tonight. Because as nervous as I am to be crowned King of Alastria and the Celestial Court, the question I'm prepared to ask my crossed star is far more important to me than any royal title. And though I'm confident I already know what her answer will be, part of me fears that I have somehow misread her intentions.

Thankfully, I don't have much longer to agonize over what's to come. A cheer sounds from beyond the threshold, and I recognize that as our signal. Lyanndra tucks her hand back into the crook of my elbow just as the doors part, revealing the interior of the throne room.

It seems like all of Alastria is packed into this vast space. Demigods stand side by side with their Starless counterparts, clapping as I lead my crossed star across the marble floor. The chips and divots from our battle with Kartas are repaired, erasing any trace of chaos and treason. Black banners etched with the new golden sigil of our joint power line the walls. My chest warms when I realize that Lyanndra can't seem to take her eyes off them.

We proceed to the dais, where the golden throne awaits. Torran stands before it, leaning heavily on a gnarled cane. I was worried he may not recover fast enough from his injury to preside over the coronation, but he pulled through with only a slight limp to show for it. Not bad for an old Demigod.

Lyanndra and I step up onto the dais. She lingers at my side as I turn to inspect my assembled court. I search the faces of the crowd, some grief-stricken part of me hoping to see the familiar brown eyes and tousled hair of my cousin, but of course Kartas isn't here. I burned his body atop a pyre of black flame in the courtyard and spread the ashes across the training grounds.

It's what he would have wanted.

Torran catches my eye, distracting me from my ghosts, before he redirects his attention to the crowd. "Good people of Alastria!" he intones as he addresses the room.

Silence ripples out at his words, allowing space for anxiety to twist through my bones once more.

When he's sure he has everybody's attention, Torran continues, "We are here today to witness the coronation of Syran, Lord of the Midnight Flame. Like his father before him, he will rule, unchallenged, by the will of the stars."

Lyanndra shifts almost imperceptibly beside me, and I'm suddenly aware of several eyes flashing toward her. Does anybody really think she would relegate me to my father's fate? Tamping down the anger that rises in me at the impudent thought, I remind myself that, by the end of this night, nobody will ever be able to question her loyalty again.

Torran faces me. His blue eyes are solemn and comforting. "Wield your blade," he instructs.

I do as he asks. The steel grates against its sheath as I pull my sword free and plant the tip in the marble at my feet. I kneel before it with my head bowed to the hilt and my eyes cast down to the ground. From this angle, I can only see my subjects' shoes beneath the hems of dresses and the edges of cloaks.

"Syran, do you swear to protect the kingdom of Alastria and uphold her laws?"

"I swear." My voice echoes off the marble walls and rolls through the room in a powerful, decisive wave.

"Do you swear to honor your people, both the wealthy and the poor?"

Torran and I practiced these lines a thousand times in the last few weeks, and I always answered him in the same, prescribed way. Now, I deviate from the script and vow, "I swear to honor all of my people, both the Demigods and the Starless."

Shocked whispers flurry up from the crowd. I can practically hear the admonishment Torran will give me later after the festivities are in full swing, but nobody can undo the words I have just pledged myself to.

The old Demigod clears his throat, once again commanding silence. When everybody is appropriately hushed, he imparts the last line. "Do you swear to give your life in the name of Alastria?"

I do not hesitate in my strong response. "I swear."

"I bestow upon you the sacred crown of Alastria. It is said that your forefathers before you fashioned it from the fallen stars. Do you accept this burden?" Torran asks seriously.

"I do," I proclaim.

A heavy weight circles my head as he rests the crown atop my flaming hair.

"Then rise, Syran, Lord of the Midnight Flame, King of Alastria and the Celestial Court."

Raucous applause erupts in the throne room.

For the first time since the start of the vows, I lift my gaze to look upon my people. Though my loyal knights made short work of Kartas' supporters after the failed coup, I was worried that my blatant show of unity would upset some of the gathered crowd. But all I see is joy and exuberance as the Demigods and Starless cheer side by side.

I climb lithely to my feet, careful not to disturb the crown that rests on my temples. The weight is strange and unfamiliar. It's a burden that I'll grow used to over time.

Torran motions for me to sit on the throne, but I don't heed his quiet request. Ignoring his puzzled look, I instead hold up one hand, silencing the crowd.

"I do not take the burden of this crown lightly," I begin once everybody has settled. "My father's rule was marked by blood and ash. Alastria lost countless sons and daughters to his foolish war, and to those who would follow in his footsteps. And while some of us may carry the sins of those who came before us heavy in their hearts, we will *not* repeat them. Today marks the birth of a new path forward, one of peace and prosperity." My heart pounds wildly in my chest as I muster up my next words, the ones I've wanted to utter for so, so long. "It is an honor to be your king. I wish to lead us into a better age, and I can ask for no better woman to stand by my side than my crossed star." I pivot away from the crowd to face Lyanndra, who stares up at me with questions brimming in her hazel eyes. I drop to one knee before her and hold out my left hand. I breathe out the next words, terrified that she might say no. "From the moment we were crossed, I have been yours. Will you do me the honor of being my queen?"

A thousand thoughts scurry through my mind in a chaotic tumult. Will she reject me? Have I overwhelmed her by asking in front of the entire court? Logically, I know she already announced her intentions of ruling by my side weeks ago when we declared victory over Kartas in his attempt to usurp the throne. Since then, she's given me no indication that she's changed her mind. Yet, adrenaline still surges through my blood as I anxiously await her answer.

After what feels like forever, Lyanndra shifts her golden helm to sit beneath her right arm and then places her left hand in mine. The metal band of her ring is warm against my skin.

"I will," she says. "I have always been yours."

The stars were right all along.

CHAPTER 43

I've never felt this way before.

Wanted.

A strange sort of warmth seeps into my bones as yet another courtier approaches our table in the ballroom. It's only been an hour since we left the throne room, but it already feels like we've talked to a thousand people in that short time. I barely process the newcomer's congratulations to Syran on his ascension to the throne, or his well wishes for our formal betrothal. Like the others, he rambles on endlessly about how, of course, the union is only natural, given the bond of our crossed stars, but that it's still quite a bold statement for a Demigod king to take a Starless woman as his queen.

I don't care what he, or anybody else, thinks. My armor is impervious to thinly veiled disapproval and muted insults. All that matters is that Syran sits proudly by my side, his hand curled tightly around mine as he rubs soothing circles against my knuckles with the pad of his thumb.

We're finally given respite from the courtiers' long-winded drivel when the feast commences. Servants place dozens of steaming golden dishes down on the long tables that line the room. Mouthwatering smells waft up from the lavish plates, and I'm suddenly reminded of how ravenous I am. It's not until I've served myself a heaping portion of the delicacies around me that I realize that these are all my favorites. Did Syran really pay attention to my eating habits over the last several weeks I spent with him in the palace?

One glance at his smug face confirms my suspicions. "What?" he asks when he realizes he's been caught. "Would you prefer roasted rabbit? Or some jerky, perhaps?"

I roll my eyes, but I can't keep a small smile from dancing across my lips.

Syran grins, looking awfully pleased with himself. "Eat," he murmurs quietly. "You'll need that energy for later."

"And what happens later?" I question innocently, though I think I have a pretty good idea of what my crossed star has in mind.

He leans back in his chair with his hot green gaze locked on mine. "I was hoping you might congratulate me on my new royal title," he replies. "*Thoroughly.*"

"Perhaps," I tease as I bite into a tender piece of duck. Flavor explodes in my mouth, and I have to fight to keep the ecstasy from showing on my face. After years of eating fire-roasted game and endless cauldrons of stew, I don't think I'll ever get tired of the palace fare. I've always had a large appetite, which is a problem when food is scarce, but is a boon to me now as I sample each of the spectacular dishes laid before me.

Syran's hunger seems to be of a different sort. His eyes never stray far from me as I dive into my plate. Every so often, he pauses in his interest to pick at a leg of chicken or a roasted potato. But even as he drinks, he surveys me over the edge of his goblet like I might disappear if he looks away.

When my plate is empty, he tugs on my hand he still holds beneath the table, urging me to my feet.

"If we leave now, everybody will assume we've gone to lie together," I mutter under my breath.

Syran smirks. "I'll be fucking you into my silk sheets this evening regardless," he shrugs. The words instantly ignite a fire in my core.

His grin widens at the blush that creeps up my cheeks and he adds, "Let them talk. This night is ours."

I have nothing to say to that. If I really wanted to argue, I'm sure I could think of some witty quip to throw his way, but the truth is that I want to go with him now and keep him to his heated promise, even if I have to hold a knife to his throat to do it. So I stand at his side and wait impatiently while Syran addresses the room.

"Good people of Alastria, we bid you goodnight," he declares. "The hour grows late, and we are weary after such a momentous day. Stay and feast until the wine runs out, in honor of our united kingdom."

Even pickled in alcohol and stuffed with fine food, the courtiers have enough manners to clap politely and save their gossip until after we retreat from the party.

I allow Syran to guide me from the ballroom and through the blissfully empty corridors. Everybody is still at the feast aside from the servants running food up from the kitchens, and the marble halls are awash in moonlight. As we turn down one particular passage, I recognize where we are. A wicked idea strikes me.

Grinning in the semidarkness, I tug my crossed star off course toward a closed doorway. He throws me a questioning glance, but whatever he finds on my face encourages him to follow me. We slip inside the room, shutting the doors firmly behind us.

Terraces of books rise up before us in a silent watch. Colors fracture across the marble floor as moonlight cascades in through the high stained glass windows. The library is by far my favorite place in the palace, but today, I haven't brought us here to read.

I lead Syran over to one shelf in particular.

"You kissed me here," I murmur as I push him up against the place where he caged me in with his arms all those months ago.

"I did," he agrees hoarsely. "And you smacked me with a book."

"I did," I echo.

"Are you going to do it again?" His tone is teasing, but I can hear the naked need hiding behind his words.

"Maybe." He shivers against me as I run my hands down his chest plate and trace the bottom edge of the metal with curious fingers. "Or perhaps I have something else in mind."

A thrum of anxiety chases my excitement as I think about what I'm about to do. We've had plenty of time to ourselves in the last few weeks, but there's something we haven't yet tried. I heard fellow soldiers talk about it so reverently over shared campfires, and now I want to give Syran that same pleasure. But what if I do it wrong and he hates it? I'll be absolutely mortified.

But the potential for failure doesn't stop me from trying. Syran's eyes flutter closed as I reach for his trousers. It's a bit of a challenge to unlace them in the dark, but at last, my fingers close over the velvet length of his cock, and his breath hitches.

I drop to my knees before him.

"What are you doing?" he gasps as I stare up at him. The moonlight throws his features into shadowy relief, reminding me of the night he first took me in our dream.

"Isn't this how you're supposed to worship a king?" I challenge.

He starts to reply, but I don't give him the chance. I lean forward and close my mouth around his cock.

Syran's reaction is immediate. He hisses in pleasure as I swirl my tongue experimentally, tasting salt and desire. When I start to move, his hands fly up to tangle in my braid in a silent plea to continue.

The sound of my lips massaging his cock is sinful. Wetness pools between my legs as his groans echo salaciously through the empty library. His hips push forward to meet me as I take more and more of him, coaxing him toward his edge.

Just as I think he's about to unravel, he pushes me gently, but firmly, away from him. I sit back on my haunches and wipe my mouth on the back of my hand as I stare up at him expectantly.

He tucks the evidence of his desire back into his trousers and laces them hurriedly with shaking hands. I worry that I did something wrong, but he dispels that anxiety with one hungry look.

Before I can react, he seethes forward and scoops me up, tossing me over his shoulder like he did in our dream. I yelp in surprise at the sudden movement, which only seems to excite him further.

"Do you know how good that felt?" he growls as he whisks me out of the library and into the abandoned corridor. "Do you know how hard it was for me not to spill myself in your wicked little mouth? Why would you punish me so?"

I flash him a pleased grin even though I know he can't see it at this angle. "Would you rather I threw another book at you?"

He chuckles darkly, and the sound goes straight to the place between my slick thighs.

The journey up to his chambers seems to take forever. When we finally burst in through the door, I'm squirming with need in his iron grip. He tosses me down onto the bed like he did the first night we were crossed and advances on me with all the grace of a flexing serpent.

He pins me down with the weight of his body, his fingers coiling around my wrists. Our armor scrapes as he kisses me fiercely, drawing a wanton gasp from my lips.

There are far too many layers between us. I can barely feel the friction of his hips against mine through the tarnished metal and dragonhide leathers I wear. Syran seems to come to the same conclusion because he sits up and releases me in favor of removing each piece of my ensemble with well-practiced ease. He chases each reveal of my skin with searing kisses that leave me arching and panting in their wake.

Finally, I'm naked beneath him. The night air licks at me as he quickly strips and tosses his armor down with mine in an abandoned pile at the bedside. At last, he rests against me, his swollen cock teasing my entrance.

Syran's eyes capture mine, a shining green to my hazel. "Did you mean it when you said you'd be my queen?" he asks softly. I'm surprised to hear the vulnerability that lingers in his voice, especially juxtaposed to his heated gaze.

How many times does he need to hear it? Was I not clear enough the day we felled the usurper and put a stop to his coup? I intend to rule by Syran's side, not because the stars willed it so but because I *want* to.

Because I want *him*.

So my answer comes easily. "Yes," I say firmly. "I will be your queen."

Triumph sparks through his emerald eyes as he thrusts into me. I gasp at his sudden roughness. This isn't just lust, I realize when he pulls out until only the tip of his cock remains inside me.

He's *claiming* me.

I cry out as he slams back into my slick heat. Pleasure mingles with delicious pain as he does as he promised, fucking me into the luxurious fabric of his sheets while he drives me toward sweet oblivion. I clutch him desperately, curling my nails into the smooth skin of his back. I don't care if I make him bleed. I don't care if it hurts him. All I want is for him to keep going, to show me that he is as lost to this as I am.

And when I finally shatter beneath him, I howl out his name for the moon to hear.

His hips stutter as he, too, finds release. His teeth clamp down on the tough muscle of my shoulder, hard enough to leave a mark. And then he stills, and his eyes once again seek out mine.

"I meant what I said, Lyanndra," he growls. "Now that I have you, I will never let you go."

Something *more*, something beyond lust and the carnal hunger for his body, floods through me. It's new and delicate, and I don't dare give it a name.

Not yet.

But I feel it all the same as I press a hot kiss to the corner of his parted lips.

"Chase me," I plead, "wherever I go. To the very stars."

He tilts his forehead down to meet mine, our noses touching as he stares down at me with eyes as fathomless as the heavens. And when he makes his vow to me, I know with frightening certainty that he means it down to the fire in his soul.

"Forever."

EPILOGUE

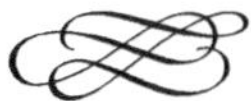

Ressa

Syran doesn't love me.

He doesn't.

He doesn't.

I've known it for a while, ever since he threw me down here to rot in the dungeons with the rats and criminals. But the bitter taste of his deception still will not leave me, and I savor it now on my tongue as I picture my former betrothed in my mind's eye.

The red hair, the strong jaw, the perfect nose, those endless green eyes–all of that was supposed to be *mine*.

Not hers.

I snarl into the murky corner of my cell at the thought. How dare that horrible Starless whore come between us? I picture her too, but my image of her common features and disgusting armor is far less flattering. What makes her better than me? Why would he want her more?

My thoughts scrunch into an indecipherable tangle as I ruminate and seethe. She should be down here instead of me. I should be the one in Syran's bed, where, as I overhear from the guards, he takes her every night.

I don't even want to think about what they must do together. It must be a dismal chore for poor Syran to bed such a lowborn wench, yet I can't seem to tamp down the jealousy I feel at the thought of her fornicating with him in such a manner.

"That should be me," I hiss out into the empty air of my cell.

Never once did Syran take me to his bed. He touched me, yes, and I certainly did some unladylike things to him on more than one occasion, but he never laid with me.

Not like he's doing with her.

And I know he is because the guards talk.

Not to me, of course, but to one another when the nights are long and tiresome. They gossip worse than the ladies of the Celestial Court, who are famous for clucking around like a pack of mad hens. And while I would never stoop so low as to join such uncouth conversation, it would be foolish of me not to listen every now and again.

So I've heard the knights chatter about how Syran moons over the Godslayer and shows her off on his arm, as though she's some wondrous prize to celebrate rather than the monstrosity that she is. They talk about her like she's beautiful, and those are the words that drive me into the worst fits of rage.

Because she's not.

She's *not*.

Not like I am.

I squeeze my eyes shut and shake my head. My dark tresses hang limply around my face, and I grip them now, wondering what it would feel like to tear the Godslayer's hair from her scalp. There are a thousand other horrible things I'd like to do to her, and I'm sure I'll dream up a thousand more before my mind is satisfied.

But I can't do any of them in here.

Why has Syran exiled me to this wretched place?

I hate him for it.

This vile cell is no place for a lady of the Celestial Court. I'm forced to wear a plain gray shift that is suited only for the poor and the wretched. The guards feed me regular meals of bread, dried meats, and hard cheeses. There is no wine, only water. Somebody comes twice a day to empty my chamber pot, which is an indignity all to itself. Each night, I lie on a lumpy cot with only a thin wool blanket to cover me, and I dream of Syran's black silk sheets and the silvery gauze of my bedspread.

Are my rooms still here in the palace, with all my precious possessions waiting for my eventual release? Or have they been purged and gifted to somebody else?

Fresh anger sweeps through me at the thought. I bare my teeth and snap them into the darkness.

How dare Syran do this to me?

I curl up on my side on the cot and listen to the sounds of the palace's underbelly. Other prisoners mumble and curse, but I ignore them. I would never speak to anybody of such low stature. Instead, I focus on the low hum of conversation between the guards who don't sound particularly happy to be here on this night.

"Do you think the kitchens will save anything for us?" one asks. Since I can't see him, I picture him as very tall with a long nose that pokes out through his helmet.

"Fuck all, if I know," a second knight replies. This one is probably fat, I decide arbitrarily.

"I heard from the last shift that the king already left the feast," the thin one muses. "Took the Godslayer with him, all subtle like."

His companion laughs, even as I seethe. "I would too, if I had a lady like that. She's a right beauty, even if she scares the stars out of me."

I let out a low hiss into the darkness. I hate it, *hate it*, when they talk about her like that.

Like she's better than me.

But still, I listen because there's nothing better for me to do.

"You owe me ten pieces of gold, by the way," the first guard comments.

"How's that?" the fat one rebukes.

"I said he'd propose to her at the coronation, and he did. You said he wouldn't because she's Starless. Ten. Pieces. Of. Gold."

"Well, what did she say? You wagered that she'd have to accept too."

"Of course she said yes, you fool!"

I slam my hands over my ears to block out the rest of their conversation. I don't want to hear this. I *can't* hear this.

Syran has asked the Godslayer to be his queen.

She will sit on the throne instead of me.

She will forever share his bed instead of me.

She will bear his children instead of me.

I'm going to have to kill her.

Syran will go mad, but he deserves it for what he did to me. I loved him, and all he ever did was use me. Even now, he doesn't have the decency to end my suffering. Instead, he locks me up and ignores my requests for an audience, prolonging my torment. This is his own special torture for me, and he must know it. Why else would he forsake me like this?

Part of me regrets not allowing Kartas to finish what he started. He promised me so much–*too* much, I remind myself. He was just as bad as Syran, but he was stronger than me. If I hadn't intervened, he would have struck down the Godslayer. Syran, even mad, would have been mine.

I desperately wish I could turn back time, but I know that what's done is done. All I can do is move forward.

All I can do is plot my revenge.

The time will come when I'm free of this cell, and I can take my anger out on the Godslayer. She might be stronger than me, but I'm smarter. I know the Demigods, and I know the inner workings of the Celestial Court better than anybody else. I will turn the kingdom against her, and, when she's at her weakest, when she's lost every-thing, I will strike her down.

The thought of her hot blood frothing at my hands makes me grin. Someday, that will be a reality.

Worked up by my fantasies, I realize that I've inadvertently chased sleep away. I open my eyes and stare into the corner of my cell. The darkness there lingers like Syran's midnight flame, black as pitch and full of poison.

But then the shadows shift, and I think I see something glint within.

An eye? Two?

Yes.

Yes.

I sit up, intrigued. There's no fear—I'm far past that now. I'm filled only with cool interest as I trace the strange, dark outline that coalesces against the shadows.

The form does not move. It simply watches, blinking slowly every few seconds. I squeeze my eyes shut, and, when I open them, the shape is still there, staring.

Perhaps I've gone mad. I've been here for so long that I can barely keep track of the days, let alone the weeks. For all I know, a year has flown by in this dark and fetid place. A person could truly lose their mind down here, and though I feel sane, I pose it as a distinct possibility.

But then the figure speaks, and I know that I have my wits about me.

"Lady Ressa," it hums. The voice is thin, like it's come to me from a great distance.

I cock my head. "What are you?" I ask, for I know from the way my skin creeps that this visitor is not of the natural sort. If this is Demigod magic, I have never seen the likes of it before.

"A friend," the dry voice slithers.

Kartas was the last true friend I had, and even he betrayed me. And I'm not foolish enough to think that any of the other courtiers were truly fond of me. They were all too busy backstabbing one another to develop any deeper connections.

Suspicion drips from my words as I challenge, "Why should I believe you?"

The thing in the corner blinks. "Because we want the same thing."

How dare this stranger presume to know my desires? I want to snap and rage, but I remember my gentle manners and push the anger down to inquire, "And what is it that we both seek?"

The form grins, exposing white teeth that shine out of the darkness. "Your freedom," it croons.

Freedom.

Freedom.

I can practically taste it on my tongue. I think of the sunshine and the fresh air in the world above, of the smells and the sounds, of the Godslayer's blood on my hands, and Syran's body against mine.

"But it comes at a steep price," the voice warns, snapping me from my dreams.

Nothing comes for free, I suppose. But what could be worse than this? So I prompt, "Name it, and perhaps we shall strike an accord."

The thing's grin widens.

"The Godslayer," it says. "I want her head."

Perhaps we want the same thing after all.

ACKNOWLEDGMENTS

A massive thank you to Lianne for allowing me to borrow her name, and to my amazing editor, Amy, for her fantastic support.